T0165459

Secret of the Laurel Crown

Andrea MacVicar

ISBN: 978-1-4497-2290-6 (e)
ISBN: 978-1-4497-2291-3 (sc)
ISBN: 978-1-4497-2292-0 (hbk)
Library of Congress Control Number: 2011913127

WestBow Press books may be ordered through booksellers or by contacting:

WestBow Press
A Division of Thomas Nelson
1663 Liberty Drive
Bloomington, IN 47403
www.westbowpress.com
1-(866) 928-1240

Printed in the United States of America

WestBow Press rev. date: 9/15/2011

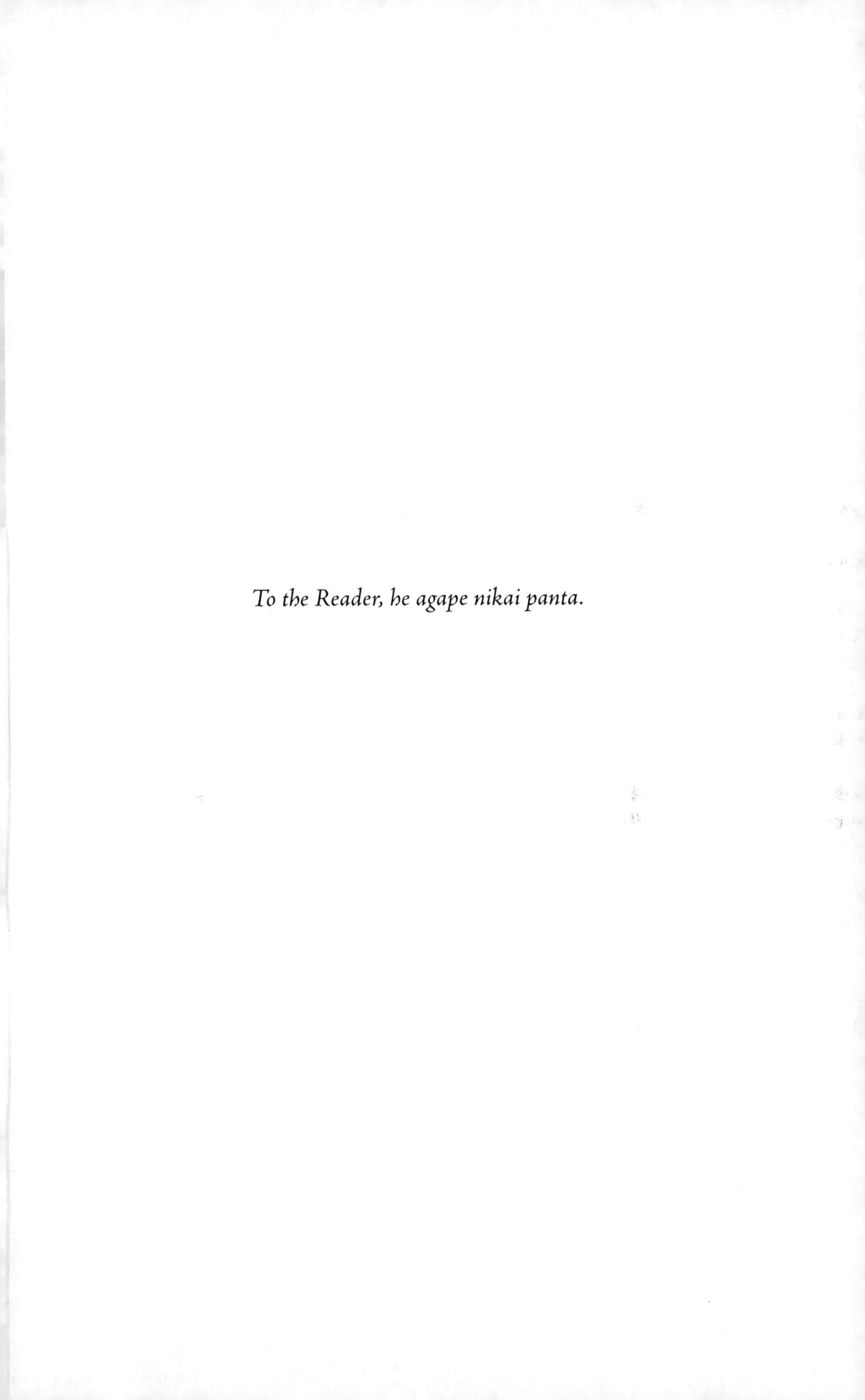

To the Reader, he agape nikai panta.

Chapter 1

the puzzle

The seventh-grade gym locker room was crowded with chattering girls. The bell rang. In ones, twos, and threes, they drifted into the gym. Carolyn waited until everyone was gone before she pulled off her brown sweater and plaid skirt. She sat on the bench, ripped the Velcro wrap from around her left ankle, and unlaced her black shoes. Deliberately, she dropped each shoe so that the thick, hard, rubber soles would make loud *thunks* on the tile floor.

Out of the corner of her eye, she saw something brown skitter across the cracked white tile and disappear under the rusty edge of a locker. It took a moment to register in her brain the name of the creepy, crawly thing. A centipede.

Ew!

She picked up her shoe.

Another one followed the first.

"Gotcha." She smacked it hard.

She looked at the squish on the bottom of her shoe. Wipe it somewhere.

"Don't leave a mess for someone else to clean up." She heard her mother's voice in her head.

"Yeah. Okay." And then realized she had answered as though her mother was still alive.

She limped to the sink and turned on the water. She watched the centipede remains go down the drain. *Well,* she thought, *so has my life gone … down the drain. And, I made it happen. It took one second. Just one.*

"Carolyn Farmer?" Yolanda's voice bounced around the locker room. "Better get your buns out of there. Ramrod-Riguez's taking attendance."

"Yeah. Okay."

Back at the locker, she pulled on the navy shirt with RH in gold letters and the pleated gym shorts. She pushed her feet back into her shoes, lacing the left very tight for support. The Velcro wrap around the left ankle was next. Looking down, she thought about the cool sneakers all the other girls wore. *Someday, I'll be out of these black horrors and into something beautiful,* she promised herself.

By the time she entered the gym, the class had already circled the track a couple of laps. Rodriguez frowned; she pointed and then thumbed at her to join in the lap.

Okay, Ramrod. Got it.

She waited until Yolanda ran past, widening enough space to slowly ease in.

One and a half laps later, the calves of her legs began to ache. And at three laps, both shoes weighed a ton while the Velcro wrap strangled her left ankle.

"Oh, have mercy," she groaned. *Legs, don't fail me.* One more lap and her body screamed: stop! While her mind repeated: *I must keep going. I must. I must.* The words pounded with every aching step.

Suddenly the left rubber sole stuck to the varnished floor, sending her sprawling, spread-eagle down the track. Her chin, elbows, and knees hit the hardwood with a thwack.

"Ohh," she groaned, tears of pain springing into her eyes.

Several of the girls giggled as they went by.

"Come on," Yolanda said, running past her. "Get up. You can do it."

"Mind your own business," she mumbled under her breath. "Easy for you to say. You've got a beautiful body to push around."

Rodriguez came over and bent down. "You okay, Carolyn?" She helped her up.

"Yeah, I'm fine."

"Here, let me have a look." She lifted Carolyn's chin. "You've got a bit of a bump, but there's no skin broken." Her fingers pressed around Carolyn's kneecaps. "How does this feel?"

Carolyn gritted her teeth. Don't cry, she commanded herself. "I'll be okay."

"We can call your grandmother to take you home."

"Gram isn't home. She's working. And she doesn't drive."

"I can't send you home unless there's someone there. It's school policy. Who's at home after school is out?"

"Oh, that's Mr. Reed. He lives next door. He kinda looks after me until my older brother, Jimmy, comes home after practice. But I know he's not there until later. Today is Friday and he belongs to a club... stamps, I think."

Rodriguez gently guided her to a long bench. "Here, sit down until you feel better. Nothing's broken. No cuts. When you get home, put some ice on your knees and ankle." She patted her on the back. "Don't be discouraged. It takes time to recover from an injury like yours. You'll be fine tomorrow."

Carolyn leaned against the cool beige tile wall surrounding the gym. Every muscle in her body throbbed. She closed her eyes, pushing the ache of tears down into her throat. She took in a deep breath, blew it out her lips, and then swallowed hard. *I will get through this day. I* will.

After a hot shower in the girls' locker room, she hurt all over. But the absolute worst was this: she knew how she looked in the mirror. In a couple of hours, a big purple bruise would be on her chin instead of a red patch. Ugly neon purple turning into ugly yellow. It would probably take a couple of weeks, maybe more, to disappear.

She knew she had two things going for her in the looks department—her light blonde hair and flawless complexion. Her mom had always commented, others too, about her beautiful gray eyes. But how she wished they were a deep blue. Deep blue was glamorous with blonde hair. *Why couldn't I've inherited my mother's blue eyes instead of my dad's gray?*

Her wet hair dripped onto her sweater. Again she toweled her hair, trying to make it look decent. Her natural curl always frizzed when damp. And straight was in, not frizz. *Come on, think something good. Think something positive. It's Friday. Only three more hours in this concentration camp. Then breakout time.*

"I have some makeup you can use," Yolanda said. She touched Carolyn's arm with her compact. "It might help cover it up."

She was in no mood for conversation, or for any kind of help, especially from her. "Um, thanks, but no thanks," she mumbled, lightly pushing the compact away. "It's probably the wrong color." She forced a polite smile.

"Hey Yolanda, you're wastin' your time talking to *that* one." Jennifer tossed her towel into the laundry basket. "She's a loner."

"Hey, yourself. MYOB. I'm just trying to be friendly."

Carolyn's stomach felt like she had swallowed rancid milk. "Hey, don't fight over me. I'm fine, really."

"Well, okay. I just thought ... just trying to make you ..."

"Your charity mission?" Carolyn asked. "You think I need you to feel sorry for me?"

"Look. I was only trying to help. I know about your accident ... your parents and all. Word gets 'round."

"Yeah. Well, my life is none of your business, either."

"Like, I'm done tryin'. An' like they say, 'Don't call me; I'll call you.'" Yolanda pitched her towel in the basket.

In the mirror, Carolyn saw the obscene gesture directed at her from Jennifer and chose to ignore it. As quick as she could, she balled up her towel and sank it in the basket. She smiled in triumph at the score. She picked up her pack from the floor and slung it over one shoulder. Without looking at either one of the girls, she limped out the door as fast as her pain would let her.

The rest of the afternoon was a nightmare. Every part of her body was on fire. No matter how she tried to position her left foot under her desk, the shoe grew heavier, squeezed tighter. The Velcro gnawed at her ankle with sharp teeth.

By the final bell, she could barely swallow the sharp rocks that pressed against her throat. She gritted her teeth. *I* will *not cry*. She pushed against the classroom door and limped out into the hall. She could see Yolanda by the outside doors talking to a couple of girls from the gym.

She focused on the door, shutting them out of her view. Still, she would have to walk past them. Thud. Step. Their conversation died. Thud. Step. Thud. Step. And she was past them. She pushed against the heavy oak door. Outside, she breathed in the crisp October air. On parole for two days.

On each side of the alley shortcut from Roosevelt High, the red brick of the boarded tenement houses rose like prison walls. Rough, curling plywood covered windows and doors. Weeds grew between broken concrete chunks. Her shoes crunched on gravel mixed with broken glass, fallen bits of plaster, and wood.

Empty. They're all empty, she thought. *People lived in them once. Where did they all go? The people had blown away, just like Mom and Dad. Wherever they went has got to be better than here.*

She shivered and pulled her backpack around to protect her chest. Her blonde hair whipped and parted in the brisk wind. She turned the corner of her street where large maple branches creaked overhead, and their red leaves sailed past her.

The twenty duplexes stood in rows like half-gallon milk cartons, exactly alike. Built during the Depression, some were neat and clean. Others looked like torn boxes ready to be thrown away.

At the beginning of the row, she paused and turned her back to the wind. The tears she had jammed down all day erupted like a geyser.

Her mom's smart-phone pics of their past life in Seattle slid through her mind—her orderly, everything-in-its-place bedroom with its blue chintz-flowered drapes and matching bedspread, the dining room with her mom, dad, and Jimmy laughing, eating, talking about important nothings.

That was a million years ago.

The wind felt colder from the tears on her wet sweater.

After several minutes, her storm passed. As she slipped her right arm out of the pack, she turned to face the row of duplexes. Under her breath, she started counting them while fishing the backdoor key from the pocket of her skirt.

With a sigh of relief, she unlocked number ten and entered the warm kitchen filled with the fragrant scent of molasses. She dropped her pack on the kitchen table and picked up one of Gram's oatmeal cookies from the plate on the counter. She went to the fridge for milk.

The note on its door read: "Carolyn, I'll be home before seven. Heat up the tuna casserole. Make a salad. Don't forget to do homework. Remind Jimmy he has football practice early tomorrow morning. Love, Gram. PS, There's a surprise on your bed."

Well, it was Friday. She didn't have to think about homework until Sunday night. She leaned against the counter, munching the cookie and taking sips of milk.

The chill was off her. She looked at the kitchen clock: 4:00 p.m. She figured, at most, it was fifteen minutes to a half hour to relax, maybe even take a short nap, before Jimmy came home. Another bite, a sip, and suddenly she realized she was completely exhausted.

Forget the ice on the ankle or anywhere else. I'm dead. Bed, don't fail me now.

The stairs were like climbing Mount Rushmore. As soon as she was through the door, she ripped off the wrap and unlaced both shoes.

"Oh, man," she said with a sigh, dropping her body onto the bed. Her head hit the corner of the shoe box set on her pillow.

"What?" And then she remembered: "PS, There's a surprise on your bed."

Taped to the lid was another note.

> Carolyn,
>
> I bought this at a garage sale. I know how tough life has been for you these past months. I thought this might help make a sad girl smile. The woman who sold it to me said the pieces are all there. She told me she had tried to put it together many years ago, but it was too hard. There's some kind of secret message with it, but she could never find out what the message meant and what it had to do with the puzzle. When your mom was your age, she loved to do puzzles.
>
> Love, Gram

Actually, there were two additional surprises in the note. First, Gram couldn't possibly know she loved puzzles. They had never discussed it. And second, she didn't spend money on what she called "unnecessary, foolish things." "Money doesn't grow on trees" was one of Gram's favorite sayings.

Reading the note again, she looked over at the small walnut desk where her mother had carved her initials and done her homework years ago. It wasn't hard to picture her mother at the desk. From old photos, her mother at thirteen looked exactly like her. She could imagine where the bed legs had stood from the marks on the wood floor, and why her mother loved purple and wore the color often. When new, the faded wallpaper of lilacs and green vines must have matched a bedspread and curtains on the one window of the room.

Her heart warmed. In some mysterious way, working on the puzzle would be like plugging into her mom's presence.

Now two narrow folding cots, each with a thin mattress, were pushed up against opposite walls. In the Detroit duplex, two days after they had first arrived from Seattle, her brother took white chalk and drew a line on the wood floor between to dive the room.

"Pick your side," he said.

She did, grateful he thought of the idea. His side was always a mess, crammed with his junk into every inch. They agreed he wouldn't come into her clean space and she wouldn't cross the line to ever go into his mess.

After neatly rolling up the Velcro inside one of her shoes, she slid them under her bed. She lifted the lid of the box and dumped its contents. Five hundred pieces of the jigsaw puzzle tumbled out onto the worn yellow wool blanket. Brown, beige, cream, black, pink, and combinations of these colors spilled in front of her, creating a multicolored hill on yellow ground. As she pushed the pieces aside, a folded parchment—its edges ragged with age—caught in a small hole.

Picking it up carefully, so as not to tear the creases, she unfolded it and read the words in faded black, handwritten script: *"He agape nikai panta. The Laurel Crown shall choose the wearer. Be warned. Beware of the Baal contract."*

That's weird. Slowly she tried to sound out the funny words. "Hee a gape nigh kay I pan tah. Baa all." Was the secret message about the puzzle? Maybe the message had nothing to do with the puzzle. Somebody from a foreign country could've put it into the box later on. But why? And who?

"Oh, come on," she said aloud. "What's the diff? It's the puzzle that counts." She put the paper back in the box.

Without a hint of the subject, she knew the puzzle would be quite a challenge. She would have to use her detective skills in trying to put it together. Start by separating the pieces by color.

With intense concentration, she examined each one. Some felt softer than others in her hand, and warmer too. She put one of the cream-beige pieces on her cheek next to her ear. It was as smooth as baby skin.

"Mademoiselle Carolyn Farmer. *Mon amie,* I beg your help." The silky, feminine voice rolled the r's.

"Uh, what?" She responded in shock at hearing the voice and her name. She looked around the room. Everything was normal. But the piece next to her ear grew warmer.

"Hurry, Mademoiselle. Make me whole. The Laurel Crown beckons you."

"What'd you say?" Like a racer waiting for the gun to go off, she held her breath—her body motionless for an answer. Silence.

Chapter 2

the cellar

"Hey, sis." Jimmy's voice jolted her. At fifteen, his voice had deepened to sound like her father. Sometimes it flashed her back to her dad, squeezing her throat for a few seconds.

"Sorry I scared you. You were a million miles away." From the hallway he flung his football shoes. They fell on the floor an inch inside his line before he entered.

"Man, am I pooped!" He swung his canvas gym bag and football helmet on top of the desk like bags of potato chips.

He looked at her from across the room—his gray eyes a mirror image of hers. Flecks of dirt from his blond hair added tiny black dots to his freckled face.

"Whatcha got there?"

"A puzzle. Gram gave it to me. Came in this old shoe box. Must be five hundred pieces."

"Don't expect me to help you put it together." He dismissed her with a wave of his hand. "I got homework and I'm beat after practice. And no way are you going to use *my* desk either." He flopped on his unmade bed and folded his arms behind his head. "It can't be tied up for some fool puzzle."

"Did I ask you for anything?"

"No. But I know you. You always need some kind of help. So count me out."

They glared at each other.

Names like *stupid* came into her mind as she wanted to yell at him. But her horrible day had ended on a good note with the puzzle. *And I won't let my dumb brother mess it up.* She dropped her gaze.

He propped his head on his elbow. "Know what the picture is?"

"There's some kind of old paper in with the pieces. I read it, but it makes no sense." She took it out and showed it to him.

"Must be some kind of a joke." He handed it back to her.

She nodded. "Yeah, probably. I'm going to keep it anyway. It might mean something later. But I won't know what until I find a place where I can lay out the pieces."

"Are you deaf? Like I said, you can forget about using *my* desk." He rolled over, his back to her.

"*Your* desk? Ha! That belongs to both of us. Just 'cause Mom and Dad are gone, don't mean you can take over me."

"Listen, *little* sister. I can do what I want on my side. The desk's on *my* side. Got it?"

"It's mine too. Gram said it's for both of us … for homework."

"A puzzle ain't homework. A puzzle takes time. You gotta lay it out and leave it there." He rolled over, turning his back to her. "Forget it. Find someplace else."

"All you care about is football and girls," she mumbled under her breath.

"Say what?"

"Just … all you care about is *you*."

His bed creaked as he rolled back and glared at her. "Listen, you care enough about yourself for the both of us."

"Oh, yeah. Well, things didn't happen to you. They happened to me."

"You mean things like us bein' hit by a truck? Almost getting killed?" He ran his fingers through his hair. "You mean, like Mom and Dad dead? That happened to me too. I was in the backseat with you when we got hit."

"But the police didn't have to use the jaws of life to get you out. You got off without a scratch. You didn't have to stay in the hospital for months, trussed up like a chicken in a butcher shop. *You* went to the funeral. *You* had a chance to say good-bye to them. I didn't."

Her voice was shrill. "You had Gram to help you pick the caskets. You had Gram beside you at the cemetery. All *I* got are the pins in my ankle and the pictures and the obit in the newspaper. *You* got the real memories. *You* got to cry."

She glared at him. "Gram came to the hospital after the funeral. Where the h were *you*?"

"I hate hospitals."

"Yeah. Well, I know just *how much* you care about me. Zilch. Zero. Nada."

"Listen. Who started the argument? Who was whiny baby asking to stop every ten minutes on that trip to Mount Rushmore? Who was the one Dad looked at in the mirror to *shut up?* It was *you.* He looked in the rear view at you. Not me."

"And Gram still lets you do what you want," she said. "You get away with everything. I'm still hobblin' around."

"You wouldn't hobble if you'd exercise. You blame everybody else for your trouble."

"No. I don't." She emphasized each word separately.

He rubbed the back of his head. "It was nobody's fault. It just happened."

"Yeah, like I tell myself that a hundred million times. But things just don't happen. Not those kind of things anyway."

"Let's skip talkin' about it. Life goes on. There's nothin' we can do about the past. They would've wanted us to be happy. Make somethin' of ourselves. Be proud of us."

"Well, big jock, big cheese, you think you're really somethin'." Her words were coming between quick angry gasps. "I just hope someday you'll know what it feels like to be trapped like I was. Then you'll want my help ... you'd give anything for it." Her voice quivered. "But I won't be there for you, bro. I'll be gone!"

"Oh, bug off."

She was not going to let him have the last word. "I'll be gone, you'll see."

"Uh, huh." He turned his back to her.

"Burrpth." The raspberry sound was her last word.

With an angry fist she punched her pillow into a ball, propping it behind her and the wall. She lay against it. Her lids, her body grew heavy ...

"He agape nikai panta. Escape with me. The Laurel Crown awaits you."

Instantly she was awake. She looked over at Jimmy snoring lightly. He hadn't moved. Did *I dream her voice? Hey ... a ... gape eh ... That was on the paper?*

She lifted the lid and stared at the writing. Still made no sense. She put the same piece to her cheek. It softened and warmed.

"Mademoiselle Carolyn Farmer." The feminine *r* rolled like a French purr. "Sweet child, *mon amie*, do not alarm yourself. Fear not."

She gulped. "Wha … what did you say?"

"Mademoiselle, I come not to harm you. I come to bring you to your destiny."

"Who are you?" she whispered, her fingers trembling against the soft piece.

"Disclosure cannot be obtained until I am free. Escape with me and you will be free from the entanglements of your life. Fear not me. Fear those, should you tell, who will think you insane. Put me together. The essence of time is ever fleeting. Seize the day, Mademoiselle. *Carpe diem*."

Suddenly the piece was slick, hard cardboard.

She held it to her lips. "Tell me who you are."

The only sound was Jimmy's snoring.

She held another piece near her ear.

Nothing.

Another. Again nothing.

Then with both hands she scooped up a couple of piles and held them against her pounding heart, waiting for them to soften—to hear something. They remained hard cardboard.

She looked around the tiny room.

For sure, getting out of this box would be the ultimate. Where is my life exactly? Nowheresville. That's where.

But she came for me? Maybe from another world? At least, someplace else. Hey, take me there! Every second outta here would count high on the Richter scale of great. Yeah, carpe diem. *Grab the opportunity.*

"Hey," she whispered. "Whoever you are, okay."

The problem is, where can I work it? Gotta find a place.

She dropped all the pieces back in the box and slid it under her cot.

It took a couple of minutes to loosely wrap the Velcro around her left ankle and slip into her shoes without tying the laces. She eased her body down the stairs as quickly as she dared. Climbing down a mountain could be more dangerous than going up.

The kitchen still smelled like molasses. The pink Formica table intended to seat two was piled with books, keys, an arrangement of pink plastic roses, yesterday's newspaper, a stack of mail, and the plate of cookies. With two of normal appetite and one like an industrial vacuum sucking every particle of food in sight, the size of the fridge was totally inadequate.

She shoved bottles and cans aside until she found the casserole. The old stove was a two-top burner. She lit the gas in the small oven below and put the casserole inside.

In shifting the pile from the table to the pink counter, she realized, even if Gram wanted to, letting her use the kitchen table was impossible. It was the only surface in the whole apartment that was ever clear of anything. And then only for a few minutes at any time.

She sighed. *Oh, crud. Got nobody who has room.* Suddenly she thought, *Wait. Maybe there is someone. Maybe, Mr. Reed.*

She rapped twice on the kitchen wall, paused, and then rapped three more times. In a few seconds she heard the same sequence of knocks from the other side.

Half a minute later, she opened the door and looked up at the tallest man she had ever seen.

At six foot eight, Mr. Reed had to duck even lower than Jimmy to enter the kitchen. In denim coveralls, his thumbs hooked in chest straps, and his brown eyes twinkled down at her behind horn-rimmed glasses. His black Afro with sideburns connected to a couple of days growth of beard. Gold-capped teeth made his grin friendly, inviting.

"Missy, what's happenin'?"

"I kinda got a problem. I was wondering if you might know where I could get some space. I need some place to work."

"Is that all?" He stopped smiling. "Here, I thought it was some kind of emergency. You were suppose' to use our signal if you needed help."

"Oh, I do need help. You know how jammed we are. I need a place to work for a special project."

"What kind of project?"

"Oh, um ... very special. Oh, please. I need some place real private, real bad."

"The only place I got is my root cellar, but it ain't heated. Up 'til today, weather's been good an' warm. Weather turns, it can get cold and damp real fast in a basement. Not too healthy to stay down in the damp too long."

"Pretty please. I promise I only need it for a short time. And I'll be careful to dress real warm."

Mr. Reed rubbed his stubbled chin thoughtfully. "Well, if it's okay with Eunice, it'll be okay with me."

"Great, thanks!" She paused and licked her lips.

"Yes? You need somethin' else?"

"Do you have an old table," she hesitated, "and an old chair I could use? You know, something real old … um … no good … you know, you might throw away?"

"Missy," he said with a laugh, "you remind me of your ma when she was your age. Always busy working on some special game or other. Tell you what, maybe I can come up with somethin'. How about a butcher's table? And a real old foldin' chair? Why, they're so old you'll have to scrub 'em down. If you clean 'em, you can have 'em."

"Great!" She clapped her hands. "Thanks so much. Um … can I start right away? I mean, will you let me come over right now?"

"What's your big hurry? I told you, ask Eunice first."

Her thoughts raced. *Can't wait for Gram to come home. Gotta start working right away. Time is of the essence.*

She put her hands on her hips making herself as tall as she could. "Jimmy's home. And if Gram *trusts* me to fix dinner, I'm old enough to be left in charge of things. And if it gets cold like you said, the faster I start, the better it'll be for me 'cause it's a school project. And … and there's no place I can work on it on our side, so it's *very* important I start right away. I have to work on it the whole weekend. Monday it *has* to be turned in."

"Well, I don't want to get in the way of your education. Can you wait until I round up the table and chair?" He rubbed his chin thoughtfully. "Now considerin' I got to do all the give'n in this here arrangement, I expect some kinda payment."

She didn't know what to say. She didn't own a penny. How could she pay him anything?

He laughed. "I suppose I could hurry it in ten minutes for the price of some of your grandmother's cookies."

Relief swept through her. "Sure. I'll give you all we got."

"Ya' got yourself a deal. I'll meet you 'round the cellar by the trap door."

His eyes twinkled. "It's creepy down there. Ya' might change your mind after you see it. But if you're sure, I'll see you in ten. Just don't forget to let Eunice know where you are."

Ten minutes later, carrying a plate of cookies and a large paper bag filled with cleaning supplies, she followed Mr. Reed down two narrow, concrete block steps into a dismal cellar. A small amount of late afternoon light slanted in through the open trap door, casting creepy shadows against the dark, dirt walls.

After her eyes had adjusted to the gloom, she could see the basement was clean. Still, the room smelled of damp and mold. She stumbled on the irregular dirt floor, bumping against the steel legs of a butcher block table, tipping over the wooden folding chair leaned up against its side. He grabbed her to keep her from falling.

"Careful. The floor slopes down a couple feet. Ya' gotta watch your step. When the day's cloudy, it gets dark down here."

A bare bulb with a chain hung from a wood rafter. Mr. Reed reached up to pull on the chain, but no light snapped on.

"Need a bulb. Be right back."

After righting the chair, he left.

With a few rays of late afternoon sunlight coming through the trap door, she could see the table would be large enough for her puzzle. And the chair would do also. She began to set out the cleaning supplies she had brought.

"Let's try this," Mr. Reed said a few minutes later. He screwed in the bulb and pulled the chain. The bare bulb swung, casting its swinging light against the dirt walls.

"Whaddya think now?"

"With the light on, it's not bad. It'll be just fine."

"To tell the truth, that surprises me. Knowing what you've been through, didn't think you'd want to be in some place dark. You know, below ground? It might be scary for you. Didn't think you'd want to stay once you'd seen it."

"Thanks for everything," she said, tight-lipped. "It's a terrific cellar."

He nodded, smiling. "I'm mighty glad you like it. Have fun." He reached for the plate. "And thank Eunice for the cookies."

After he left, she pulled a soapy wet rag, a dry dish towel, and her shoe box out of the bag. Quickly she cleaned the table and chair. When she finished, she put everything but the box back in the bag under the table. After lifting the lid, very carefully she scooped out the pieces in handfuls and piled them in the center of the table.

From the large mound, she began to sort and group by color. Dark and light brown, black and black-brown, white, creamy-beige, pink-rose, with and without markings, and those shades nearly but not exactly alike were divided and placed in smaller piles around the table. The more she concentrated, the more intensely she worked, the greater she felt the pressure to hurry. It was as if someone were standing behind her—watching her—urging her on.

When all was divided, she studied each pile.

Under the glare of the bare bulb, the dark and light brown-colored pile seemed to glow. Its soft color beckoned her to begin there. She pulled that mound closer and spread the pieces flat. She chose two. And as she worked, they grew warm in her hands. She slid and twisted and angled them. But they would not come together. She discarded one and chose another, repeating the process several times.

Snap.

Suddenly two became one.

She stared at the joined pieces. She couldn't tell what they formed.

She picked a new piece from the pink-rose group, angling, turning it this way and that. What she couldn't fit, she discarded. She continued to try to fit other pieces. One from here, one from there. And ...

Snap.

Two more matched the other two. Four became one.

She leaned back and studied the section: a brown circle with white in an almond shape, surrounded by light brown with a black arch. A black arch over an almond shape with a brown circle, surrounded by white.

She studied and studied and ...

An eye.

The black arch was an eyebrow. The brown circle was an iris. The almond-sized shape was the upper and lower lids surrounded by coffee-cream flesh.

As she watched, the colors deepened.

Slowly the curved, jigsaw seams began to fuse until they disappeared, leaving no trace of the cardboard edges.

A black fringe of lashes grew and curled as the softened lid quivered slightly over the iris.

It blinked.

She froze.

No. I must have blinked.

The eye blinked again and gazed back at her from the table.

Her body pounded with shock, confusion, disbelief. It wanted to take flight. *I'm going crazy.*

Her brain answered. *Don't run. Calm down. Stay put. Remember: fear not.*

She closed her eyes and rubbed her temples and the back of her neck and shoulders. She commanded her heart to stop pounding and her body to stop trembling. After several deep breaths, she opened her eyes and looked at the puzzle.

The lids were wide open. The lashes quivered. A film of moisture grew into a large tear that spilled over the lower lid. It trickled from the left corner of the eye and ran down the outer edge of the piece and onto the table. Another tear followed with a blink. And another. Soon a small puddle of tears pooled on the table.

She understood tears. In the last months she had shed plenty of them—enough to fill the Atlantic and Pacific. She felt a kinship with those tears from whoever was in the puzzle.

I'm not crazy. I did hear her speak.

The eye blinked. Another tear ran onto the table.

"Oh, please don't cry. You must stop or you'll soak the cardboard and ruin yourself."

Immediately she thought, *That was a dumb reason to tell someone to stop crying. A person isn't made of cardboard. A person has feelings.*

"I believe you are real," she said. "Don't worry, I'll put you together as fast as I can."

The eye winked twice and closed.

She realized she had been answered.

With trembling fingers, she dried the area with the dish towel, being extra careful around the cardboard edges. And after she did this, the eye opened and looked at her.

She still couldn't quite believe.

"This really is happening, isn't it?" she asked herself more than she asked the eye.

It winked twice and then remained open.

Whoever it belonged to understood her perfectly.

Fascinated, she watched the eye watching her. Occasionally it blinked as a normal eye would.

"The rest of you has to be in the puzzle."

It winked twice.

"Well, I guess I'd better get to work if I'm going to find out who you are."

Very slowly the lid lowered over the iris.

She understood. "I don't know what you look like, but I'll try to be fast."

Because she knew the coffee-cream was flesh and the exact shape and color of the other eye, she quickly found and snapped together the left eye. She placed it close to the right one but did not join them because the bridge of the nose was missing.

She watched in amazement as the black fringe of the lashes grew and curled. The lid quivered, and the left eye blinked in unison with the right.

With the two eyes looking back at her, she became aware of how lovely they were. Their almond shapes were soft and feminine. And the eyes seemed to sparkle with warmth and appreciation.

The nose was harder to find. She couldn't tell by the shape of the eyes what the nose was like. Suddenly finding the nose seemed like the most important thing in her life. And when she finally snapped the pieces in place, and heard the sharp intake of air—*inhale, exhale*—and saw the nostrils flare with each regular breath, she felt a victorious thrill.

Spurred by success, she immediately sought the mouth. But it wasn't in the flesh-colored mound. She looked over the various colored piles.

Lips are pink.

From the pink-rose, she slid and turned and angled. And just as suddenly, the lips came together. She pressed them under the nose.

And waited.

"Say something."

Every nerve in her body tingled with excitement.

The lips remained fixed.

"Why don't you speak? Tell me who you are."

Chapter 3

Black hole

"Carolyn, you know what time it is?"

From above the open trap door, Mr. Reed's question shot through her like a bullet. "It's late. Eunice told me to get you."

"Don't come in here!" she shouted. "I'll be up in a minute."

Panic-stricken, she threw the lid over the face.

"Better get goin' *now*."

Gram would be furious. She had forgotten to write a note explaining where she was and why—something she had sworn she would always do.

As his footsteps receded, she picked up the lid.

The seams had reappeared. The partial face had turned back into an ordinary cardboard section of joined puzzle pieces.

But when she touched that section, it was soft and warm and the colors deepened.

She would think about it later. She had to leave.

Before she opened the kitchen door, she smelled the stink of burned tuna and noodles. "Oh, shoot," she mumbled. "I forgot to turn off the oven."

She watched Eunice bent over the oven, vigorously scrubbing the blackened crusts with a knife. The ragged hem of her yellow striped housecoat touched the linoleum as she shifted her thin, frail legs around the oven door. Out from a bun at the back of her neck stuck long copper hair pins. A few long strands of blonde hair streaked with gray escaped to curl over the frayed collar.

"Where have you been?" Eunice fired the question without looking up while increasing her attack on a stubborn burned spot.

"I forgot the time. I'm sorry."

"You forgot more than the time."

"I know. I'm sorry about dinner."

"You know very well you're never to leave this house without letting me know where you are going."

"I know. But I wanted to work on the puzzle ... and I found a place where I could do it ... and I forgot the time."

Eunice slammed the door shut.

"I'm very angry with you, Carolyn. You broke your promise to me. You ruined dinner and made a mess for me to clean up." She squirted detergent into the hot water filling the sink. "If I have to buy a new dish, you'll do a lot of extra work around here, young lady."

Carolyn held her breath. She recognized those gray, almost black storm cloud eyes. *I'll do anything you want, just let me keep working on the puzzle.*

"I know what you're going through, Carolyn, but that doesn't excuse you from your responsibilities. I gave you that puzzle hoping it would cheer you up ... give you something to do. You haven't made much of an effort to get to know anyone at school." Eunice sighed. "Frankly, I don't know what to do with you ..."

Here it comes.

"I don't want to confine you. You spend far too much time in your room as it is ..."

Whew. Just slid into major cool. I can still work it.

"However, there are consequences to wrong actions. Tomorrow you will scrub the oven ... and wash ... and polish everything else in this kitchen until it shines. Do you understand?"

"Yes'm."

"And this will never happen again, right?"

Be really, really sorry. If she gets an inkling of how easy the punishment is, she'd change it. Besides, I'm guilty. I did forget.

"I'm really sorry about dinner ... and everything. Anything I can do?"

"What happened to your face?"

"Huh?" And then she remembered.

"Oh, it's nothing."

"Did you fall?"

"Yeah."

"Well?"

She recognized the tone. An explanation had to be forthcoming.

"It happened in gym class. I was running and I slipped." She shrugged. "It's nothing. It's okay."

"No, it isn't. Dr. Snider's shoes will have to do for awhile longer. You know, money doesn't grow on trees."

"I know. It doesn't matter."

"Yes it does. I was young once. I know how important it is to be like the girls in your class. I want you to feel good about yourself."

Change the subject. Get her to think about something else.

"You make the best molasses oatmeals in the world. Mr. Reed loves your cookies. He wanted me to thank you."

Eunice's voice was sharp. "I wondered where they went. Next time, ask me before you give them all away. I don't mind your sharing. I do mind your leaving none for us. And don't forget to ask him for the plate back. Tomorrow I'm cleaning Mrs. Anderson's house, so I won't have time to get it before dinner tomorrow night."

"I'm sorry. I wasn't thinking. I wanted to do something nice for him."

Eunice put her hand on Carolyn's shoulder. "I know. Next time, just leave some for us."

She turned Carolyn around with a gentle shove. "Go set the table. Get out the eggs and sausages I've been saving."

Eunice took a frying pan out of the cabinet. Soon the delicious smell of spicy, sizzling meat erased the burned fishy odor.

Carolyn watched her expertly crack an egg with one hand, cleanly splitting the shell in half. The yolk and white neatly slid down the side of the pan.

Six eggs later and not a broken yolk or a shell fragment.

"Gram, you could get a job as short-order cook," she said, handing her a fork. "You'd make a lot more money than house cleaning for Mrs. Anderson."

"I'm too old to work in a hot kitchen all day. And cooking for three is different than cooking in a restaurant." With the fork, Eunice whipped the eggs into a froth and rotated the pan so the eggs cooked up the sides.

"After you put the bread and butter on the table, go upstairs and get Jimmy. Tell him dinner's ready."

"Jimmy!" she yelled.

"Honestly, Carolyn. Why can't you do what I ask?"

He came into the kitchen, drying his wet hair with a towel. Wavy strands dripped water down his freckled cheeks onto his wide shoulders.

"Man, that smells good. "

"Go back upstairs," Eunice commanded. "Finish drying your hair and put on a shirt. Your mother taught you better than to come half-naked to the dinner table."

Later in bed, Carolyn dreamed a giant, glistening centipede with countless legs was chasing her around an ice-coated track. Its head was a snake, mouth open, fangs ready to sink into her flesh. Desperately she tried to run away. But her feet were like lead. In slow motion it kept coming closer, closer ... Her left foot slipped. Down, down she tumbled, into a bottomless black hole.

Her body jerked her awake. She gasped for breath, her heart pounding.

She felt Jimmy's hand on her shoulder. "Hey, sis, take it easy."

She groaned, "Oh, I'm so sorry. It was my fault."

He patted her. "It ain't nobody's fault. It was an accident. You were dreaming. Try to get some shut-eye. I've got early practice tomorrow. Give us both a break and go to sleep."

She heard his cot creak as he rolled over.

Sleep?

The day's events and questions rolled and heaved like the sea in a hurricane through her mind. *Why did they have to die? Why does bro' hate me? Who's behind the eyes? Escape to what?*

She punched her pillow flat and covered her head. *Why is my life such a mess?*

Finally, hours later, she fell asleep.

Chapter 4

Gazellia

The light of dawn cracking through the Venetian blinds on the window woke her. The house was quiet.

Jimmy and his football gear were gone.

It would take only a few minutes to make sure the puzzle was okay. Guessing what the weather was like outside, she slipped on her brown sweater and heavy denims for warmth. Shoes and Velcro ankle wrap were next.

The air was crisp. The birds were chattering and singing.

Behind Mr. Reed's duplex she opened the cellar door and remembered the two cement block steps. With hands outstretched in the dark, carefully she inched her feet down the dirt floor. She judged correctly the distance to the bulb chain. She stood on the chair and pulled it. She could see exactly where she had left off. The printed eyes, nose, and mouth were in the same position.

She stared, hoping—

The seams didn't disappear.

She sighed. Yesterday she believed a miracle could be possible. Yesterday there was someone in the puzzle. There was someone who needed her. Like herself, there was someone waiting to be freed.

Now she wasn't so sure. The puzzle looked like any other she and her mother had once worked on.

She sighed again. Loneliness and the terrible day must have taken a toll on her mind.

Listlessly she pushed a coffee-cream piece back and forth. For the longest time she stared at the multicolored piles she had painstakingly sorted the afternoon before. It really had all come from her imagination. But that doesn't make it a bad puzzle, she finally decided. Just enjoy it for what it is.

Before she closed the cellar door, she looked back at the partial face.

"See you later. Gotta keep my promises to Gram."

By 11:00 a.m. the linoleum was waxed, the cabinets cleaned, the silverware polished, and the glasses shined. The table was set for dinner and the fruit basket filled. She was done.

The late morning sun streamed into the cellar and warmed the dirt room. The atmosphere was considerably more pleasant than at dawn.

For the next two hours she slid and turned pieces, chose and discarded. Successful on occasion, she pressed into place several coffee-cream pieces. She filled in cheeks, chin, and forehead. The oval face of a young woman in her midtwenties emerged. Her full pink lips were perfectly balanced by her large, almond-brown eyes. The face was complete except for her hair.

She guessed by the woman's eyebrows that her hair must be in the brown-black pile. It didn't take long before she laid a braided crown of black hair into its correct place.

She returned to the coffee-cream pile for the neck. And because she was familiar with each piece from that pile, she quickly assembled and connected it to the chin.

The head and neck were finished.

Carolyn relaxed. She propped her elbows on the table and studied the face.

It wasn't beautiful by TV-model-star standards, but it was lovely. She had seen ladies' faces like it in classical paintings in an art museum on a school trip. Some of the women in the paintings had Egyptian-looking features, others had European. But the face in the puzzle had a combination of beauty that could not be defined by continent or culture. She was a blending of all that was natural and beautiful—but not from any specific country that Carolyn had ever seen.

She wondered if the face was part of a larger scene. Perhaps the puzzle picture was a copy from an old master. There might be others in the puzzle. Was this the face of a maid or of a royal lady?

While she pondered this question, the seams began to fade and the colors of the print deepened. The lashes grew and curled, lids quivered, and the brown eyes sparkled. Within the flat cardboard a lovely three-dimensional face came alive. The braided head moved. The full lips moved. "Mademoiselle, be not afraid—"

Carolyn reacted like a hand touching a hot iron. She jumped away, tipping the chair backward onto the dirt floor.

"What you are beholding is true. I am not an apparition." The voice was sweet, melodious. "Come, sit yourself down. We must continue our quest to restore my person."

Awestruck, speechless, Carolyn stood trembling as she stared at the moving head in the puzzle. Very carefully she touched the face.

The flat cardboard yielded slightly under her fingertips. Unaffected, the head tilted and moved as if its 3-D image was projected from somewhere inside the table top.

"Mademoiselle Carolyn, your touch is as light as a hummingbird's wings. My choosing you is fortuitous. Come. Continue your work."

"How do you know my name?" She was surprised her dry lips could form the question.

"My dear, remiss I am." The head tilted forward. "Good manners must prevail. I am Gazellia."

"Uh ... what?"

"G-a-z-e-l-l-i-a. Think of a gazelle and then add an *ee yah*." The melody slowed with each syllable. "Guh-zell-ee-yah."

"Gazellia," Carolyn repeated feebly.

"Say it with confidence."

"Gazellia."

"*Très bien*. That has a firm ring to it."

"What a weird name."

"Fleet as a gazelle, I am. Thus, my name."

"How do you know my name?"

"A truthful tale of woe without considerable earth time to answer. Know this, Mistress: the speed with which you restore my person, thus shall your question be answered."

"But ... like, who are you? You speak French and a funny kind of English. Where do you come from? How did you get in there?"

Gazellia smiled. "After I am together explain I will, what I can. Of utmost importance is the rest of my body. *Carpe diem*."

Carolyn righted the chair and sat down.

"Well, you can start by telling me what the rest of you looks like. Like, you know, describe yourself. Are you sitting? Standing? What are you wearing?"

"Prisoner I am by command. Knowledge of my body in this confinement is unavailable to me."

Carolyn leaned forward. "You can't you feel where you are ... where your body is?"

"Not until I am all in place."

"But, then ... you must be a mechanical doll ... or machine ..."

Gazellia's smile was gone. Her nostrils flared, her eyes flashed. "Must you impose more suffering upon me by accusing me falsely? Must every question be answered before I am set free?"

"I just wanted to know about—"

"Fully human I am. I am a preserved, Baal contract-maintained, earth-born-human. I am more than four hundred years old. I am in service to MV Enterprises, Incorporated. At present, the history of my imprisonment will not be disclosed."

Carolyn's mind reeled. Four hundred years old ... under Baal contract ... something about MV. What was that?

Then she remembered the parchment warning: "Beware of the Baal contract."

"But you really didn't answer—"

"*Regardez*. Consider ... your comprehension of the who and why of me is no greater than before. Your first task is to put me together. I shan't reveal more until you do."

What Carolyn heard was unmistakable: no questions, no argument.

But how fast can I work? Hundreds of pieces remain.

"I don't know how long it will take me. Yesterday I spent hours just doing your eyes, nose, and mouth. I'm not very fast. I don't think—"

"Mistress Carolyn, you must abandon delays. Time is of the essence for both of us."

By midafternoon, Carolyn still hadn't been able to join one to another. Her seat was numb, her back stiff sore. Her stomach growled.

She stood, stretching her arms above her head.

"What hinders your work?"

"I'm tired and hungry."

"You have put forth great effort these last hours."

"Can't seem to get anything to fit."

"Some food and a short rest should refresh you. In an hour you will return, ready to begin again." She nodded. "You have my leave to depart."

But as Carolyn closed the trap door, she thought, *Hey, don't count on me doing any better. I've tried every piece, every which way I can think of. It's impossible to put you together in one day. Two weeks, maybe three—that's more like it.*

Back at the kitchen table, she rested her numb left leg on the opposite chair seat. The thousand jabbing needles were beginning to leave. With a tired sigh, she unscrewed the lid of the peanut butter jar and automatically knifed out the sticky butter. She slapped it in the center of a slice of bread, rolled it up, and took a bite from its end. Then she remembered the milk. It was in the fridge. She would have to get up.

Forget it, she decided. It wasn't worth the effort. She took a McIntosh apple from the fruit basket on the table. The moisture in the apple would have to do against the sticky peanut butter. In a few minutes the soothing mixture and her exhaustion combined into a potent drug she couldn't resist. I'll just rest my head on the table for a minute.

"Hey, sis."

His words came through a thick fog to register in her brain.

"Kitchen looks great." He shoved aside the place settings and dumped his gym bag and helmet next to her.

Should I tell him?

"You look beat. You okay?"

He picked up her apple and took a large bite.

"Didn't get much sleep last night, that's all. And I'm tired. Like ... too many things been happening to me lately."

"Like what?"

She shrugged. "Oh, nothing."

"You sure?" He pushed her leg off the chair and sat down.

"Do you really want to know?"

"I asked you, didn't I?"

"Well ... it's that darn puzzle."

"Yeah? What about it?"

She gave him a long, searching look. *Take a chance.*

"It talks to me."

"What?"

She saw his face register a mix of *maybe you're lying, but maybe not?*

"I know it's hard to believe, but it's true."

"Aw, come on." He stopped chewing and frowned at her.

"It *is*. The puzzle is a she with a beautiful face and black hair, she's hundreds of years old, and her name is Gazellia."

"You got brain drain."

"Do not. Why would I make up such a story? I can prove to you that she's real."

"Oh, sure. Uh, huh." He got up. "That I'd like to see."

"But I can prove it. Come on. I'll show you."

He followed her into the cellar.

She pointed to the head on the table. "See, there she is."

He peered at the flat section.

"Pretty, all right. But she looks like an ordinary puzzle."

"Young sir, ordinary I am not."

He gasped. Like a bullet fired from a gun, he was out the door and gone.

"Jimmy, wait!" Carolyn yelled. "She needs our help."

She turned to the 3-D face. "I'll be right back."

Carolyn slammed the kitchen door hard and glared at him leaning against the counter. "Man, are you a rabbit ... or what?"

"I ain't getting into any voodoo witches brew. You can take that invitation, if you want." He slipped his right arm through the neck strap of his helmet. "Count me out of your kind of trouble."

"Listen." She grabbed his arm to keep him from reaching the gym bag. "Just give me a minute and listen."

He looked at the kitchen clock. "Okay. One minute."

"Look, I know I've been difficult as a sister for some time. But really, I think with your help we could find out what this person ... this female wants. Remember, Gram gave me the puzzle. And Gram would never give me anything that would be harmful in any way. Right?"

"Not buying what you're sellin'."

She crossed her arms the way her mother used to whenever matters were to be taken seriously. *Give it your best shot. Use the absolutely right adult words.*

"Think of it this way. We would all benefit greatly should we discover a phenom of some kind. We are a family. Let us work to benefit everyone who lives here."

"You're full of it. You ain't Mother."

"Come on, bro. I need your help. What've you got to lose?"

"Plenty. Like I want to mess with a spook?"

"Big cheese in a freeze. Big cheese in a freeze," she sing-songed.

His face flushed. "Cut it out!"

"Gimmie some scissors," she sang.

"Not funny."

"You're just scared."

"Am not."

"I dare you to come back with me."

She rubbed one index finger over another, pointing them at him. "Wait 'til I tell everybody at school you're a coward over a puzzle."

"Oh, yeah. And who do you know that I'd care about what you'd say?"

She realized she didn't have an answer to his question. She didn't know anyone he knew. In fact, the only one she knew was Yolanda. And no way would she tell her she had a brother. Might lead to something icky-sticky between them two. Bro and Yo—how yucky *that* would be. She took a deep breath. Stay cool, like it's not important.

"Okay." She shrugged. "You win. Like I said, all you care about is football and girls."

She shoved his helmet and gym bag off the table, sending the peanut butter jar and knife skittering across the linoleum.

"Hey!"

In her mother's tone, she said, "You know better than to put your stuff there."

Like a surgeon placing instruments, she rearranged the place mats, plates, and silverware.

"Gazellia is no ghost. She said she's a prisoner. I, for one, want to find out why. Aren't you the least bit curious?"

Spreading her fingers, she measured precisely the distance each water glass was to the left of the plate.

"What a story you could tell your girlfriends if you freed her. And, you'd get more publicity than if you'd won the state championship all by yourself. Think about that."

Carefully, she picked up the peanut butter lid from the floor.

Bro and Yo—not a bad idea after all. Might go for it.

"There is somebody who might think you're real terrific. She's in some of my classes. Real, real pretty and an athlete, a kinda jock like yourself. But not a jock. Classy girl. Now *she* would be *impressed* not by your biceps but by something so sci-fi spectacular, that is, *if* you'd help me free some four-hundred-year-old lady … and when you'd introduce sci-fi lady to your new girlfriend, how could any classy girl resist you?"

He bent down. "Here, let me help you." He scooped up gobs of peanut butter and glass with the knife and deposited the mess in the garbage can under the sink.

"See, that's what I want. Your help. And … you'd be a hero. Think of the media blitz. Facebook. YouTube. A movie, maybe. Money in it, maybe."

His gray eyes scanned her. "Ya' think?"

"Why not? Hey, I'd let you take all the credit."

His hand reached across the table to hers. "You gotcha yourself a deal. I'll help you, you'll help me."

Chapter 5

together

In the cellar, Carolyn looked down at Gazellia's angry, pinched face.

"You are not as I had hoped. You abandoned me to wait in this accursed state for hours."

"Who are you?" Jimmy asked.

"Master Jimmy, no explanation will be forthcoming until I have been freed."

He leaned on the table to steady himself. "How do you know my name? No one has said my name."

"Yeah, I did, when you high-tailed it out the door," Carolyn reminded him.

"Oh … yeah."

"He's my brother."

"Ah. Très bien." The lips became a full curve upward. "Time is of the essence. You may proceed."

"I'll work from the other side of the table," he said.

For the next three hours, they were a successful team. One by one, the sections grew larger and larger. Pink-beige with curving white streaks became a lacy bodice. The lacy bodice was attached to a skirt made of yards of sheer, silky pink-cream chiffon. Flowing pink chiffon sleeves fitted and covered parts of arms that snapped into graceful hands.

In front of Gazellia's face she held up a section that seemed unrelated to any part on the table. "What's this?"

"That is my foot."

"It doesn't look like a foot."

"It is in a toe shoe."

"You're a ballerina?" Jimmy asked.

Gazellia nodded. "*Oui.* If you would be so kind as to connect both, I would be most grateful."

He snapped the left toe shoe to her ankle. Within seconds, he attached the other one. Except for several background and edge pieces, her body lay in three large sections.

"We're almost done," he said.

He gathered the scattered left-over pieces into a small pile.

"Excellent. *Merci, mes amis.*"

Easily, Carolyn joined the upper and lower body. Ever so gently she slid the head closer to the rest of Gazellia's body and pressed it onto her shoulders.

For a second the seams reappeared. As though stuck in a single frame in 3-D, Gazellia stood *en pointe* in an *arabesque*. Another second's pause, and all the seams fused. The colors deepened. Ever so slightly, her left leg lifted higher behind her. Slowly she arched upward from the waist. Her graceful arms waved skyward. Spread fingers curved like feathers. The gossamer pink-cream chiffon began to move. Swiftly she turned. And as she did, her chiffon skirt became a pink froth fluttering in a wind she created as she spun.

She rose and dipped, twirled and jumped in an ever-increasing complexity of steps. And as she danced, her limbs lengthened. She grew taller, larger. The butcher block table creaked and jiggled under her full weight. The wind from her whirl caused the chain to swing inches above her head.

Suddenly she leaped from the table, alighting on the dirt floor as buoyant as a loose pink feather. In a classic ballet curtsy—arms open, head tilted, right leg slightly bent and positioned directly behind the left—she regarded them with the assurance of a well-done performance.

A stunning silence followed. Carolyn didn't realize she had held her breath until it whooshed past her lips. She looked at Jimmy who stood transfixed, his mouth open and his pupils gray pools of shock.

This was no ghost—but flesh and blood. A gorgeous ballerina with dark flashing eyes and slender, graceful limbs stood in front of them.

"Whoa! Total awesome," Carolyn cheered, clapping wildly until her hands stung.

Fingers against his front teeth, Jimmy whistled again and again.

"Merci. Thank you," Gazellia acknowledged with a deep curtsy. "Wonderful it is to be whole."

"You're wonderful. How do you do it?"

She laughed. "With practice, Mademoiselle."

"Not the dancing," Jimmy said. "The way you grew. You went from a flat puzzle of eighteen inches to a woman almost six feet tall. Just how did you do that?"

"By the power of love. I regained my normal height because I was freed by the person I believe the Laurel Crown chose."

He scratched his head. "I don't understand."

"Limited you are by lack of knowledge."

"Inform me. I put you together."

For a moment, Gazellia hesitated, her body stiffened with tension.

"Mistress, Master, duty bound I am not to break the legal clauses of my contract. The endangerment to my life and limb ... and my return to MV Enterprises hinges on my discretion to keep my promises."

"What are you talking about?" he asked.

Carolyn elbowed him. "Can't you see she's upset?"

"I want to know who she is. What's wrong with that?" He ran his fingers through his hair in frustration. "At least tell us who you are."

"Yes, Mistress, Master. I can reveal the history of myself."

"Can you forget the Mad-mo-sell, Mistress, Master stuff?" Jimmy asked.

"However impolitely you have spoken, I shall be gracious to address you both by your familiar names. Do you wish me to continue?"

"Oh, yes ... please," Carolyn said.

From under her silk bodice, she pulled out a gold chain. Its links were small and fine. At its end dangled a round gold pendant.

After she scooped the yards of chiffon under herself, she sat on the table. Slowly, she creased the silk on her lap, making a series of chiffon pleats—her face solemn.

"Oui," she said finally, sliding the pendant on the chain back on forth. "'Tis safe to tell this part."

"I was born a peasant's daughter in the year 1571, somewhere in the Rhone Valley in France. I do not know the exact month."

"How can you celebrate your birthday if you don't know the month?" Carolyn asked.

Gazellia chuckled. "Mon amie, at the time of my birth, the month was, how do you say, immaterial. It was *très importante* that I lived. My mother died at my birth."

"Sorry, I didn't know." Carolyn frowned. "But if you didn't have a mother, who took care of you?"

"My father. He was a tenant farmer who worked in a vineyard to gather another man's grapes. He did the best he could until I was seven years old. Then—"

"We lost our mom too," Carolyn interrupted. "And our dad."

"Hey," Jimmy said. "Let her get on with it. It's *her* I want to know about. You can tell about us later."

"Sorry," Carolyn said. "Please go on."

"Then in that year there was a mistrial ... a cold wind that brings a sudden freeze to the crops. The grapes were destroyed. *Mon Dieu,* it was a terrible winter. Many starved to death. My father knew I would not survive 'til spring. He decided to leave me at the convent of Sainte Clare. There, I would be fed and cared for."

"I know what a convent is, but what's a Sainte Clare?" Carolyn asked.

"They are nuns with a special calling ... a type of organization which was founded in France centuries ago."

"Did your father come to visit you when things got better?" Carolyn asked.

"I never saw him again."

"How awful. You were in a kinda prison, abandoned just like me," Carolyn said.

"You lie. Gram and me, we do everything for you." Jimmy jerked his thumb at Carolyn. "Don't believe her. She's no prisoner."

"Well, I feel stuck like one."

"Miss Pity-Party. That's you. That's all you—"

"Mon Dieu," Gazellia waved her hands at them. "I thought you desired to know about me."

"Yeah, you're right," he said. "Go on."

"At the convent, the Sainte Clare nuns were kind and I learned to love them. They taught me to read and write. Though the work in the fields was hard, at one point I considered becoming a Poor Clare. But I did not."

"How come?" Carolyn asked.

She smoothed out the creases she had made in the chiffon.

"Because one cold March night, Lady Francoise entered my life and changed it forever."

Carolyn lightly cleared her throat. "Um, can I ask some questions? I mean, not to interrupt or anything. But ... You know you really are ... I mean take time getting used to."

Gazellia smiled. "Oui, mon amie. Expecting too much too soon for you both, perhaps. You may ask, since you have done so politely."

"Okay," Carolyn said. "Who is Lady Francoise?"

"She was a distant cousin of Gaspard de Coligny who was assassinated by Henri Duke de Guise at a wedding feast. A bitter religious and civil war commenced, killing thousands."

"Man," Jimmy said. "Not a good start for a marriage."

"She was not the one who was killed. Gaspard was because of religious differences."

"Sounds a lot like what we have today," Jimmy said. "But we're supposed to accept one another, aren't we?"

"Oui. But acceptance or respect for another, not always a human trait."

"What did this lady, whatever her name is, have to do with you?" Carolyn asked.

"Lady Francoise. Never shall I forget her name. For twelve years she had fled from religious persecution because of that name ... though she forsook royal politics or any of the strife raging in France."

"So, she was innocent? Right?" Carolyn asked.

"Oui. She was." Gazellia rubbed her forehead. "Please, let me continue."

"Sorry," Carolyn said.

"I think I was about eighteen years old when she beat on our convent doors. She begged the sisters for sanctuary. And for several months they hid her in the bell tower until Henry of Navarre, who later became King Henry IV of France, offered her protection and a home."

"So she was really like, in prison," Carolyn said.

"'Tis true. My heart reached out to her during those months in the bell tower. So sad, so lonely she was. It was my duty to serve her meals and we became friends. She told me about Paris court life ... its pageantry, its music and art, its gossip and intrigue, and the lords and ladies of royalty and wealth ... before her troubles began."

"Living in the past," Jimmy said, "never gets you anywhere. Best to move on and not look back."

"Hey, bro. That's easy for you to say. Nothing happened to you."

"Oh, yeah, you—"

"Mes amis, could you not stop arguing for a few minutes?"

"Yeah, sorry," Jimmy said. He elbowed Carolyn. "We won't again."

"Oui. I continue. Wondrous were her stories. Convent life paled in comparison. I felt stifled and ignorant. She promised if ever her fortunes were restored in Paris, she would send for me."

"In 1589, when King Henry IV brought religious tolerance and peace to France, he invited Lady Francoise back into his court.

"You must have missed her. I know how it feels to lose your friends," Carolyn said.

"Then perhaps, my dear, you will understand what it is to long for a better life. After she left the convent, I dreamed of nothing else but her promise for five long years. I was twenty-three when she sent for me to be her personal maid."

"I bet you were excited," Carolyn said.

"Thrilled, my dear. The day I left the convent is etched in my memory. It was warm, sunny ... a good omen for my glorious adventure ahead. But the sisters fussed over my decision."

"Why wouldn't they be happy for you?" Carolyn asked.

"They warned me I was not suited for what they termed 'the worldly life.' But my mind was set on my dreams."

"I think that's cool," Carolyn said.

Gazellia smiled. "They must have thought it *cool* also, because at my departure they presented me with this gold medallion."

The light from the bulb reflected gold orbs on the dirt walls.

"It's beautiful," Carolyn said.

"It must be worth a lot," said Jimmy. "You said they were poor."

"'Tis true, poor by choice they were as nuns. Withal, when a maid chooses convent life, a dowry is required as a token of her promise in marriage to God. A few Poor Clares rejected their wealth for a life of poverty and chastity. Hence some of their dowry gold was melted to provide this keepsake given to me with their love."

She tenderly rubbed the medallion.

"'Tis priceless beyond gold value. Its words are my protection."

She leaned over to show it to them.

"Regardez, on the one side, the date I came to Sainte Clare, and the words in French meaning 'Never forget us.' And on the other side in Greek, "He agape nikai panta." In over four hundred years I have never taken it off."

"Wait, I know those funny words," Carolyn said. "They're on this piece of paper." She pulled off the lid and unfolded the parchment. "What do those words mean?"

Gazellia cupped the medallion inside her palms and bowed her head. "It translates: 'Love conquers all things.'"

She lifted the medallion, kissed it, and held it up to the light. "Regardez the engraving of Laurel leaves underneath the words."

Carolyn squinted at the design. "It looks like a crown."

"Oui, the sisters of Sainte Clare passed down its legend. They believed it to be true."

"What legend?"

"Hold it," Jimmy said. "Let's not get off the track here. What about the warning?"

Carolyn handed Gazellia the paper. "Written right there," she said, "is the warning, 'Beware of the Baal contract.'"

"Upon my soul, I do not know the mystery of how the parchment came into your hands. It is a warning I did not heed. Thus my predicament. It need not concern you."

"Aw, come on," Jimmy said. "Let's have it all. The whole story. Yours and the paper." He pointed to the pieces on the table. "Without me, you'd still be in there."

Gazellia nodded and slipped the medallion under the chiffon, yet kept her fingers pressed against it. "Life in court was beyond what I had imagined. For two years I lived in the palace and served Milady."

Carolyn saw Gazellia's lips quiver slightly. She's holding something back.

"You can tell us your secrets. I think you're beautiful … and …" Carolyn looked at Jimmy. "Whatever you say, will stay with us, we promise. Right, bro?"

"Depends on what she says. Anything spooky gets told above ground."

Gazellia smiled. "I do not think you would be able to convince anyone of my story, Jimmy. It is not for you I have come. I have come for Carolyn."

"What?" Carolyn said. "What do you want with me?"

Gazellia pointed to Carolyn's feet. "You have an injury that can be healed. It is a promise from the legend of the Laurel Crown. I have come to take you to your destiny. Freedom from fear and pain."

"There's no way my sister is going anywhere with you." Jimmy shook his index finger in front of Gazellia. "And if anyone is going anywhere, it's you going back where you came from."

Gazellia gently pushed his hand away from her face. "A caring brother would want his sister to be free, just as I hope to be when we both return to prove the legend."

"It's confusing … I don't know what to think … believe … I mean …" Carolyn frowned. "What or who are you? Why me? How did you get into the puzzle? Why should I go with you?"

"Because, my dear, what you have hoped for, longed to have again, is love. The legend promises a love that can conquer all things. And the knowledge of this love, this power, belongs to the one who can learn the secret of the Laurel Crown."

"But … I don't know how to figure out my own life. I mean … so … why me?" Carolyn asked.

Gazellia stood and shook out the creases in the chiffon. "Helpful it might be to share one more part of my story with you. Then perhaps you will believe I understand your heart and desire to live your life differently." She gently touched Carolyn's shoulder. "A few more moments of patience, I beg you."

Chapter 6

In Prison

"Okay," Carolyn said, "as long as you clue me in to why it's me you're after."

"Because I can understand your pain, mon amie." She pointed to Carolyn's feet. "It all started with shoes."

"Huh?" Carolyn frowned. "What's shoes got to do with do with it?"

Gazellia smoothed a stray hair into a braid. "With your kindness, I shall try to explain.

"At the convent I would wear sandals in the winter to protect my feet from the cold stone floors. Otherwise, I went barefoot. You may observe, I am not a tiny woman.

"Once in court, I was obliged to wear shoes matched to my maid's uniforms. The largest pair of ladies' shoes were two sizes smaller than my feet. They were instruments of torture. Off they came whenever the situation allowed."

Hey, she does understand. "I know what you mean," Carolyn said.

"Thought you might, my dear," Gazellia said. "To go on ... one night there was a grand palace ball. In the royal changing room, the ladies would need wig repairs and fresh gowns for the overnight affair.

"Between changes for Milady, I thought, no harm in my slipping away for a few minutes to catch a glimpse of a handsome count dancing with a countess.

"Down the corridor past many doors, the orchestra was playing. Oh, lovely it was ... the rugs soft under my bare feet as I waltzed closer to the ballroom."

No, she doesn't understand. I can barely walk.

"You could dance on sore feet?" Carolyn asked.

Gazellia nodded. "Watched Milady dance numerous times. I copied whatever moves she made."

"What's the point of all this?" Jimmy asked.

"'Twas a minute in time that changed my life, like any life can be changed in a minute," Gazellia said.

"Yeah, like Mom and Dad," Carolyn said.

"Come on," Jimmy said. "Tell it already."

"Oui. When the music stopped, I heard angry voices coming from down the hall. Lady Francoise was arguing with a man. I pressed my ear to the door and heard her shout, 'King Henry is my Lord Protector! Never would I injure the king. I could not do him such dishonor. I will personally inform His Majesty of your attempt to discredit my good name.'

"When she opened the door, who was more astonished—she or I—I do not know. Milady told me to forget what I heard. Upon my soul, I promised I would.

"One week later at three in the morning, royal guards burst into our apartment. They were led by the man whose voice I heard through the door. He accused us of treason … of plotting against the king. She and I protested, but he wouldn't listen.

"The guards bound and gagged us. They forced us from the royal quarters down into the castle dungeons. We wound around too many stairs … I lost count of the levels. I could hear the rats, see their shadows scurrying over the wet stones away from the lit torches."

"Whoa," Jimmy said. "Now this is getting more interesting."

"Will you stop already," Carolyn said, "and let her tell it?"

Gazellia sighed and closed her eyes. "Merci. Our fetters cut, we were shoved into a tiny cell. We slept on one narrow cot covered with dirty straw.

"Once a day, a bowl of porridge, a bowl of water, and a lit candle were slid through a slot under our wooden door. To keep the days, I marked the wall with sooty wax."

"Uh …" Carolyn started, but she changed her mind. Lips zip.

"In two weeks Lady Francoise fell ill. I nursed her best I could. Mon Dieu, there was naught I could do. Upon the daily ration, I screamed through the slot for a doctor.

"A short time later two guards took Milady out on a stretcher.

"I pleaded … I fought to be taken with her. They shoved me back into the cell."

She wiped her forehead with the edge of her chiffon skirt.

"Dungeon time is endless … without hope. In that rat-infested, filthy hole, I lost reason … longed for a quick death. Then what I thought was a miracle, happened."

She took a deep breath.

"On the other side, I heard tapping … scratching, digging sounds. I used the water bowl to scrape away the dirt between the stones with its sharp edge. My hands bled at first but after three, four days grew calloused.

"At last … a rush of cool air. And a hand reached through the hole. I laughed. I cried. Madly I clutched his hand—"

"His?" Carolyn asked.

"Oui. 'Twas a man's hand. We began to dig frantically to make the hole larger."

"Didn't you say anything? Didn't you ask him who he was?"

"My dear, comprehend my weakness … my terrible physical condition … my desperation. No strength to talk … I was near the end of my existence."

"Sorry." Carolyn felt a hot blush creep up her neck to her cheeks. "I really am dumb."

"Do not concern yourself. My time it was, not yours."

She paused, wiping away a drop of perspiration from her upper lip. "It took us a week to make the hole large enough for him to crawl through—"

"What did he look like?" Carolyn asked.

"What difference does that make?" Jimmy said. "You wanted me to stay out of it. Why don't you do the same?"

"Just curious. That's all."

"He was a few years older than you are now, Jimmy. He told me his name was Claude. He said he had been in the cell next to mine for six months … imprisoned for sorcery."

"He was a witch?" Carolyn asked.

"Men aren't witches," Jimmy said. "They're wizards, right?" He turned to Carolyn and said, "See, it was witchcraft that put her in that puzzle. I told you she was a spook of some kind."

Gazellia's eyes flashed with anger. "I am not a spook, a ghost, or an apparition. The woman who stands before you is a flesh and blood person."

"Yeah. Right." Jimmy's voice was filled with sarcasm. "Come on."

Gazellia held out her hand. "Feel my skin, touch my fingers, young sir."

Jimmy didn't move.

Carolyn reached forward and gingerly rubbed the top of Gazellia's hand. "It's like real."

"Okay," Jimmy said, also touching Gazllia's hand. "Okay, so you're human. For now, I buy it." He let go. "But—"

"Well if that guy wasn't a wizard," Carolyn interrupted, "who was he?"

"Mon amie, in that moment, I cared not who he was. I cared only to be freed." She patted Carolyn's hand. "And, now, grateful I am to be out of prison because of you, my dear. And because of you doing me this most fortunate favor, I shall return the favor by taking you to the most precious, beautiful gift I have ever known ... the Laurel Crown."

She grasped Carolyn's shoulders. "The mysteries of the universe are directed for the outcome of good for those who are chosen to learn that love conquers all things. I believe you are the chosen one I was sent to find. Therefore, now that I am free, we will go to where the crown is waiting for you."

"The only place *my* sister is going is home with me!" Jimmy stood on the cement block in front of the cellar door, his arms across his chest. "Nobody leaves until I say so."

Carolyn felt Gazellia's fingers tightened around her shoulders as her words became more intense, emphatic. "My dear, your brother cares not about what is best for you."

Ya' got that right for sure, Carolyn thought.

"I have come to take you to your destiny. A destiny that will challenge you, inspire you, and make every dream you have ever had come true. I believe you have the key to unlock the secret of the Laurel Crown and free yourself from your prison."

"Hey!" Jimmy yelled, grabbing the inside latch to the door with his right hand. "Nobody leaves without my say so." He shook his left finger at Carolyn. "Don't believe that spook. She's a liar. *She's* the one who doesn't care about you. I do!"

"Mon amie. Look to your future. You can become whatever you desire." Gazellia lightly touched Carolyn's cheeks. "Think, my dear, about walking without pain. Perhaps even dancing. Think about a life so splendid, so filled with new discoveries, you will never be the same. Come with me to a glorious new adventure. Do not be afraid." Her fingers caressed Carolyn's chin. "I have your best interests at heart."

In the pit of her stomach, Carolyn felt a pull of hope.

Escape from her life in a box with her annoying brother. Escape from the rules and regulations of Gram. Escape from the past and her guilt. Move forward into something better, something wonderful—*exciting.*

Carolyn saw Gazellia's eyes become pools of warm chocolate with the promise of sweet surprises. "Mon amie, you have been chosen for greatness. In the land of Double Suns the supernatural will become natural. The possibilities are limitless as to what you can accomplish. Fear not."

"Don't listen to her!" Jimmy yelled, waving his left arm at Carolyn. "Come here! You know you can't do anything without my permission. You're going nowhere. And that's *final.*"

Going nowhere, Carolyn thought. *Nowheresville. That's where I am now. But does it have to be that way? And since when does bro control my life? Or Gram? It belongs to me.*

"What do I have to do?" Carolyn asked.

In two steps, Jimmy grabbed Carolyn's arm. "No way. You're goin' with me. She can go back where she came from." He pulled her away from Gazellia. "We're leavin, now!"

Carolyn wrenched her arm free. "I'm going. And you can't stop me."

"Oui, leave this to me." Gazellia smoothed her bodice and shook out her skirt. "Fear not, Jimmy. Your sister may return to you if she wishes. You cannot keep your sister from her destiny."

Quickly Gazellia lifted her skirt and embraced Carolyn in yards of chiffon.

In less than a blink of an eye, they vanished, leaving the stunned Jimmy standing in the cellar.

Chapter 7

MV Enterprises, Inc.

Carolyn dropped out of the earth and into a silent void. Covered in chiffon, she could feel Gazellia's arms and fabric tight around her. She had no sensation of spinning through space.

"Fear not, Carolyn. I have you."

You're kidding, she thought. *I hate feeling my heart pound.*

"Prepare. We enter. Mon amie, I must let you go."

Carolyn smashed into a hard surface that shattered into a million splinters, stinging her exposed skin like fire ants. Spinning, helpless to swat them away, finally they sailed past her, disappearing into the void.

Suddenly she was pushed down a long, black, furry chute. Over and over she tumbled, finally landing on her back in a clump of tall grass. While her mind roller-coasted, looping upside down and over, she tried to still her churning stomach. Determined not to be sick, she breathed deeply.

The ground felt cool, damp; the grass smelled fresh, green. Like summertime. Brightness poured through her eyelids. She shielded her eyes between a crack of fingers and looked up at two orange discs in a purple sky. The ground seemed to tilt when she tried to get up.

"The land of Double Suns or am I seeing double?"

"'Tis Double Suns."

"Feels like real dirt and grass."

"Oui." Gazellia stood, brushed herself off, and pulled out a couple of dried blades from her hair. "Conditions were duplicated to provide an environment most familiar to humans. On different planets, various surroundings are programmed to provide the right kind of security for other species."

"Other *what?*"

"Species. My dear, surely you know there are galaxies and planets with forms of life elsewhere? Duplication of earth-likeness has been made to specification on Double Suns."

"What'd we crash through?"

"The invisible security dome that protects this valley. One could say we crashed through the back door. For certain, Mauvais knows we have arrived."

The roller-coastering stopped enough for Carolyn to sit up.

"Who?"

"Mauvais. Pronounced, Maw-vay. This is her domain."

As Gazellia leaned down and tightly gripped her hand, Carolyn saw the same sad, haunted look as when she had talked about Lady Francoise.

"Mon amie," she whispered, her voice husky with affection. "Believe my true heart. Believe I care about you. You have freed me, and great hope I have that you shall discover the secret of the Laurel Crown. In my heart of hearts, my hope for true freedom lies in you. And there are others who are waiting to be freed. My survival and yours depend entirely on God's protection and your courage. My dear …" Her fingers tightened. "I beg you … trust me. We have need of each other."

Trust and *need*. Two words with intense meaning. Not even her mother used them to ask for her help. And now, look at who was asking—someone who had lived more than four hundred years. Someone who could dance more beautifully—was more beautiful than anyone she had ever seen. Why *wouldn't I trust her? She doesn't think I'm a loser with a handicap. We got each other out of a trap. My life will change totally because of her.*

She squeezed Gazellia's fingers to assure her she understood.

"Bravo." Gazellia helped Carolyn up. "We shall proceed."

While Carolyn brushed off her denims and pulled her sweater down around her waist, she wondered why Gazellia was nervous. She keeps looking up as though she knows we're being watched. But there's no one around. Just us.

"What's wrong?" Carolyn asked.

"Do not concern yourself. I assure you we will be welcomed."

Out of the cool grass, the suns beat down on Carolyn's fair skin. It was hot and she pushed up her sleeves. With the palm of her right hand shading her eyes, she scanned the horizon. From her position on the grassy knoll, she could see a two-story cranberry-colored brick building in the far distance. On its flat tile roof, a red flag atop a tall pole flapped in the breeze.

She was too far away to read the lettering between the first and second floors. Tall, trimmed shrubs obscured the bottom of the first-floor windows. Surrounding the rectangular building was a high wrought-iron fence. There were letters on each side of the two-story, arched double gate in front of the entrance. Even from a distance, Carolyn could see its ornateness contrasted sharply with the plain red building.

"How far is it?"

"Less than a mile. If you are ready, we will start walking."

"What happened to flying? Why can't we go like we came?"

"I am as mortal as you."

Carolyn had never heard *mortal* used in ordinary conversation. But she knew that word from church. Was Gazellia saying that they could die here? She shivered in the heat. No, she dismissed the frightening question. *I've misunderstood. Gazellia has already lived beyond four hundred years. Didn't she say I've been chosen for greatness? And a minute ago, didn't she ask for my trust? And didn't I give it? What kind of a friend would give her word and so quickly take it back?*

Disgusted with herself, she slapped off the bits of grass clinging to her jeans and sweater. "Yeah, I'm ready," she said.

The hill was steep. And the tall grass hid many holes and rocks. Every time she fell, Gazellia would stop and help her up.

When they reached the arched double-iron gate, she was a wreck. Weed stems and dirt clung to her clothes. And her knuckles were skinned and raw. Her feet burned in her shoes.

Behind the gate, the two-story building was bigger than any downtown bank or library she had ever been in. It towered over shrubs and trees. On one side of the gate, thorny iron branches were forged into a capital M. On the other side, the branches formed a capital V. Several large iron cobras snaked among the branches.

Carolyn licked her sore lips burned by the suns. It was then she realized the sign on the building was in French.

"What does that mean?"

"It translates: 'The School of Special Arts, Lady Mauvais Vallee, director.' Mauvais Vallee is the administrator, principal and director. She supervises all activities and classes. We will be staying here for awhile."

School. Like a bomb, the word exploded in her brain. More hateful girls. A hundred boys like Jimmy. Nobody cares whether I live or die. She recoiled.

"No dumb school. No way. You can't make me go there." She spun around. "Take me back. Now!"

"My dear … mon amie …" Gazellia put her arm around Carolyn's shoulder and gave her a slight hug. "I understand how you must feel." She patted her arm. "Think of it as your new adventure … beginning your new life. And remember what I told you: there is a gift awaiting you."

"You *don't* understand."

"Mistress Carolyn, your new life awaits you." Her voice was sticky, smooth honey. "One beyond any dream you could ever dream. Hot and tired you are because you have walked a long way. Once rested, your good nature will return."

Carolyn felt icky from Gazellia constantly rubbing her shoulder.

"Stop it!" She pushed her hand away. "What's the matter with you? What don't you get about *no?*"

Like an army recruiter in a commercial, Gazellia addressed an unseen audience. "This is a wonderful, magical school. You will be taught special arts, you will see supernatural events, enjoy riches and comfort beyond your imagination. Here at MVE, you will experience all that immortality can give you. Have courage to discover your destiny. *Attendez,*" she cheered, "the universe is yours for the taking. Be all you were meant to be at MVE."

"But—"

The honey was gone. Her voice dropped to a desperate whisper, "My dear, think about a new body. The ugly shoes gone. Think about being more beautiful than any woman you have ever seen. Think about being famous and rich. No worries about money ever again. Think about that. This school will teach you how to achieve all that your heart has ever desired."

Scaredy cat. Pity party. Quitter. Loser. The names Jimmy called her popped up in her mind.

No, I'm not, she answered his voice in her head. *I dreamed about being out of the box. And here I am. What's to keep me from being rich and famous? More gorgeous than Yolanda? Who's there to stop me? Jimmy? He isn't here.* She patted her chest to calm her heart. *Chill girl. Chill.*

"I'll give it a go," she said.

"Excellent. A wise decision."

Gazellia pressed down on a cobra's head.

Both sides of the gates swung smoothly inward into a large formal garden. Junipers, yews, and various evergreens were trimmed in cones and square-shaped hedges. They were planted in a pattern—diagonal, crisscrossed, and parallel to each other.

"Looks like a maze," Carolyn said.

"'Tis that."

She followed Gazellia into the first opening in the hedge. A few steps inside and she was unable to see anything over the high greenery except the path directly ahead.

Whenever Gazellia came to a fork, she didn't hesitate in choosing one. At one particular juncture, there were three choices.

"How do you know which way?"

"Many an hour I have spent walking here, considering my past. Every bush, every hedge heard my prayers, saw my tears asking Milady to forgive me."

"Do you think she did?"

"Mon amie, if there is a heaven, she is there. If the sisters are right, she has forgiven me. 'Tis myself I cannot forgive."

"Yeah, I know what you mean."

High above the hedges adjacent to the building, Carolyn saw a white dome with a black iron weathervane. She pointed to it. "What's that?"

"'Tis the gazebo where the Laurel Crown is encased. At the appointed time, I shall take you there to your destiny."

An adrenaline rush shot through Carolyn's body. "What's wrong with now?"

"Obliged I am to introduce you to my benefactor, the honorable Mauvais." She put her finger to her lips. "Hush, question me no more," she whispered. "First, Mauvais and the school. Then, what shall be, will be."

Okay. Lips zipped.

The hedge path led to a wide sandy courtyard that extended the full length of the building. And from there, cobblestones led directly to the front door.

Triple wide and half again as high as any door Carolyn had ever seen, it was completely mirrored with no hinges, handle, or lock. It reflected them perfectly without its silvered surface catching one glaring ray of the suns.

Beside her, Gazellia squinted into the mirror. Her breath made a ring of moisture on the glass. Quickly she licked a finger and slicked each dark eyebrow.

"Regardez, honorable Mauvais, the fair maid, Mistress Carolyn Farmer. The New One is exceptional. Consider, I have returned. Let us enter."

Carolyn spit on her hand and carefully rubbed around her bruise at the dirty smudge.

With a shock, she suddenly realized the hedges were in front of her. She was on the other side of the mirror looking at Gazellia still peering into the door, not realizing she had been transported. "I'm in here!" she shouted. "I've been—"

"Welcome, New One." The eerie words echoed from all directions at once.

Carolyn spun around into total blackness. She pressed her back hard against the door. A terrible fear overwhelmed her that if she moved one hair's breadth, she would disappear into nothingness—never to be found again.

"I am your host, Mauvais Vallee, the administrator and principal of this school." The vowels slithered endlessly in metallic echoes of sound. "I welcome you as a prospective student and member of my company."

Perspiration stuck Carolyn's sweater to her back. "Where are you?"

"You are not in good condition." The words thundered through unseen walls and ceiling.

Her trembling legs unable to hold her up any longer, Carolyn slid down the glass door.

"You are tired from your long journey. You will be taken to your room where you will rest and recover." It was a command.

"I'm not moving one inch without Gazellia." Carolyn's voice cracked. "Not … not one inch."

She could feel a presence carefully measuring her resistance. She flattened herself against the glass with all her strength.

"We will become better acquainted after you have rested."

A moment later, she felt Gazellia's breath in her ear. "Are you all right, Carolyn?"

She nodded, unable to moisten her lips to reply. *What grand adventure is this? So far, I'm spooked out of my mind. I have to get out of—*

Gazellia put her arm around Carolyn's shoulder. "Have courage, Mistress, your good fortune lies ahead."

The minutes ticked by. Carolyn felt strength returning to her legs and body. Her mouth was wet enough to speak. "I think I'm okay."

"Très bien, my dear." Gazellia placed her hand under Carolyn's arm, lifting her to her feet. "Mauvais, how do you expect us to find our way?"

"You know the way," the voice echoed.

"Oui, but we cannot see it in the dark."

A lit crystal globe, the size of a medium cantaloupe, materialized in front of them. It hovered over their heads, illuminating a grand hall.

"Whoa." Carolyn squinted in the light. Like a high flyer who had missed the trapeze and found the net, she was saved.

"It's a palace."

Carolyn could now see the gilded chairs and tables that lined the hall. The legs, arms of chairs, and tabletop edges were carved with leaves and fruits. They gleamed in the light from the highly polished veneers of walnut, cherry, and mahogany. Atop the tables were numerous porcelains of various periods and countries.

Some carved high-backed chairs were upholstered in green, blue, and gold velvet, others in red silk with the MV logo in black stitching. Oil paintings hung in silver and gold frames on the walls. As the globe rose to lead the way, three immense cut-glass chandeliers glittered like diamonds, their prisms casting miniature rainbows on the high, curved ceiling.

"We are pleased you have decided to accept our hospitality. Follow the light to your rooms."

They followed the globe past three doors. Mounted on each door panel was a polished brass cobra's head. Its mouth open, a brass ring hung from its fangs.

At the fourth door the globe stopped. From the center of the crystal, a ray of light shot out, causing the ring to rap against the door panel three times. Smoothly the door opened into an enormous bedroom. It was decorated in the same elaborate style and with similar furnishings as the hall.

On a raised platform in the center of the room stood a huge four-poster bed with a canopy of red silk. Its tall, walnut carved posts almost touched the curved ceiling. A red silk bedspread hung in rich folds to the floor. In the center of the spread, the letters *MVE* were embroidered in gold and black satin thread. Surrounding the initials were black satin-stitched branches and cobra heads.

"Wow. Will you look at that bed!" said Carolyn.

"I heard it was a gift from King Baal to a princess as a reward for her loyalty."

"A real princess?"

"Truth be told, I am not certain."

"So who cares if it isn't true," said Carolyn. "I, for one, am going to believe a princess slept here. Who else could have owned such a bed?"

"May your sleep be sweet, and blessed may your dreams be."

"You mean ... that is my bed?"

"Oui, mon amie. An honored guest you are for as long as your invitation lasts."

"Really?"

She walked across the green marble floor over the burgundy rugs to the platform. She stepped up, and with arms outstretched, nose-dived into the coverlet. Sinking into the soft, smooth satin, she sighed. "Oh, man, I've never felt anything so beautiful."

Her body melted into the silk. She yawned.

Gently Gazellia shook her. "My dear, sleep must wait. Follow the crystal to your changing room and bathe."

"Do I have to?"

Gazellia nodded and motioned to the crystal.

From where it had been hovering near the ceiling, the globe sailed to illuminate a side door.

With every muscle complaining, she followed the crystal through a dressing room into the main bath. A whiff of roses awakened her tired senses. The fragrant steam filled the bathroom from the water in an old-fashioned, gold-plated tub with claw feet.

She tested the water with a finger. The temperature was perfect. Quickly she undressed and eased her sore body into the warm water. With a tired sigh, she leaned back in the curve of the tub—glad she had given in to Gazellia's order.

The globe hovered several feet above her head as she washed with rose-scented soap and dried herself with a thick, red towel. When she reached for her jeans, the crystal bobbed in front of her face. It moved in such a way that she guessed it wanted her to follow.

In the dressing room it stopped in front of a walnut armoire—a large chest with doors. She opened it and found red silk pajamas exactly her size.

She slipped into the pajamas, picked up her shoes, and limped back into the bedroom.

Gazellia had pulled back the coverlet.

She folded her Velcro wrap inside her left shoe. After placing both shoes on the platform, she climbed into bed. Without a word, Gazellia tucked the white satin sheets around her. Before she was finished, Carolyn was asleep.

Chapter 8

power

Carolyn slid her body against the smooth satin sheets. Every muscle ached. At the sound of her movement, the ball dropped from the ceiling to hover inches in front of her face.

For a moment she didn't know where she was. *I'm dreaming,* she thought as she rubbed her fingers over the silk.

She pressed her nose into the soft feather pillow. The smell of roses engulfed her senses. She took a deep breath. *Umm. How nice. It's not quite like a hug from Mom, but it's close.* She covered her eyes with the back of her hand to shut out the light. *Umm. Go away.*

The crystal grew brighter and continued to bob up and down.

No matter which way Carolyn rolled, she couldn't shut out its light.

"Go away." She tried to wave it off.

"Jimmy, cut it out. Get lost. Not funny."

The light intensified.

"Hey!" she shouted. "Get outta—"

Her eyes flew open. She squinted into the light. *Some alarm clock. Let me turn you off.* As soon as she reached for it, it circled, bobbing around her head, just inches beyond her fingers.

"Okay. Okay. I'm up."

Immediately it dimmed.

"What *do* you want?"

It lifted and soared to a small dining table in the far corner of the room. The table was set with china, silverware, and glasses. A red linen napkin was neatly folded on the dinner plate. The globe bobbed to indicate it wanted her to sit on the high-backed chair.

Suddenly she realized she wasn't just hungry, she was ravenous.

"Great." Her stomach growled in agreement. She sat down, unfolded the napkin, and placed it on her lap. There was nothing on the table but the setting.

She smelled the blueberry pancakes before she saw them materialize on her plate. A six-inch stack of cakes with hot steam rising appeared before her. At the same time, a stick of butter on a silver dish and a silver container of syrup appeared as well. She watched as milk and water filled two glasses from the bottom up.

"Neat trick. Thanks."

Very quickly she spread the butter, poured the syrup over the cakes, and dug in. The butter, hotcakes, and syrup melted in her mouth.

Umm. Good as Gram's? Yeah, maybe even better.

Intent on stuffing pancakes into her mouth, she didn't hear the door swing open and click shut.

Gazellia kissed her lightly on the cheek. "Good morning, my dear. Eight earth hours has made for pleasant dreams, I hope?"

Carolyn nodded, her mouth full. She noticed Gazellia's face was serene, confident as if nothing had upset her the day before.

She had changed from her pink chiffon to a floor-length, sky-blue silk dress. White lace trimmed with sparkling crystals and seed pearls was sewn around the collar, sleeves, and bottom of the full skirt. Blue silk-covered high heeled shoes, embroidered with crystals and pearls, peeked out from under her skirt. Her black braids had seed pearls and crystals intertwined in her hair. The gold medallion hung from her neck. Tiny rainbows and orbs of light danced off the walls and ceiling from the crystals and the medallion.

Carolyn took a swig of milk. "Man, I slept like dead. But now I'm alive. As my mom used to say, 'I'm up and at 'em.'"

"Très bien." Gazellia held out her hand to Carolyn. "Come. It's time to get dressed and then meet the director." She snapped her fingers at the crystal. "Finished we are."

The globe flashed and instantly everything disappeared.

Carolyn patted her stomach. "I hope what's in here doesn't vanish."

Gazellia laughed. "No, mon amie, what is in your innards is permanent."

She snapped her fingers to the crystal. "Clothes for the guest."

Rays flashed over the bedspread. Instantly silk underwear, a white slip, and an ankle-length dress of green satin, trimmed with lace, crystals, and seed pearls, appeared. Beside it appeared a lustrous strand of pearls and a long green silk ribbon. On top of them all lay a wide, white silk sash edged with lace.

Carolyn had never seen a dress so beautiful. She touched the green satin and pearls. Smooth. Soft. Wonderful.

"I will attend you," Gazellia said.

"I've got morning mouth and I need to wash up."

The globe sailed to the bathroom door. A few minutes later, she returned and took off the pajamas. After Gazellia slid the green satin smoothly over Carolyn's arms, she tied the wide sash into a large bow behind her back. Then she pulled the ribbon through Carolyn's blonde curls.

Carolyn fingered the smooth white pearls around her neck. She looked down at her shoes. "Why didn't it make matching shoes for me?"

"I cannot fathom." She stepped back and appraised Carolyn. "Mistress, you are beautiful."

"Let me see."

Carolyn looked around. "How come no mirrors?"

"I cannot answer." Gazellia lifted right arm. "Come, place your hand on mine and walk beside me. Your new life awaits you."

Carolyn took a deep breath. My first step to a new beginning. She placed her left hand on Gazillia's arm. "I'm ready."

The crystal led them down the hall, past several doors, and stopped. The ring in the cobra's head rapped three times and the door swung inward.

Nothing could have prepared Carolyn for the kind of room she entered. It was five times the size of the bedroom. The first half was a sitting room filled with similar ornate furnishings and decorations: carved chairs and tables, brass ornaments and lit candlesticks, paintings in gold frames, fancy bric-a-brac on tables and shelves. And the thorny branches and winding cobras were stitched on red silk wallpaper, window draperies, and table coverings.

At the far end was an aviary. Up through a hole between the M and V in the marble floor tile, an ancient apple tree grew two stories high. Its shiny red apples were like Christmas balls hanging from old gnarled limbs. Live birds darted among the shining green leaves and apples. Finches, swallows, sparrows, cardinals, and doves cooed and called, sang and cawed, blending together to make raucous sounds. The apple tree spread its branches over a gold throne carved with the MVE logo and cobra heads on its arms and back.

As they approached, a dazzling image appeared on the gold throne. At first, the sight was so dazzling, so shining, it was difficult to see what or who the image was.

Awed by its splendor, Carolyn watched the image form into a woman. Completely covered in a silver lamé gown, sparkling with diamond studs, a woman sat immobile, hands resting on the gold cobras' heads.

No super model or Hollywood movie star that Carolyn had ever seen could compare in beauty to the dazzling woman on the gold throne. Her hair was copper colored. And on her head was a ruby crown. This shining creature, sitting as if on a stage in a spotlight, lifted her hand. As a white dove flew from a branch to perch on her finger, a thin silver chain appeared around its neck. One hand held the chain, while the other stroked its back.

As Carolyn received the full effect of sparkle and light, Mauvais nodded to her. "Welcome, New One. Welcome."

It was the same echoed sound she first heard when her back was pressed against the front door.

Though the perfect lips—redder than the apples—mouthed the words, they did not seem to come from the gorgeous apparition. They echoed from throughout the room as if a hundred amplifiers had been hidden everywhere.

"We are Mauvais." The dazzling woman lifted her hand. Instantly the silver chain disappeared and the dove flew back to an apple branch.

Mesmerized, Carolyn thought, *She is a goddess.*

Black eyes, deeper than a wintery night, scanned Carolyn from head to toe.

The birds were suddenly still, as if their invisible silver chains had tightened around each one's neck.

Gazellia coughed nervously.

The cold stare shifted.

Immediately she curtsied, bending her body low. "My Lady Vallee, this is Mistress Carolyn Farmer." Her voice trembled slightly.

"You were correct, Gazellia. This New One has recovered and is presentable. This pleases us."

With a queenly wave, she motioned Gazellia to rise.

Although Gazellia obeyed, she did not look up but kept her head bowed as she stood.

Carolyn didn't know what to believe—what she saw or what she felt. The dazzling, perfectly formed goddess woman glowed like an angel. Yet, there was something ominous about her. And her presence was like her voice: it seemed to be coming from everywhere in the room—like powerful, cold electricity. Before she could think further, the midnight eyes appraised her.

"We judge we have a great deal of reeducation to perform on your behalf. Much effort will be necessary to complete you as planned."

From the pause, Carolyn knew she was supposed to say something. She had better respond.

"Yes'm."

"Good."

The birds sang and whistled and chirped.

"As the director of this school, we promise you will more than learn; you will be changed. MV Enterprises has researched the most successful method of education and reeducation. Each student's mind is resurfaced in the mind-set method. All doubt, confusion, and fear are eliminated. You will acquire the security of knowing the correct goals of the company. The right goals of the company are the right goals for its members. You will learn correct thinking and perfect obedience."

Carolyn didn't know what the mind-set method was. But she did understand Mauvais to say that all doubt, confusion, and fear would be gone.

Now that was a great idea. Eliminate doubt and she would always be sure how to act. Eliminate confusion and she would know for certain exactly what to do and say all the time. And if the first two, doubt and confusion, were gone, why then there would be no more fear. Never being scared or nervous, no matter what happened, would be wonderful. She was amazed at the simplicity of it all. Whatever the mind-set method is, I'm for it, she decided.

"We see you are pleased. That is excellent. You are going to be a fine example of the quality specimens produced by our school."

Carolyn smiled. She glanced at Gazellia, expecting to see gladness on her face. But Gazellia's head was still bowed, her profile unreadable.

"Has Gazellia informed you that you are to receive a gift?"

She hesitated, not knowing how to address a goddess. "Yes'm."

"You may call us Mauvais. A privilege we give to the members of our company."

Carolyn wondered about the "we" and "our." She looks like a single person. But now's not the time. Ask Gazellia later.

"Yes'm … uh, Mauvais, Ma'am."

"You will soon become a member of our company family. You will get used to calling us Mauvais." The corners of her lips curled upward.

"You will also learn to curtsy properly when addressing us. However, at present, you are a guest. We never expect perfection without training. Therefore you are excused from uncouth behavior. This will all change, we guarantee it."

The voice paused and this time Carolyn knew what to say. She bowed slightly, "Yes, Mauvais."

"Good, Carolyn Farmer. You learn quickly."

She clapped her hands and the crystal came near.

"Take Gazellia and bring back our gift," she commanded.

Without lifting her head, Gazellia followed the crystal ball out the door.

Carolyn looked at the goddess sitting under the tree. Suddenly she realized with amazement that there were no bird droppings. The floor, draperies, throne—all around the tree were spotless. And the birds moved where they perched but did not fly within the branches. Are they real?

Mauvais rose from her throne, gliding like a queen over to Carolyn.

Up close, her presence was even more powerful, electric. However, Carolyn noticed, while Mauvais's body was as perfect in form as any woman would want to be, she seemed stiff. Then she remembered her third-grade math teacher who everyone called Mizz-Freezer. She taught them with the same kind of imperious, cold distance. Okay, so she's not warm-fuzzy, like Ramrod-Riguez is on a good day. So what?

Mauvais pointed to an ornate chair. "Come. Sit here, New One. We shall become better acquainted."

She did so, thinking, *Relax. Ease back. Be friendly.*

Mauvais reached down. Instantly a silver chain appeared in her right hand. She pulled on the chain and a robin flew from the branch to her hand. "On earth, have you not wished to hold one?"

"Yeah. When I was very little, Mom and I'd feed the pigeons in the park. I'd try to catch them. She used to laugh ... and we'd run after them together."

"Hold out your hand."

The robin flew to Carolyn's outstretched finger and cocked its head at her. Gently she stroked the red feathers on its breast. It was warm, alive under her fingers. "It's real."

"Of course. Notice his feather-colors are bright. He is a male." She twisted his chain around her finger. "Consider, this is for his protection. Without it, he would hurt himself. Here he is free to enjoy the best we have to offer. On your earth you cage your birds. But we are more gracious in caring for those who give us pleasure."

She leaned forward, her lips hinting a slight interest. "Tell me, New One. How do you like your room?"

"Really cool, fantastic." Carolyn continued to stroke the robin.

Mauvais's smile broadened to reveal perfect white teeth. "We are pleased. It is our best guest room. And how was your breakfast?"

If I say, "Really cool, fantastic" again, she'll think I've got brain drain. Sound like Mom.

"It was delicious. How did you know my favorite was blueberry pancakes?"

"Our advanced science and technology allows us to have extensive files on all our guests. For example, you live with your brother Jimmy and your grandmother Eunice Page. We know your parents were killed in a car accident. As a result of that collision, you suffered substantial, painful trauma to your legs and left ankle."

Carolyn was stunned. "You know all that about me? How?"

"Our methods, our scientific technologies, are far ahead of your earth systems. Here you will learn, even discover your true self. Your true purpose. Here you destiny lies, and your future begins with a gift. One which will help you accomplish all you have dreamed."

As if on cue, the door swung open. The crystal soared to the ceiling as Gazellia walked toward them. She held a silver and gold box encrusted with diamonds and multicolored gems. On its lid the MVE logo was inset with emeralds exactly the same shade of green as Carolyn's dress.

"You must release the robin to accept our gift."

Like a moth to a flame, like iron to a magnet, Carolyn felt a pull so strong, so exciting, she could hardly wait to put her hands on it. Quickly she threw the robin up in the air. His chain disappeared as he flew to a branch.

"Present the New One our gift."

Carolyn's heart hammered. The box itself seemed priceless.

Gazellia gripped it tightly and stepped back.

"Give her the gift."

"No." Gazellia shook her head emphatically and looked at Carolyn. "The gift meant for you is in the gazebo. This is not the gift I intended for you, my dear."

"What you intend is of no consequence." Mauvais's black eyes focused on Carolyn. "What is inside the box will give you power."

Chapter 9

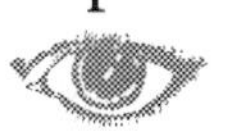

the shoes

Mauvais motioned to the crystal, indicating she wanted it to take the box out of Gazellia's hands. From the crystal a ray streamed directly to the box.

Gazellia curtsied deeply, covering it with her upper body.

"Mauvais, I returned to you with the New One. Please, consider my loyalty."

Carolyn was surprised by her sudden change of expression. Clearly Gazellia was trying to appease Mauvais. But why doesn't she want me to take the gift?

Her head bowed, Gazellia continued. "Please ... consider, gracious I have been to you. Please, consider to give Carolyn your gift without any conditions. Please, do not force her to sign the Baal contract for her gift. Once freed from the puzzle, I could have escaped. Instead, I have brought you the one who might be able to wear the Laurel Crown."

Mauvais snapped her fingers. And the ray was disconnected from over Gazellia's body.

"Because you have returned to bow down in our presence, we will consider your request." In a queenly gesture, she indicated she wanted Gazellia to rise. "However, you have misunderstood my intentions completely. The Baal contract protects all who are members of our company. Carolyn is offered a gift of priceless value. This is a gift of power to control her body against the force of gravity. Our gift is simply a small token of what awaits her after she signs her contract."

Gazellia stood, holding the box tightly against her chest.

"New One, we created this gift for you. It is your destiny to use it. What is inside will change your life forever."

But again, Gazellia shook her head—more emphatically than before.

Though Carolyn didn't understand what was happening, she trusted Gazellia more than she trusted Mauvais. "Maybe I can have it later?"

"No," Mauvais waved and a ray jerked the box out of Gazellia's grip. "You will take them now. They were made for you."

The box hung suspended inside the light stream in front of Carolyn. A force field of desire radiated from the box to her heart. She had never wanted anything as much. She looked at Gazellia. "What should I do?" she pleaded.

"Take it!" the echoes thundered.

"Mon amie, only receive the gift under one condition. That at any time in the future, return it you may to her without penalty. Or, if you choose to keep it, it is yours to use however you wish."

Immediately Carolyn understood. The gift had to be without strings. It had to be hers completely or not at all. "I will take it if I can do whatever I want with it," she said, with confidence.

"Done," boomed the voice. "But it is the first and last bargain you will ever make with us."

She pointed to the crystal. "Let Gazellia's interference be recorded."

"And the subsequent agreement between Mauvais and Carolyn," Gazellia said, smiling in triumph.

"Open your gift," Mauvais commanded.

Carolyn reached into the beam and pulled it out. She turned the box, admiring its silver filigreed sides of vines. She lifted the curved gold, jeweled-encrusted lid. Inside, a pair of red satin toe shoes rested on white silk.

"Ohh," she sighed. "Ohh, they're beautiful."

"Put them on, New One."

"But I can't wear these. I can barely wear my own shoes without hurting."

"Did you not ask for new shoes to go with the dress we provided?"

"Well, yes. But how did you know?"

"We know all that goes on in our domain. Nothing can be hidden from us."

Mauvais pointed. "Those have been created especially for you. You must put them on to know what they can do."

Carolyn sat down. She unwrapped the Velcro and unlaced her shoes.

The red ribbons streamed to the floor as she forced her toes into the narrow flat tips.

Gazellia bent down and neatly crisscrossed the ribbons around each ankle. She tied a small half bow and tucked it under them near the inside of the ankle bone.

"Stand up," Mauvais said.

The unbending steel plates in the arch of the shoes hit the marble floor with loud clunks. Carolyn felt like a flat-footed duck waddling about in the rigid shoes. Her squeezed toes protested their discomfort.

"I feel stupid. And they hurt."

"Gazellia, show her what to do."

"This is the way, my dear." Gazellia arched her right foot, lifted it, and in a swift and graceful movement stepped out. She then repeated the sequence with the other foot. "And left, right, left, right—" She danced in a small circle. "Now you try it." She took Carolyn's left hand to give her some balance.

At the instant point of contact between the floor and the tip of the right shoe, Carolyn plugged into a force field of power that surged up her leg and into every part of her body. She spun and twirled and leaped across wide areas of the room. She was an electrified, human dynamo of energy.

The shoes had wings. She was an eagle soaring on a warm updraft between mountains, circling higher and higher. Then she was a hummingbird flitting from flower to flower, sipping the sweet nectar of each. Then she was a dove, joyously flying from branch to branch. Her heart sang as she flew, light as a feather, dancing around the room.

"Enough."

No. I want to go on forever.

Mauvais clapped her hands.

She fell, an eagle shot in midair by a hunter. Her bottom hit the hard marble.

She was furious. "Why'd you do that? Why'd you make me stop?"

"Because you do not know how to control the shoes. Until you do, they are still under our command."

"What do you mean? Are they mine or not?" Carolyn asked.

"Mauvais, remember your agreement," Gazellia said.

"Remove them."

The moment Carolyn put the shoes on the floor they began to twirl and spin and leap by themselves. It was as if an invisible ballerina were dancing in them.

Mauvais clapped her hands and they dropped to the floor.

"They are yours to command according to our bargain. Focus your mind, every thought, on the shoes. Concentrate. Will them to move."

Carolyn centered her whole being on them.

It was the ribbons that moved first. They rolled themselves up into each shoe. She concentrated on the flat toes and visualized the heels rising, their arches bending. And they lifted. She saw them on a screen in her mind pirouetting—doing grand leaps. Whatever combination of steps she pictured, they did.

"Bravo," Gazellia said as she applauded. "You did it."

Carolyn relaxed. "That's hard work. It was easier when I was in them."

"When you were in them, New One, we had the power to move you. Subsequently, according to our bargain, we relinquished our power over the shoes. We see you have learned how to command them. Well done. You learn quickly."

"And they will dance whenever I choose, no matter where I am?"

"You have absolute power over them. On your feet or off, they will obey you."

But doubt registered in Carolyn's gut.

Cool? Hmm ... maybe not. The "we" that controls the birds. The "we" that controlled me in the shoes. How much is really from me and how much is from her? Or ... them? Should I trust the shoes? Or the questions in my mind? Well ... I'll take them now and find out later.

She picked them up.

"We are pleased you have decided to accept our gift. There are other wonders awaiting you. Stay awhile as my guest."

Mauvais waved. A cardinal flew from a branch and perched on her finger. While she stroked his feathered back, the silver cord appeared around his neck.

"There will be a gathering in your honor, New One. We wish you to meet the other members of our company. When you do, you will realize what opportunities await you. You may rest and refresh yourselves until the crystal alerts you that your attendance is required. Ask it for whatever you need."

As Carolyn watched, the edges of her body began to dissolve. Dazzling, shimmering, she melted into the throne.

"You are dismissed. The crystal will show you to your rooms."

The cardinal flew out of the pool of light and landed on a branch before he disappeared entirely.

In the hallway, Carolyn sat on one of the gilded chairs. She positioned the toe shoes so they would fit back in the box. After running her fingers over the stones and filigree, she closed the lid.

"This is some gift. The box has gotta be worth millions? Right? I mean, even without the toe shoes."

"Mon amie, the value of the box is small in comparison to the power you have to control inanimate objects."

"Yeah. It's like magic."

"The sisters always said, 'Faith can move mountains.' My dear, whatever you can dream, whatever you can visualize, is possible."

"Like I did dream myself out of the box I was in. It can happen. Here I am."

Carolyn hesitated, not quite knowing how to ask the questions about all the doubts that had gone through her mind. She looked at her old shoes in Gazellia's hand.

"It's just … I don't know … something about Mauvais … and the 'we,' 'our' stuff that makes me wonder if taking the shoes is the best thing to do. I mean, you seemed really down about it at first."

"Concerned I was about your agreeing to accept a gift without the promise it would belong to you. To do with it whatever you wished."

"The shoes are really wonderful and magical and fantastic … but when I take them off, I'm still the same. I want to be something terrific without them."

"What changed your mind?"

"I don't know. I guess it was the birds. And when you helped me understand there should be no strings on the gift. Well, I know they're mine … but they aren't me. I'm no ballerina."

"You know what, my dear? It takes a very special person to recognize the value in being oneself. You have proved me right to bring you here. And now I want to show you the gift I had in mind. We are not going to our rooms."

She handed Carolyn her shoes. "Come. Put them on, because we are going for a walk through the maze."

When Carolyn stepped outside, she had forgotten how bright and hot it was. Fortunately there was a slight breeze. She took a few long, deep breaths and stretched her arms toward the vivid purple sky. Gazellia did the same.

"Come." Gazellia pulled Carolyn into the hedges. "*Allez,* I have a wonder to show you. This is the gift I had in mind for you."

Chapter 10

the legend

It was cooler in the greenery. Even though they were in a maze, Carolyn knew they were walking in an ever narrowing circle.

"This is what I wanted to show you," Gazellia said as they cornered the last sharp turn.

On a sandy clearing stood a white gazebo—its dome supported by twelve columns. Iron-carved vines and MVEs covered the columns and spread around the rim of the dome, creating six arches. On its top, an iron weathervane with the initials MVE, pierced by an arrow, turned in the slight breeze. Three benches in the same iron design were bolted to the round cement foundation.

Underneath the dome, exactly in its center, Carolyn saw a closed glass trophy case on a green marble stand. Inside the case, suspended on three silver wires, hung a crown of gold and emerald-encrusted leaves. Inlaid with precious faceted emeralds, each leaf was layered into a circlet. So faultlessly were the emeralds fitted into the gold that it was impossible to detect any separation between the stones. It was a masterpiece of art, simple and flawless.

"It's beautiful. What is it?" Carolyn asked.

"A special award called the Laurel Crown."

She pointed to one of the leaves. "Are those real?"

"Oui, real gold, real emeralds."

"It must be worth millions."

"Priceless it is."

"Does it belong to Mauvais?" Carolyn asked.

"No. Though she claims to own it, it can be owned by no one."

"Does she ever wear it?"

"No. She tried but cannot. In Double Suns, no one has been able to wear it."

"Why not?"

"The crown chooses as it wills. Countless many have tried to unlock its secret. 'Tis for this reason I brought you to here. "Come, Mistress. Sit."

Their skirts rustled like the sound of autumn leaves blowing across the bench.

"The story of its resurrection power has been told throughout the universe. This is the legend of the Laurel Crown:

"Once upon a time, a king had a beautiful daughter. She had many suitors, but none were acceptable to her father. Time passed and the daughter grew older and was losing her youthful beauty. She kept begging her father to allow her to marry. Finally he consented. But the truth be told, he had decided to never let her marry. He was not going to share her with anyone.

"In order to appear honorable to keep his word, he devised an evil plan to invite contestants to compete in a series of physical trials he believed no suitor could survive."

"Sounds like a fairytale," Carolyn said. "Only instead of a wicked mother, like in Cinderella, it was a father. But fairytales are silly, really. Kids grow out of 'em."

"Oui." Gazellia pointed to the crown. "But this legend really happened. And you need to know why this is such a special gift. 'Tis the reason I brought you here. And, mon amie, why I have pinned my hope upon it and you as well."

She patted Carolyn's hand. "I know 'tis a long story, but 'tis very important ... essential to your future. Perhaps even our fate. Please, let me continue."

Find out what the 'tis is all about. Carolyn nodded.

Gazellia smiled. "Merci. Since he believed his daughter was no longer young and beautiful, he was fearful no suitor would come forth. So he decided to add to her dowry of certain fertile lands within his realm, a costly symbol of victory. This extra prize had to be grand.

"Forthwith, the king hired a craftsman, a master jeweler to the palace, and introduced him to his daughter. During the next few weeks the princess and the craftsman had many discussions as to what the symbol should be.

They decided on a jeweled circlet of laurel leaves based on the award given to the winners of the ancient Greek Olympics.

"As the work progressed, their friendship turned into love. Most natural, the servants, guards, and chamber maids gossiped.

"The king's heart burned with rage. He commanded the artist to give up the princess. Instead, the craftsman demanded that he be allowed to compete.

"When the king informed his daughter that her lover desired to compete, he assumed she would be thrilled. Instead, she was terrified. In truth, she knew her beloved had no skills for battle. He was an artist, not a mercenary or soldier. He would surely die.

"Therefore, she decided she would rather fight alongside him than live without him. Without telling her beloved of her plans, the night before the trials she bribed a guard to steal a warrior's sword, armor, and helmet.

"In the morning, the king sat high in his royal box overlooking a large arena. With flags flying and trumpets blaring, ten warriors, the jeweler and the princess disguised as warriors marched before the king.

"A flag was lowered and the twelve ran to the first trial—a steep 115 foot-high mound of fresh dirt. The ten stronger warriors easily scrambled to the top. But for the last two the climb was tough. Halfway up, the jeweler recognized the princess. 'What are you doing here?' he asked, after they had helped each other to the top.

"She answered, 'I have come to fight—for without you, my life is worthless.'

"'Tis true for me also,' he said. 'Henceforth, we shall always be together.'

"Below them, on the other side of the mound, was a deep pit. Embedded into the pit bottom were tall, upright stakes sharpened to points. In their rush over the top, four of the twelve warriors had tumbled into the pit, impaled themselves on the stakes, and died. Several warriors, seeing what had happened, laid a narrow pole over the stakes.

"The princess watched them swing, monkey-style, to the other side. 'I do not think I have the arm strength,' she said.

"He said, 'I have an idea. I will tie your hands around the pole with your belt. Then you can hook your knees around the pole and, by sliding hands and knees, upside down, you will get across. And I shall do the same.' They did this and safely crossed the pit."

"Whew," Carolyn said. "Did the king know it was his daughter?"

"No. He did not recognize either one. At the end, he congratulated the eight, amazed they had survived. He announced a final winner would be selected by hand-to-hand combat to the death the following morning. He then invited the eight to a palace banquet. There, he hoped, they might fight among themselves.

"That night the jeweler and princess disguised themselves in loose fitting tunics and masks. They acted like the other warriors with loud talk and boasts of conquests in battle. They also pretended to get drunk on the dinner wine.

"After dinner, the six real warriors began quarreling as to who would win the following day. 'Why wait for tomorrow?' asked one.

"'Why not settle it right now?' asked another.

"An hour later, five lay dead and one was left. He was the biggest, the strongest, and most cunning. 'Which one of you is next?' he growled. 'Tonight I shall have the lands, the prize, and the princess.'

"'Stop!' cried the jeweler, trying to stall for time. 'The king has deceived you. There is no prize and no princess.'

"'Liar!' screamed the king. 'Fetch the Laurel Crown. Find the princess,' he commanded the guard.

"A few minutes later the guard returned. 'Your Majesty,' he said. 'Here is the Laurel Crown, but Her Highness is not in her royal apartment.'

"The king shouted. 'Search the palace grounds! Find her!'

"'There is no need, Father,' said the princess as she took off her mask.

"The king was astonished. 'Daughter, why were you dressed like a warrior?'

"'I entered the contest to die beside the one I love. Tomorrow I shall once again compete beside him.'

"'Who is he?' asked the king.

"The jeweler pulled off his mask.

"'You know very well who he is, Father,' she replied. 'He is the one who made the Laurel Crown.'

"'I will not allow you to do this,' declared the king.

"'You have no choice,' she said. 'You have the great honor of your great name to consider. As a great king you have already spilled much blood. What does a little more matter?'

"This last question pierced the king's heart, breaking it into a thousand pieces. His selfish plan had trapped him into destroying the very one he had loved the most. 'How could I have been so blind? So stupid?' he asked himself. 'No. I won't allow this to happen. The trials are canceled,' he said. 'I command you all to leave the palace at once.'

"Before the guards could move to protect the king, the warrior lifted his bloody sword and pressed its sharp point against the king's throat. 'Not so quick, Your Majesty. You can keep your great honor and your great life,' he sneered, 'if you do not deny me what is rightfully mine by combat. The Laurel Crown and all you promised shall be mine. Take care, Your Majesty. I have many friends, greater warriors than I, who will seize your kingdom should you fail to keep your word.'

"He turned to the jeweler and said, 'Enjoy your last night for tomorrow you die.' And with a mocking laugh, he strode out of the dining hall.

"'What am I to do?' moaned the king.

"'Marry us now,' replied the jeweler.

"'Yes, Father,' she said, 'please, marry us.'

"The sorrowful king, now knowing he wished his daughter's happiness above his own, agreed to marry them. He called in a legal scribe to witness the marriage. And within the half hour, the jeweler and the princess retired to her royal apartment as husband and wife.

"Withal, through the night the king sat on his throne thinking about what he had done. He deeply regretted his deceit and selfishness and the purpose for which he had made the Laurel Crown. In the dawn's light he knelt, and with tears streaming down his cheeks, head bowed, he prayed:

"'Greatest Majesty, I have put my daughter's life in jeopardy. You know I love her more than my kingdom or myself. Please forgive the evil I have done and for the lives I have destroyed because of my hatred. Please save my daughter and her husband. Tomorrow, let me die in their place.'

"He placed the crown on his throne. 'Almighty Creator, I dedicate this to you to change what was meant for evil to be used for good. Greatest Majesty, you choose the one to wear this crown. I place their lives and mine under your protection and will. Thank you, Loving Creator, for hearing me. Amen.'

"Then the king commanded the scribe to engrave the Greek words 'He agape nikai panta' on the backside of a leaf."

Wow. Some story.

Carolyn looked through the glass. It looks real enough. Wonder what it feels like on? "Um," she started to ask. But then—zip lips.

"There were many more in the arena than the day before. Word had spread about the fight at the banquet, the challenge by the warrior, and the marriage. Some of the king's subjects were in fear, wondering if the king might also lose his life. Others were excited to witness the outcome of such a momentous event. But as the crowd silently waited, the broken-hearted king could not give the signal for the combat to begin.

Time passed and the sun rose. The crowd grew restless—booing, hissing, shouting for action. And the warrior at the far end of the arena began to pace. Still the king could not give the command.

"Finally, the warrior pulled his sword from its scabbard and ran toward the royal box. 'If you do not give the signal,' he shouted, 'I will send my henchmen to take hostages! You will keep your word or your subjects will lose their lives.'

"The king looked out over the crowd and saw many men dressed in armor among his people. He had no choice but to give the signal.

"In the arena the princess and the jeweler clasped hands. 'Our love will live on, no matter what happens in the next hour,' he said.

"'I promise we will always be together,' she vowed.

"The warrior began to taunt the jeweler. 'Come coward,' he yelled. 'Come and meet your master.'

"The jeweler unsheathed his sword and with the princess walked to the center of the arena.

"The warrior smacked the shoulder of the jeweler with the flat of his blade. 'Let's see which one of us will have your wife tonight.'

"This made the jeweler furious. He stabbed the warrior through the elbow.

"The crowd cheered. And the king brightened. Perhaps there was hope after all.

"But the warrior was well-trained and experienced. He had received worse wounds and won.

"Every time the jeweler swung, the warrior dodged and ducked. In this way he played with the jeweler like a cat playing with a mouse before the kill.

"By early afternoon, the jeweler was ready to collapse. Panting, shaking, unable to lift the heavy sword one more time, he shouted to the warrior, 'You shall never have my wife, the lands, or the Laurel Crown! You will not live out this day!'

"This prophetic message so angered the warrior that he promptly struck the jeweler in the throat, killing him instantly. With his bloody sword held high, the warrior turned to the king. 'The victory is mine,' he gloated. 'Give me the Laurel Crown.'

"The princess saw her husband's blood running down the warrior's arm. 'Upon my oath,' she promised. "Naught one breath shall I take in rest before I cut your head from your neck.'

"'No!' shouted the warrior. 'I will not fight for what already belongs to me. I will take it instead.' And straightway from where they had been standing in the crowd, fifty men drew swords. Forthwith, thirty more surrounded the king's royal box and his guards. Henchman on each side of the king placed their blades across his throat.

"'A king's word is his bond!' the warrior shouted. 'Bound you are to keep it, or I charge you with treason and your people will be my slaves. Your daughter will be my concubine—never my wife. I will have what you promised or your kingdom will be in service to me.'

"The princess knew the situation was hopeless. Her subjects, innocent people, could be enslaved or killed. She had no choice but to lay down her sword. 'Willingly will I serve you, if you will release, not harm my father and my subjects,' she said. 'What my father has promised will be given to you.'

"The warrior motioned for his men to withdraw. 'I have kept my word,' he said. 'Now do what is right and give me what I have won.'

"The king held the circlet high over the warrior's bowed head. 'Whoever can wear this crown is the true victor,' he said.

"About four inches above his head, the Laurel Crown became firmly fixed. The king could not lower it any farther. Three henchmen stepped forward and added their strength to try to pull down the crown. No matter the force they applied, it would not—could not—be placed on the warrior's head.

"'You have cast a spell on it!' the warrior shouted. 'You, your daughter, and everyone in your kingdom will pay for this treachery with their lives.'

"'Wait,' said the king. 'Let my daughter try.'

"When the princess placed her hands on the Laurel Crown, the gold began to glow. The emeralds sparkled in the sun. Slowly she lowered the shining circlet the remaining four inches until it rested on the warrior's head.

"Turning to the crowd, he raised his fists in triumph. '*Vic-tree. Vic-tree. Vic-tree*,' he chanted, marching around the arena.

"Brighter and brighter glowed the gold. The emeralds turned fiery red.

"Halfway around the arena, the warrior desperately struggled. 'Get it off! Get it off!' he screamed in pain.

"The Laurel Crown blazed like a hot coals.

"When his friends tried to touch it, it burned their fingers. And no matter what they used to protect their hands, the material caught fire.

"The warrior's head began to smoke. Flashes of fire shot out from chinks in his armor. The stench from his burning flesh drove his comrades away from his body. His hair, his face turned black. In a few minutes he was dead.

"The princess rolled him over and with her sword cut off his head. With the tip of her blade she pulled off the crown and held it up. 'Who wants to wear it next?' she shouted.

"Most natural, no one did. They ran from the arena and were never seen again.

"The king lifted his hands. 'We are free!' he shouted. 'Thanks to the Loving Creator who is the power behind the Laurel Crown.'

"The princess did not hear the cheering crowd. Her grief had deafened her ears to any joy. She knelt beside her husband and placed the crown on his chest. 'Oh, my beloved,' she sobbed. 'If only you could return to me. If only you could see what you have done to save my father and my people.'

"The king's heart broke to see his daughter so grieved. He knelt beside her and bowed his head. 'Oh, Greater Than All Kings, I am the guilty one. Please, take my life in exchange for his.'

"The Laurel Crown began to glow golden and grow warm. As the heat increased, the king and princess were driven away from the body. Sparks began flying from within the gold and emerald leaves. From the center of the circlet—one, then another, then another—rose tendrils of shimmering white smoke. Each strand curled around the jeweler. Its shining smoke thickened into a white radiant cloud, totally concealing his body.

"Minutes passed. And a slight wind began to move across the arena. The crowd was silent. Every eye was focused on the radiant, shimmering cloud.

"The king and the princess, who were closest to the jeweler, noticed within the cloud a sort of bumping motion. And while this was taking place near his arms and legs, slowly, slowly the tendrils uncurled. In the exact same way in which they had curled around his body, they reversed into the Laurel Crown, disappearing into its center. The jeweler stretched and yawned as if awakening from a deep night's sleep.

"First shock, disbelief, amazement, and then joy beyond words exploded in the heart of the princess. He was alive. He was well. He was whole.

"They hugged and kissed and laughed and cried. Nothing could ever separate them again.

"The king too was overjoyed. He ordered a month's holiday for feasting and dancing and singing. He proclaimed that that day was to be celebrated every year as a thanksgiving—a memorial to the miracle that had happened.

"As to the Laurel Crown—a place of honor was built for it. For many generations it was displayed by the descendants of the royal family. And then, for an unknown reason, it disappeared and reappeared in various places. How it came to be in Mauvais's possession I do not know. Many have tried to learn its secret by attempting to wear it. None here have been able to do so."

Carolyn lifted her hand. "Can I ask a question?"

Gazellia laughed. "Oui. I have finished the story."

"Is it real?"

Gazellia lifted the glass case. "Oh, you can hold it. It fact, I can take it out for you." She unhooked the circlet from its wires and handed it to Carolyn.

The Laurel Crown was light, and at first it seemed fragile. Carolyn held it carefully, fearful she might drop it, or it might break. She rubbed her fingers over the surface of the emerald facets and around each gold leaf. It seemed brand new as if it had been created hours before. She tipped the crown and saw the engraved Greek words. "Did you try it on?"

"Oui. Mauvais and every member has had an opportunity to try. None have succeeded."

"But that doesn't explain *why* you or Mauvais can't wear it."

"It does not."

Carolyn turned it round and round in her hands, feeling awe, amazement, reverence, wonder. She tried to imagine fiery sparks and smoke pouring from its center. *Do I dare try it on?*

"Fear not. Everyone else has."

Carolyn raised it above her head, slowly lowering it, expecting at any moment to feel an upward force. But it did not resist. She eased the sharp metal over her forehead and temples. At certain places the cold points jabbed her scalp and behind her ears. She waited to feel heat, electricity, something. Nothing. She tipped it forward to make it more comfortable. It was as light to wear as it was to hold. "Well, how do I look?"

Gazellia's face flushed pink from shock. Her brown eyes were saucers. Her chin quivered with astonishment. "Oh ... oh ... Mon Dieu." Bursts of air popped through her open mouth. She grabbed Carolyn's shoulders with such force that Carolyn winced in pain. Repeatedly she kissed her on both cheeks, shaking her hard and bouncing her up and down. "Oh, my dear, mon amie. I knew it would be you. I knew!"

"But ... but ... nothing's happening ..." Carolyn stuttered, holding onto the crown to keep it from falling. "Nuh ... nuh ... nothing happened."

"Something will. I guarantee as soon as Mauvais sees it on your head, something definitely will happen."

"Uhh ... say ... maybe we should put it back where it belongs. I mean, well ... it probably looks silly on me anyway. And ... uhh ... I don't know how to work it."

Gazellia stopped her from taking it off. "My dear, you must understand. The Laurel Crown chose you. From the countless many who have tried it, it is you ... you are that special one chosen to wear it. A great honor has been bestowed upon you."

"But why? I'm nobody. Nothing special at all. Because of me, my parents died. And my brother hates me. Why *would* it choose me?"

"Perhaps it knows your heart better than you do. The sisters used to say, 'From a pure heart blessings flow to others.' Perhaps it has a purpose for you that you do not yet know. Whatever the reason, it means for you to wear it."

Chapter 11

tea time

On the way back from the maze, Carolyn kept touching the crown on her head. Imagining the legend, she saw the beautiful princess and handsome craftsman kiss. *Happily ever after—now that's the way a good fairytale should end.*

She thought about the princess. Was it possible to love someone that much? Enough to be willing to die? She shook her head. Living for love was great, but dying for it was something else entirely.

"A franc for your thoughts."

"Huh?

"Pardon. A penny for your thoughts."

"Oh, I was just thinking about … things. Do you think there's any truth to the story?"

"In my heart of hearts I believe it to be true. 'Tis the reason I kept seeking with great hope the person who might be able to wear it." She patted Carolyn's cheek. "And thrilled I am it is you."

"But how come it *is* me?"

"At the convent I was taught that God moves in mysterious ways. The fact that I came to you in the puzzle, and you were God's instrument to free me, led me to believe you might be the one."

"But you knew my name."

"When your grandmother bought the puzzle, she talked about how much your mother loved them, how she hoped her granddaughter Carolyn would too. And later in your room, I heard you and your brother talk."

Carolyn chuckled. "You mean fight."

"That is of no consequence. He will prove himself to be a fine brother, whatever you think of him." She sighed. "My dear, you are the fortunate one to have a brother who cares. I was an only child. And one abandoned by my father. It took many weeping nights for me to accept what he did."

"What makes you think he cares about me?"

"He cares enough to argue. Sometimes the person who irritates you the most is the one you care the most about."

"For sure that's Gram. And all her … dumb old rules. I just can't keep 'em … can't please her no way, no how, no matter what. They're rid of me and they'll be glad about it."

"Even if that is true, the crown has purposed you for a journey you are destined to take."

She rubbed Carolyn's shoulder. "Whatever the future holds, you are a part of my life now, and, whether you wished it or not, the crown chose you. You will have to do your best whatever comes. This truth I have learned: there are some things deep inside that one can know, without the ability to explain how one knows those certain things."

She lightly brushed her fingers near Carolyn's ear. "When you placed a piece of me there, in my heart of hearts I knew to trust you to put me together. For many years I prayed to be set free. Why the Laurel Crown chose you—"

She stopped walking and thoughtfully pursed her lips. "I wonder if that is part of its secret power."

"What do you mean?"

"In the legend, the king dedicated it to God. Remember it was to be a symbol of victory over death. He agape nikai panta. Love conquers all things. Obviously it is going to use you in some way."

"But I can't do anything."

"Receive the gift. At present that is all that is necessary."

Through a slit in the air above their heads, the crystal ball suddenly appeared. It bobbed in front of Gazellia's face.

"Come," she said. "The members have been prepared to entertain an honored guest. What they do not expect is one who wears the Laurel Crown."

Carolyn's heart flip-flopped. Her mouth was suddenly dry. "What do you think will happen?"

"I cannot know. But whatever happens, remember it chose you."

As they approached the mirrored door, they paused. For the first time

Carolyn could see how she looked. The green silk dress was as beautiful on her as she had imagined it. But it was the crown that took her breath away. Nestled in her blonde hair, the green and gold glowed and sparkled like a halo in the sunlight.

Is this beautiful girl really me? She touched the mirror. And it reflected her movement. She stepped back to admire herself. *Yeah, it's me, all right. She looked down at the Velcro wrap and shoes.* It was as if a part of her was still ugly, a reminder of what her reflection said she no longer was. *If I put the new shoes on, I can will my feet to glide across the floor perfectly—matched to my new, beautiful self.*

The gems on the lid were cool under her fingers. "I think I was wrong about these."

Quickly Gazellia prevented Carolyn from opening the lid. "Mon amie, do not change your mind. Your wearing the crown will be quite enough to impress Mauvais. You are most beautiful. Do send the box back to your room."

"You really think I should?"

"The sisters believed 'tis in your heart the spirit of truth lives. 'Twas your heart that told you the power behind the shoes was a deception."

"Yeah. It was like I knew in my gut you were right, warning me something was wrong about the shoes. But *now* it's *my* mind that controls the shoes.

"You have been given the power over them. But in your heart of hearts, would you not prefer to stay true to yourself ... who you are without pretense? Your first instinct to say they were a 'cheat' was correct. Later, if you still wish, I will teach you to dance. My dear, I promise we will dance together."

How cool is that? Gram would be blown away to see us dancing together. Could jog rings around Yolanda and Ramrod.

She lifted the box toward the globe. "Put this in my room."

Instantly it was absorbed and both disappeared.

Gazellia knocked. "We are ready, Mauvais."

Before Carolyn realized she had moved, they were back in the hallway in front of an open door The crystal materialized and led them through.

It was as if a seventeenth-century French painting had come alive. The ceiling was painted with pastel flowers, woodland scenes, and animals of every kind. Handsome men and exquisite women, talking, laughing, gesturing to one another, were scattered in clusters around an immense ballroom. Their conversational hum was pleasant and inviting. The women were dressed in the finest of gowns and jewels. The men were in brocaded suits with diamond stick pins holding cravats on silk shirts. The gilded mirrors reflected every color Carolyn had ever seen in her life in the fabrics, jewels, lace, and furnishings.

She glanced sideways at Gazellia as she whispered, "Isn't this the room we were in earlier? The apple tree is gone and so are the birds."

There was no response. Her face was expressionless.

The crystal bobbed. It wanted them to move farther into the ballroom.

As they walked, Carolyn noticed all the men and women were in their midtwenties—like Gazellia. Maybe it's just their bodies, she thought. There might be somebody my age on the inside. But it *would* be totally cool to be twenty-five forever.

The crystal continued to lead them to the center of the oval room. Conversations stopped as they passed by. Soon the only sounds in the room were the occasional rustling of silk and satin and swishing of lace fans.

Carolyn could feel every eye on her. She reminded herself she looked as lovely as anyone else. *I am the honored guest,* she thought. *I look like a princess. I shall act like one.*

Slowly, minimizing her limp as best she could, she walked past the clusters of ladies and gentlemen to the far end of the room.

The crystal guided them to a long, oval banquet table covered with white lace. A centerpiece of red roses, pink carnations, and various green foliage was arranged in a large silver bowl. The centerpiece stood between two six-pronged golden cobra candelabras.

On the polished mahogany table, platters of assorted tea sandwiches, bowls of chocolates, and *petit fours* were arranged among napkins, plates, and silverware. At one end of the table a handsome man in a white brocaded suit poured tea from a silver teapot. His black, curly hair softly touched his gray silk collar. His skin was translucent—the color of the porcelain tea cup he held in his slender fingers. As he offered the cup filled with tea to Carolyn, his blue eyes gazed at her with piercing energy. His sensuous lips curved into a charming smile.

A thousand butterflies took off inside her. She wanted to say something totally awesome.

"Cream? Sugar?" The questions were asked in a deep, rich baritone.

With a start, Carolyn realized, she hadn't moved. Embarrassed, she cleared her throat. "Thank you," she said, taking the cup and saucer with both hands in order not to spill the tea.

All she could feel was the beat of a thousand wings fanning the hot blush rising in her cheeks.

Gazellia pushed her slightly forward. "Claude, I wish to introduce you to our honored guest, Carolyn Farmer."

He put his right hand across his chest and bowed in acknowledgment.

"Claude was the prisoner in the cell next to mine."

"Which was fortunate for me. For we have had a friendship spanning many centuries."

"I'm pleased to meet you," Carolyn said. She was glad her voice sounded steady. "I heard how you dug through the stone wall."

"Ah, you've been told how we met." He dropped a couple of sugar cubes and carefully poured the cream into Carolyn's cup, never taking his eyes off her face.

Carolyn hesitated. Could this perfect take-your-breath-away-dude be a wizard, like Jimmy said? Or, she glanced at Gazellia, was he her lover?

Gazellia chuckled. "Mon amie. Your face reflects questions. You have my permission to ask them."

"Okay," Carolyn said. "Here goes. Were you in prison for being a wizard? And, um, ... after you got out, did you guys, um ... you know ... love each other?"

Claude cleared his throat. He looked Gazellia. "No, we were never lovers. We are friends. What you would term in your century, *like brother and sister.*"

Carolyn's heart skipped a beat. "Um ... that's nice." *Nice* is such a stupid word. "Um, I mean I'm glad, you're—"

"Friends?" Claude laughed. "Perhaps it would be helpful if I explained. Gazellia and I were accused of being traitors against the king and, therefore, imprisoned, awaiting execution. We were guilty, of course."

Gazellia sighed. "During those years, King Henry had many enemies. Milady would have nothing to do with internal politics of the court. But because of her family name and her protection from the king, certain people wanted to use her. And they did through me."

It took a few seconds for Carolyn's brain to wrap around "traitor." That doesn't compute. Gazellia is awesome. Can't be. Her mind searched for better word. "You mean you were a spy?"

"'Tis true. Ashamed I am to confess, I dropped secret messages from one part of the palace to the other. Both sides employed me. Neither danger nor consequences to Milady or to the king entered my brain. Money was my desire. Considerably paid I was for the secrets I heard in confidence from Lady Francoise." Lightly she touched Carolyn's arm. "Mon amie, do not think too badly of me. That was then. This is now."

Claude slid the plate of sandwiches toward them. "How much does she know about the contract? Did you tell her I put the note in the box?"

Carolyn heard Gazellia's voice drop to a whisper. "I have only told her as much as she can comprehend right now. She never would have come with me if I had told her everything."

Stunned by this whispered conversation, Carolyn's confused mind filled with questions. *What are they talking about? What's this got to do with the legend? And me? Now the wings fluttered for a different reason: fear. Oh, Jimmy, why didn't I listen to you?*

Claude pointed to the crown and leaned toward Gazellia. "I see she can wear it. You know there will be a challenge. Mauvais is not about to free any of us without a fight. You were courageous to come back."

With a silver tong, Gazellia chose a couple sandwiches from the plate. "Can I count on your help, as before?"

"I will do what I can," Claude said.

"What about your sister? Can I count on her, and the others too?"

"I don't think so. I have talked to Lissette. Though we are twins, we are not alike in our thinking. She lives the mind-set directive and is loyal to Mauvais. However, I found three others who believe in the legend and want to be free," Claude said.

Carolyn's hands shook, spilling the tea into the saucer. "Free? Whadda ya' mean free? What contract? What's the mind-set method? Gazellia, what's—"

But before she could finish her last question, a light began to rotate from within the crystal. Claude and Gazellia stiffened, and every person, including Carolyn, turned to watch the globe move across the ballroom to the door.

It opened. And in the center of its gilded frame Mauvais stood, dressed in a tight, form-fitting black leather jumpsuit. Diamond, gold, and silver studs embellished the side seams of the skintight pants. The studs outlined the edges of the leather sleeves and neck lapels. Her copper hair was twisted high on her head set with a diamond tiara. Around her neck a diamond-encrusted MVE pendant hung on a large chain.

With her hands on her hips and her feet spread apart in silver and diamond boots, her dark eyes scanned every face. When they met Carolyn's, her mouth tightened, drawing her lips into a hard, thin line.

No one moved. Not even a rustle of silk or a sigh could be heard. A fearful electricity charged the air. Carolyn could feel its power crawl up the back of her neck. She didn't dare move against its intensity. The light from the crystal bounced off the wall mirrors.

Mauvais's boots clicked on the marble floor. Behind her two leopards followed, their black spots and amber coats sleek and tawny. In her right hand gold chains appeared, attached to the cobra collars around their necks. Their muscles rippled as they padded, one on each side of her, into the room.

Her gaze never wavered from Carolyn's face. As she approached, her pace slowed. One of the leopards rubbed up against her leg. She stopped, bent down, and stroked its side. The chain hooked to its collar vanished. She whispered in its ear. Immediately that cat padded across the room and jumped onto a silk-embroidered settee. She stroked and whispered to the other.

No longer chained, tail low, ears flat to its head, the leopard focused on Carolyn. The closer it came, the lower it crouched—a predator stalking its prey.

Terror nailed Carolyn to the floor.

Mauvais clapped her hands.

The cat stopped a few feet from her. The tip of her tail twitched; her ears flattened; her upper lip curled. A guttural snarl came from her throat.

"She is welcoming you, New One."

The cat hissed.

"Mauvais, please …" implored Gazellia, shifting her body between Carolyn and the snarling leopard.

"The New One must know who rules here."

"You do, Mauvais," she said, pressing her body fully in front of Carolyn. "You do."

"And what does the honored guest say?"

Carolyn's mouth felt like it was filled with dry cotton. She could hardly say the words. "You … do."

"Good. Good." Mauvais clapped her hands.

The cat relaxed. Her ears pivoted forward. She sauntered to the settee, joining the other leopard.

Gazellia's body also relaxed. She took a couple of deep breaths and stepped away from Carolyn.

Chapter 12

Members of the Company

"A member of my company need never be afraid of us." Mauvais voice echoed around the room. In measured strides, her hands behind her back like a general, she slowly walked around Carolyn.

"We are pleased the crown has chosen the New One. Gazellia, you have accomplished much as a loyal and trusted friend to bring such a lovely specimen, perhaps even more lovely than you were once, into our domain. How auspicious a beginning for you to have returned to us."

She turned to Gazellia with a dazzling smile. "We are quite pleased you have shown the crown to the New One. It is obvious to us all that she is a most precious person, worthy of such a gift. We are pleased you have both come to become a part of our family. The New One for the first time. And you, the prodigal friend who became special to us over the centuries, and to whom we did reward generously. This is truly a momentous occasion."

Mauvais lifted her hands in a gesture inviting recognition. "Pay attention, everyone. This is the New One. Welcome her."

"Welcome, New One," they all chorused.

"I hope you have met some of the members of our company."

Carolyn knew only one response was acceptable. "Yes, Mauvais."

"Good. It is important you become acquainted. We are a large, happy family here. The sooner you become one of us, the better."

Mauvais snapped her fingers and beckoned. At once, sixty beautiful people moved. They crowded around Carolyn with murmurs of "Hello. Delightful to have you. Pleased to meet you."

Claude's sister Lissette introduced herself. In a rose satin gown with pink pearls, her black shining curls around a perfect oval face, she was as gorgeous as he was handsome.

Compared to that lady, Yolanda's a dog, Carolyn thought.

Like a celebrity, she answered questions and asked some too. She learned there were two others from Detroit named Carlos and Raymond. One lady, Michelle, was from Seattle.

Others gave their names, but they were numbers—some mixed with odd-sounding letters she couldn't repeat or remember seconds after. It was easier to remember the American names by the colors they wore. Like, Michelle was in the yellow silk.

Carolyn also talked about the accident—how she and Jimmy had to move in with Eunice. Sharing her past melted the fear inside her. Carlos and Raymond told her how they too had been rescued from a life they hated. Michelle whispered she understood how much Carolyn missed her parents because she had been orphaned early in life. Everyone was friendly, charming, inviting—interested in everything about her.

Leaning back on the settee with a leopard stretched out on each side of her, Mauvais clapped her hands. "Attention. We must commence to entertain our guest."

A flurry of rainbow colors, and swiftly thirty men lined up chairs behind thirty ladies near the banquet table. Skirts blossomed like spring flowers in a garden—silk morning glories, rose taffetas, gold brocaded mums bloomed in lush profusion as the ladies sat.

Carlos and Raymond lifted a wingback chair and placed it behind Gazellia while Claude pulled a matching one over to Carolyn. Just as she spread her green skirt, she felt him push the chair slightly under her.

"Here," he leaned over and whispered, "is a temporary throne for true nobility."

When everyone had settled, Lissette strolled to a grand piano in the middle of the oval room. Spreading her fan with a flourish, she first curtsied to Mauvais. Then with a slight nod, she acknowledged Carolyn, turned, and, after adjusting her skirt on the bench, she began to play.

As her fingers wove a tapestry of sound, Carolyn felt every note. The rippling phrases and harmonies wove a magical design—a design that interlaced itself through Carolyn's body and completely enraptured her. She soared with every note. Her heart beat to every rhythm.

Lissette often glanced at Carolyn as she played, watching her respond to the music. With a grand flourish, her fingers flying over the keys, her eyes on Carolyn, she thundered to the end of a concerto. Before Lissette could rise from the piano bench, Carolyn was on her feet, clapping wildly.

Carolyn's head swirled with excitement. What talent! How beautiful she is! Oh, to dance to such beautiful music would be heavenly. The thrill of being a part of something more wonderful than she had ever experienced before caused her to clap and clap until her hands stung and her arms ached. "Bravo! Bravo!" she cheered with the others.

Lissette smiled graciously and bowed. When the audience quieted and Carolyn realized Lissette was going to play again, she quickly sat down. She held her breath. Her whole being anticipated the first note.

While the music surrounded and held her a joyous captive, she thought of the toe shoes and the glorious power surge through her body when she had them on. *Why did I send them back to my room? This is what I was created to do. I was born to dance—to soar like an eagle circling high on a warm updraft in a bright blue sky. I was born to fly. I was born to be free ... to be special ... and great ... and wonderful and ...* Her thoughts dissolved into the music.

Lissette performed several more pieces with equal artistry.

For Carolyn, time stopped. Thoughts stopped. Only the music was important.

She didn't realize until Lissette stood up that the final piece had been played.

Lissette bowed slightly to acknowledge the audience and Carolyn's wild clapping. With a swish of silk she curtsied to Mauvais, signaling her part of the entertainment was over.

It took a few minutes to register in Carolyn's brain that there was no more music moving through her body. It was as if someone had disconnected her from a powerful electrical current—a plug pulled from its socket. Her body ached to become one with the music again. The power to dance in her toe shoes was far beyond any pleasure she could have imagined. It was possible to fly high enough to reach the stars. When the electricity stopped, it was as if a part of her had been snatched away and she longed to have it back.

The men and women returned to chatting with each other and wandering about the room.

She leaned over to Gazellia and lifted her feet. "I can't wait to dance in my new shoes."

Gazellia whispered back, "Remember you are wearing the Laurel Crown."

Before she could even think to respond, Mauvais stood in front of her.

"I am pleased you enjoyed the program. Lissette is quite talented. No doubt you would have liked to use the gift we gave you when she played?"

Carolyn nodded. "Oh yeah, that would have been total cool, um, perfect."

Mauvais pointed to her shoes. "If you agree to stay with us, you can throw those away. You will never have to wear them again."

She started to say she would stay forever. But before she could, Mauvais snapped her fingers at the crystal.

It flashed. And a mirror, larger than a door, materialized on a platform with castors. It was framed in gilded, ornately carved wood.

"I have something to show you, New One."

Carolyn felt Mauvais's hand slip under her elbow to escort her to the mirror. It was cold but felt human.

"New One, we are like you in many respects. Consider the technology to reconstruct cells to conform to the highest ideals of beauty and talent belongs to us. Our science is far ahead of yours on earth. You are in a new realm of discovery."

She positioned Carolyn in front of the mirror.

"Stand here and see your future."

At first Carolyn could not see herself. There was a film, a kind of dust which had settled on the silvered side. She stepped closer and peered into the glass. Inside, she caught a glimpse of something moving—an outline, a shadow. She wasn't sure what it was. She was about to ask how she was supposed to see through this film when an invisible cloth started wiping the dust from inside the mirror. From the upper right corner to the left, all the way down, the wiping continued until the mirror was clean and clear.

Mauvais pointed. "Regard your future. It awaits you."

Carolyn saw a large stage in an empty theater. Down center, near the edge, an elderly, bald man straddled a chair. He faced two dancers. One was a young woman in black leotards, pink tights, beige knit leggings, and worn, dirty toe shoes. Her yellow hair was pulled back into a bun and a white sweat band encircled her forehead.

The other was a young man in a white T-shirt, black leotards, and black slippers. Both men watched the young woman dance a series of chain steps.

The man in the chair said something in French. He then gestured he wished the male dancer to join her. The couple danced a *pas de deux* for several minutes. He supported her as she pirouetted and arabesqued. They seemed very much in love. In a grand finish, he lifted her onto his shoulders. At that moment, the mirror zoomed in a close-up of the dancers' faces.

It was she. With Claude. Was that possible? Could that slender, stunning young woman be her? Half hoping, half believing, she touched the glass. Her face filled the ornate frame. There was no doubt. It *was* her. The ugly duckling had turned into a beautiful swan—an enchanting, dancing swan who thousands of people would adore.

The zoom reversed. And she watched as Claude lowered her to the stage. Tenderly he kissed her on the mouth. She leaned into him, her eyes closed, her lips responding to his. She heard him murmur, "Sweetheart, that's for luck."

"I don't believe in luck," the man in the chair said gruffly. "I believe in hard work and discipline." He got up from the chair and carried it into the wings. "I think this is the best ballet we have ever created. By tomorrow morning your names will be in every major magazine and newspaper review in New York."

He returned with a briefcase stuffed with music and papers. He walked over and patted them both on the back. "The two of you have worked very hard. Now go home, take a nap, eat lightly, and relax. I'll toast your success with champagne at the cast party after the opening performance tonight. I'll see you at curtain call."

After he had gone, Claude put his hands on her waist and lifted her, joyfully swinging her high in a circle. He laughed. "Think of the money we'll make. TV. DVDs. Commercials. Talk-show interviews. Specials. Who knows? Maybe even a movie or two. How would you like to be a movie star?"

"I'd love it," she cheered. "Hollywood, here I come."

He put her down. "Seriously, what will you do with the money?"

She didn't answer right away. She sat near the edge of the stage and slowly untied the ribbons of her toe shoes. Thoughtfully, quietly, she said, "I'm going to make sure Gram sells that old duplex and moves into a beautiful townhouse. And if Mr. Reed wants to sell his side, I'd buy one for him too."

"And your brother, Jimmy?"

"Well, since bro and Shana were married, they've had a tough time of it. Now Shana's pregnant. That college football neck injury keeps him from working full time. Neither Gram nor Mr. Reed can help financially."

Claude tenderly massaged her neck and shoulders. "You made the right decision to join Mauvais's company ten years ago. Of course, they won't know where the money comes from. Mauvais will send it to them. She is very particular about that part of our contract. She always keeps her agreement with us."

She sighed. "At first I didn't understand why my identity had to change. But I learned it makes sense. It's Mauvais's protection plan. Once I disappeared from earth, the only way I could come back and live a worry free life would be for Mauvais to change my name, my history. Not being Carolyn Farmer anymore has opened doors to many lifetimes." She put her arms around his neck. "Many lifetimes with you, my lover, my sweet …" She was whispering, her lips lightly touching his as her body leaned into him.

The zoom reversed. Her face and voice faded. The stage receded. A dusty film resettled on the other side.

"Now, New One. What do you say? It can be your future if you choose. All you need to do is sign a contract. An agreement stating you accept employment in our company. We assure you the rewards in your future life will far exceed your fondest dreams. What do you say?"

Her mind flooded. Never to be Carolyn Farmer? If I'm not, who will I be? Take care of Gram? Help bro and a wife named Shana? What was that? Fall in love with Claude? Hey, that'd be total cool. Famous? Gorgeous? Rich? Oh, yeah! Dance forever? Yes to that too. But … never go back? Never let Gram see me? Or see Jimmy again? Do I care?

The room was hushed. Even the cats were like statues. It seemed as if the whole universe was waiting for her reply.

At first she wasn't quite sure she felt the gentle squeeze around her head. Then the crown tightened again. And she was sure. *You're trying to tell me something,* she thought, surprised she addressed it directly.

Yes, came to her mind.

Suddenly the crown was heavier. *Do not sign. But do not say you will not sign. Delay.*

She took a deep breath. "Do I have to decide right away?"

Lissette and several others gasped. A nervous murmuring and shifting came from around the room. Then a long stretch of silence followed.

She didn't know what made the cats jump from the settee. They sauntered to Mauvais and sat, one on each side of her. With ears forward, they regarded Carolyn. Their amber eyes glowed as the tips of their tails twitched.

"Mauvais," Gazellia pleaded. "Please realize what a shock this has been. She needs time to think about what she has just experienced. I will explain your contract to her."

Mauvais touched the cats behind their ears. Swiftly they padded toward Carolyn. Just as quickly, Gazellia moved to shield Carolyn with her body.

The crown gently squeezed. And Carolyn realized her fear of them was gone.

Mauvais's eyes narrowed into dark slits. Her red lips became a blood-thin line.

"New One, we strongly urge you to consider our generous offer to stay with us. Surely you are wise enough to see what wonders await you here. The mirror is proof of what your future holds. Your mother and father are dead. Your past is dead. Why not move ahead into a glorious future?"

The dark slits began to glow yellow like the cat's eyes.

"We have your very best interest at heart. However, our offer is limited. There are many who would be eager to take your place. There is no offer in the whole universe to equal ours."

The red line curved upward. "We have favored you more than any New One we have invited to our school. We have allowed you to wear our crown. No guest or member has ever been given such an honor. However, we will continue to be gracious and to extend our invitation to join us by allowing a trusted member of our company to explain the details of our contract and the affection we have for our members."

Carolyn knew there was but one reply. "Thank you, Mauvais."

"You have until tomorrow morning, ten o'clock your earth time, to reach a decision."

She directed Claude to the mirror. "You will take this to our guest's room."

"Yes, Mauvais."

Her gaze had never left Carolyn. "Consider carefully your future. Gazellia is a product of our school. Her success, her beauty, her fame, her riches are her reward for signing the Baal contract. She will explain this contract to you for your full understanding. You can review what you have seen by tapping the mirror three times."

Abruptly she turned. The leopards' chains reappeared as they trailed behind her out the door.

Chapter 13

Decisions

Everyone crowded around Carolyn.

Claude was the first to speak. "You are the right choice to wear the crown. None of us would have had the courage to refuse Mauvais."

"I can't believe you would hesitate for one moment to join us." Lissette's face flushed in anger. "We are superior to all creatures in the universe in beauty, brains, talent, and ambition. How could you even think to compare yourself to us?"

"She was not being critical of you," Michelle said.

"I agree," Claude said. "Because she is the one who could wear the crown, you're jealous of her."

Lissette hit her brother's shoulder with her fan. "How dare you say I am jealous. That is ridiculous. I am a loyal member of the Mauvais company. Have you forgotten, brother, that you signed a contract of loyalty to this company? Where is *your* honor?"

"I had no choice. I was deceived into signing."

"Deceived? You were never deceived. You wanted what we all wanted ... to escape into a life which would make us rich and famous and powerful." She looked at Claude with disdain. "You've deceived yourself into thinking you haven't enjoyed all the advantages Mauvais has given you."

Her voice grew louder as she turned to address the company surrounding Carolyn.

"Take a good look at Carolyn Farmer. What do you see? A child with physical flaws. A child who will grow old and die. A child who has no talent or worth of any kind. A human like we once were. Like her, were we not rescued out of the places we hated? Did we not promise ourselves that if we ever could change our lives we would? Did we not long to be out of whatever misery we were in? How many of us would be alive in this moment if it were not for the contract? How many of us could live in a palace, be acclaimed on other star planets in the universe? You all know what Mauvais has done for you."

She turned back to Carolyn. "You are a foolish, stupid child if you do not sign a contract which will change your life, not only for the better but for rewards beyond anything you could have ever dreamed possible."

"Indeed," said a man in cream brocade.

Carolyn couldn't remember what his name was. Something with a number.

"Wait," another said. "She didn't say she wouldn't join us. She said she needed time to think. There's nothing wrong with that."

"Don't be ridiculous," Lissette said. "There is no choice but one."

"And what would that decision lead to?" Claude said. "Let's explore what signing the contract has meant to us."

"Oui, Claude is right. Think about what being a slave of Mauvais means."

"It is a gilded cage we live in," he said. "We are pampered prisoners with invisible chains around our necks like the birds. Just because we have everything material, just because we have fame, we are not free. We have no life of our own. We don't even have control over our own bodies."

"Regardez," Gazellia said. "You know my story … my trial … my punishment. Consider I was the one closest to Mauvais. Our friendship grew over the centuries. She entrusted me with many of her secrets from the time she was a high druid priestess."

"Lest you forget, colleagues," Gazellia continued, "Mauvais chooses according to her personal wishes certain favored members to retain certain parts of themselves. She gave me that very privilege. And you Claude, and you, Lissette, and a few others, you know who you are, how she breaks Baal's law of no favoritism. If the king knew she has a weakness … sympathy to any one of us … she would be eliminated and replaced."

Lissette pointed to the crystal. "You know she is listening and watching everything."

"So what, sister? We're not saying anything she doesn't already know."

"And there is nothing we can do anyway," said another lady in the crowd. "We have all signed. Our life ends if we break it. What does it matter what she hears?"

"Our hope still lies in the crown," Gazellia said. "And it has proven it can be worn and is not merely a legend."

"It has proven nothing. It's nothing but metal and stone. Just because it sits on a child's head ... an ugly child at that ... proves it is powerless. A silly myth."

"Lissette, not everyone here agrees with you," Michelle said. "I hope the legend is true. There are a few of us who believe the story."

"Yes, sister, I am one."

"You are all traitors. Mauvais has made everyone of us what we are. Which one of you would be willing to go back to what you were? Or the misery you were in? Or give up your bodies to the real ages you are?"

"Is slavery better than death?" Gazellia asked.

"To the one who is going to die, it is," Lissette replied.

Death. Die. Carolyn's stomach flip-flopped, sending nauseous, hot waves throughout her body. "What I want to know is, are you guys robots or what?"

"Like Gazellia, I am a human," Claude said.

"Then why don't you just split?" She looked at Gazellia. "Come on, wrap me up in your chiffon thing and we'll go someplace else. Back to earth, maybe. With the crown."

"You don't understand," Claude said. "Her force is very strong. Once you have signed the contract, she controls your body."

"Like what I felt when Lissette played? And when I had on the shoes? But that felt great."

"Oui. It is an invisible power that controls your body ... and can clear your mind of conscious thought."

"But how can this power control your minds? No one can tell me what to think."

"She begins by intensifying our desire to think of ourselves first. She shows us money can buy people—"

Claude interrupted. "And governments."

"Oui. We learn how to lie, steal, cheat, and do everything we can to position ourselves to control others. There is a certain pleasure in having power over others, and because they follow you, you can make them do what they don't want to do."

Carolyn was astonished. "You mean you learn how to be ... you know ... evil?

"A more suitable word is *corrupt*."

"That's a lie," Lissette said. "You were corrupt before you came here."

"You are correct, sister. However, once a member of this company, there's no hope for being anything else. We are reeducated, reprogrammed to obey without thinking. There is no right or wrong. There is one way to think—Mauvais's way. The contract seals us into a lifestyle of corruption."

"That's why the legend has brought us a glimmer of hope," Gazellia said. "When King Baal brought it here, Mauvais could not wear it. None of us could. Yet Mauvais prized it by displaying it in the gazebo. I knew she wanted to know its secret and I told her its legend."

"That proves you are a liar and a traitor, corrupt from the start," Lissette said. "You are a perfect product of the mind-set method. First, you use your relationship with Mauvais to discover her weaknesses. Second, you tell her what you want in order to steal the crown from her. Third, you did this in order to break your word, your contract. Fourth, you want to destroy the very one who took you out of prison, gave you a home, gave you a career, gave you a life ... and ... gave you the favor of her friendship. You have learned your lessons well. Mauvais would be proud of you. That is why you became a favorite."

"This is so like you," Claude said. "You twist the facts to suit yourself."

"There is some truth in what Lissette says," Gazellia said. "Mauvais did give me the favor of her friendship. When she discovered what I was trying to do she could have eliminated me. Instead, she gave me a slight chance at freedom."

"You could have gone back to Sainte Clare. She could not touch you there," Michelle said.

"Because in my heart I had hoped some of you might want to break your contract. And I believed the legend." She put her arm around Carolyn. "Special she is, born of hope for my true freedom. And I wanted to protect her." She pointed at the crystal. "Curious, it has not gone into code red. Could it be that Mauvais is afraid of the crown?"

"Mauvais is incapable of fear. She is beyond fear," said a man in blue brocade. "As for me, I like my life as it is. I agree with Lissette. There are those of us who are exactly where we want to be: serving Mauvais."

"Certainly," Claude said. "We have all made decisions this afternoon."

"Oui. We have all made decisions on whose side we are on: Mauvais's or the Laurel Crown's."

Carolyn's mind churned. Her body ached. Her emotions were exhausted. "I'm not on any side," she said. "I want to wake up from this crazy dream."

"Unfortunately," Gazellia said, "this is no dream."

"Well, I didn't ask to come. I don't know how to work the crown. I gotta be by myself to think."

The crown gently squeezed. Instantly her nausea was gone. And her mind calmed.

As if on cue, the crystal hovered above Claude's head. It bobbed twice and soared to the mirror.

"I must take that to your room."

"I don't need it to remember what I saw."

"I know. But I have to follow orders. It has to go to your room."

"Oui. Assist Claude. This will give you an opportunity to change and rest. And think. Later, if you wish, you can ask the crystal for dinner."

"Aren't you coming with me?"

"No. Mauvais and I must parley," she said in a flat tone.

Nothing more was said. Fans snapped shut, skirts rustled, and the sound of footsteps across the marble were the only sounds as the crowd quickly dispersed.

Claude and Carolyn went to the ornate mirror. It was top-heavy. He directed her to place her full weight on one side, pushing as he pulled. She pushed hard against the mirror frame with her shoulder. It wobbled until working together they were able to steady it between them.

As they rolled it out the door, he smiled at her. "We make a good team," he said.

The casters squeaked and squawked down the hall.

"Did you see us dancing together?" she asked.

"In my future it was Gazellia I danced with, not you. Hundreds of years ago I didn't know you existed."

"But ... nobody can control the future? Right?"

"It's not control. It's vision and programming."

"Huh?"

"Mauvais sees into the future. As a druid, she practices magic. As a shape-shifter she can move in many directions."

"What's a shape-shifter?"

"A special kind of entity that can change its body into any living creature but remain the same entity inside. It's the appearance that changes … shifts from one kind of creature to another."

"Like from a human to a dog?"

"Yes, like that. To disguise and hide as an animal, or something else. Mauvais has found the keys to unlock changing the cells of her body into different shapes."

"Does she think it? Like, if she concentrates really hard she can change into a flower or whatever?"

"No. If it were that simple, she would teach us all how to do that and we wouldn't have to be restored. We would just renew ourselves by, as you say, 'thinking really hard.' She has shown each of us through this mirror our future on your earth, and other planets as well. It's what your scientists call the 'string theory.' The idea of the universe exploding outward, stars ever expanding. And, depending where you are, being inside and outside of earth time. That is how we travel."

"Wait." Carolyn pulled against the mirror stopping Claude. "Gram says, 'Only God lives inside and outside of time.' He created the universe and time … and everything. This planet too. He controls the future.'"

"Maybe, and maybe not. You decided to come here."

"No. I didn't. Gazellia brought me.

"Against your wishes?"

"I didn't know where I was going."

"You wanted to escape your life because you hated it. You're no different than the rest of us."

'I didn't say I was. I just thought—"

"On your planet, it has been perhaps only seconds, minutes since you left. While in the mirror, your life and mine come together when you will be twenty-three and I'll be roughly five hundred. The exact number of years in a member's life doesn't matter anymore."

"So if I want to, I can rap on the mirror and find out who are our presidents in the next hundred years?"

"No. That's not the kind of knowledge of the future that Mauvais shows us. She only shows us a small photo, a film clip of your … my personal life."

Claude loosened his cravat. "For example, in the 2190 earth year, I will use a Gatebox, which transports me, and I will return by the same Gatebox with a specific New One. There are many entryways into this domain and the same for other stars. Those entry ways are called *worm holes*."

"Worms? In space?"

Claude laughed. "No. A worm hole is a way of describing a tunnel that can be used to time travel between galaxies."

"By the year 2500, humans will live in giant family pods that circle the earth and have satellites that map multiple galaxies. Travel to distant stars will be commonplace for humans. You know a satellite can record the smallest detail of where you live and what you do, day or night, on earth."

"Why would anyone want to do that?"

"It's complicated." He leaned against the mirror. "It's about exploring other worlds and making your world smaller ... easier for a government to control economics and social behavior. If a government can watch everything you do, it can invent ways to control your life."

He sighed. "But actually, in the timeline of when you left earth, all your present technology hasn't kept you from messing up your planet. Or, for that matter, kept you from killing each other in wars, big and small. Over the centuries, in going back and forth with new recruits from earth to Double Suns, human egos haven't evolved one smallest gigabyte. We're still the same old species that wants what we want when we want it."

"What does that mean?"

"We are born selfish. We desire to please, as Gazellia would say, *moi*. Number one. *Uno*. Me, myself, and I. That is what makes recruiting humans easy."

"What's wrong with wanting a better life for yourself? What's wrong with having nice things ... and being famous and ...?"

"Depends on what you do to get it. You heard Lissette. We are better off with Mauvais. There are definite advantages to living under Mauvais's care."

"Yeah. Like you can live forever. Have anything you want."

"Yes. That is for you to think about. Whichever path you decide: joining MVE or by going the crown's way with Gazellia and a few of us in resisting Mauvais." He smiled and bowed slightly. "It has been a delight to know you, Carolyn Farmer." He pulled on the frame. "Now, the mirror must go in your room."

With some maneuvering, they were able to position it so that when the door opened, they rolled it in. The crystal followed them.

"We'll put it in the corner, away from the bed," he said.

She remembered the front door and the ballroom. "How come no mirrors in this room?"

"Because while we are being restored, we're not to see ourselves."

She sat on the bed. "How does that work exactly?"

"Haven't you asked yourself how Gazellia or I could be still living after hundreds years?"

"Yeah, myself, but not her. Didn't have time. After bro and I put her together, she told us about herself. Where she was born. How she met you in prison ... and how old she is. Then, whoosh ... here I am."

"But you never questioned how she could remain young for so many years? With all the questions you've been asking me, I'd have guessed you're quite a curious person."

"Okay. So I didn't ask her, like how she did it. So tell me already. How *do* you live so long?"

"It's simple. In your timeline, your doctors are just beginning to understand how to perform transplants. Replacing worn-out, diseased, or age-damaged parts with new ones is being funded and supported by your private and your government's research on earth. Here, the kingdom of Baal already has provided Mauvais the technology to replace all body parts."

"But even if every part can be replaced, it would wear out too, wouldn't it? Parts are one thing, people totally being—" She couldn't think of the word he used.

"Restored?"

"Yeah. But how?"

"Suppose you could replace each part before it wore out or became diseased. Think of yourself as a living machine. The director is the mechanic. You as a member would receive periodic overhauls to keep your machinery in top running order. Also, any part that is not perfect by a certain standard would be restored. You would continue to be new, always young, always beautiful."

He approached her, slowly inspecting her from crown to shoes. "For instance, you could have new legs and feet ... or whatever you or Mauvais likes. There is a bank for each one of us."

"A bank?"

"A storage room. The place where our old discarded parts are kept. And our new replacement parts are stored there until we need them."

Her tired, confused brain registered his words. "You mean like ... pieces of humans ... or like robots? But Gazellia said you weren't—"

"We are both," he said. "The *before* human parts of me that weren't perfect. And the new parts of me that are."

Her stomach felt queasy at the thought of human legs and arms strewn about in some kind of room. Once she had seen a dog hit by a car in the middle of the street.

Ugh. Blood and guts, she thought. "Geez. How gruesome."

He shrugged. "Not really. They are simply parts. A combination of flesh cells and synthetic. Although some are all flesh, well preserved. Mauvais uses the secrets she has learned from the ancients in Egypt. You'll understand better when you've seen them."

"I don't know if I want to go."

"Every member has been in the storage room at one time or another. There is nothing to fear."

She felt the crown squeeze gently. *There is nothing to fear.* "Maybe I can see it ... I mean you ... I mean what you were ... I don't know what I mean."

"Certainly. The storage room is two doors from here. You'll understand when you walk in."

He looked up at the crystal. "You don't need to come."

It moved to the door, indicating it was not going to obey him.

"Why does it follow me everywhere?"

"It's a recording device. It transmits what you are doing, what is said, also what we are all doing with you for contract purposes."

"I don't like it."

"Ignore it. It can't do anything without orders from Mauvais. And she has given you earth time until tomorrow."

Even with the light from the crystal, the hallway was dim. Overhead only a few candles were lit in the chandeliers.

It's as quiet as a cemetery. Too quiet for a mansion filled with so many people. *They must be resting in their rooms,* she thought. *Maybe I should be resting too. But, geez, how can I pass this up?*

She followed Claude to another door. He rapped the ring three times and it opened.

Chapter 14

the storage room

Inside the storage room, Claude struck a match and lit a fat candle on a stand by the door. "Come in," he said, lifting it high. The light from the crystal dimmed.

"What's with the candle?" Carolyn asked.

"For reverence. Mauvais's idea of honoring our body parts."

"That doesn't make sense."

"Through the centuries, candlelight has represented remembering an event, like Christmas, birthdays, a special dinner or something lost. It's the only room where when the crystal dims, more light is needed."

On the back wall, rows of heads were neatly lined on floor to ceiling shelves. Along the right wall on similar shelves, sticking out of labeled boxes, were disjointed legs and arms, hands and feet—all under a cardboard sign reading: *Limbs and Digits.* To the left were the upper and lower parts of bodies, male and female. The sign above them read: *Torsos and Organs.*

Carolyn had imagined a hospital room with pools of blood on the floor under beds, rolled-up gauze, and instruments dripping with ooze in metal trays. But in the candlelight the room looked clean. Surprised, she pointed to the concrete floor. "There's no blood ... and stuff."

"No. Not here." He lifted the candle higher to spread the light. "I think we'll leave the heads 'til last."

Good idea, she thought, relieved. *No gook—yet.*

The smaller labels on the boxes were easier to read in the candlelight. From under *Limbs and Digits,* she picked an upper arm. It was a tube. All the arms were hollow. The legs were the same.

Carolyn's trembling fingers lifted the lid of a box marked *thumbs.* Inside,

hundreds of various sized and colored thumbs filled the box to the brim. Gingerly she touched one. It was soft, smooth, and rubbery, very much like the material of the baby dolls she used to play with. She checked the rest of the boxes. Hands, fingers, feet, toes—all the parts were hollow.
The torsos were arranged according to sizes. Some were tall and thin, short and fat; others were short and thin, tall and fat. There were also young and old parts in various skin colors. She was puzzled by the mix of parts. Some seemed to be perfect in shape, yet others were not.

"Didn't you say this was a bank for transplants? I mean, some of these parts aren't perfect. Why would there be old ones and fat ones, for instance?"

"I don't understand it myself," Claude replied. "About thirty earth years ago I needed a new shoulder and right arm replaced. Some transplant work takes a longer time for recovery. So during that particular stay here, I saw my older shoulder and right arm mixed in one of the bins marked, 'For Removal.' I asked Lissette about what happened to our old parts. She said Mauvais could not discard any without approval from a higher authority, which I believe refers to King Baal."

She lifted a male torso and peered down its neck. "Where are the organs and blood vessels and muscles and things like that?" she said in one breath. "Not that I want to see them."

"I don't know. I think they are reconfigured, similar to what you know as downloading a file into a computer and storing it into something else. Only Mauvais understands the technology to accomplish keeping our insides, inside us."

He's not fully human? She took a deep breath. "Are you a cyborg?"

"You mean, part human and part machine?" He frowned and shook his head slightly, "No, I feel completely human. I remember my past life and I have the same personality."

"But would you even know ... um ... if you really are still human?"

"Yes, because there is something within me that doesn't always agree with Mauvais, Lissette, and the others. Gazellia is the same way." He bit his lower lip, slightly. "The same way that Gazellia knew you could be the one to wear the crown is the same kind of knowing I'm still human. It *is* just a truth I somehow know."

"Don't quite get it ... but—"

"Perhaps this will help." He gestured around the room. "Everything here is human flesh. Mauvais has discovered how to duplicate cells. Whatever is restored is like me, only new. When I need repair the crystal puts me in a pod."

"A what?"

"Like a glass cylinder. It does this whenever I need it. Then after the part is replaced, I recover in my room. Of course, I can't see inside myself. And there aren't any mirrors in my room either."

"Does it hurt?"

"No. I follow the crystal to my room. It goes into code red and, when I wake up in the pod, I have the new part. Sometimes I'm sore. Then I have increased recovery time and therapy to use my body properly again."

"No stitches? No cuts or bandages?"

"No. Only soreness … on occasion awkwardness in learning to move smoothly again."

Well, Carolyn thought, *maybe you think you're not a cyborg, but I'm not sure you aren't one. Find out where he came from.* "How did you … um … come here?"

"I was a slave … who became a pirate … who became a mercenary who killed for money a hundred years, give or take a few decades, before I met Gazellia."

"You're older than—"

"Yes. I was a recruiter for Mauvais before Gazellia was born. Unlike Gazellia's father who cared enough to bring her to a convent, at six years old my sister Lissette and I were sold by our father into slavery to work in a strip mine digging coal. We had to carry bags of coal on our backs and dump them into wagons for our master to sell them in Paris. Mules were more valuable than we. Many died of the plague … but we survived.

"When Lissette began to blossom into womanhood, our master sold her to a brothel and me to a pirate ship. In a typhoon our ship ran aground … and being physically strong from years in the mine, I saved the captain who owned me. In gratitude he freed me. We had to eat, of course. And, in order to do so, we became hired soldiers who would fight for any country who paid us. My captain was killed in a raid, and I was caught and sentenced to be hanged within the hour. As I stood in front of the noose, the guard tying my hands behind my back whispered, 'Would you like to escape to a life beyond your wildest dreams? I have a contract. All you have to do is promise to sign it, and you will be free.'"

He continued. "Of course I agreed to sign. The next thing I knew, I was in a beautiful room like yours, in front of a table with a legal document. I read it and quickly signed. Thereafter I became a member-recruiter and through hundreds of years have served Mauvais."

"How did you land in prison next to Gazellia?"

"I was sent by Mauvais."

"In the ... um ... pod?"

"How did you get here?" Claude asked.

"Gazellia wrapped me up in her dress and we flew and crash-landed here."

"You were both transported through time and space by Mauvais's power. That's how a worm hole is used. How we move from one assignment to another."

Suddenly Carolyn was aware of the weight of the crown. In her mind, she saw the parchment and its words: "Be warned. Beware of the Baal contract."

"But I didn't sign anything and I'm here."

"Gazellia is a woman of courage to bring you without a promise or a contract signature."

He lifted the candle to indicate the crown. "We have our hope in it and you," he said as several drops of wax hit his right hand. He jerked and shook them off. "I think it is time we move along to the heads."

Carolyn took a very deep breath. Heads. Real? Not? She patted her chest to calm the heart. Okay, okay. Chill.

There were two large sections of shelves at the far end of the long room. A sign, *"Eliminated,"* hung from the ceiling in front of one large section. Over the next section the sign read, *"Current Members."*

In the *"Eliminated"* section, the first head she saw was that of a young woman in her early twenties. Her brown, uncombed hair stuck out around her head. A sad, wistful expression was stamped on her rather plain features. It was as if her head had been cut off in an unhappy midthought.

Next was a teenage boy, his complexion ruddy and covered with freckles. His blond hair was bleached almost white. He too looked sad. Third in the row, a black girl about Carolyn's age frowned angrily at someone no longer there. Her naturally dark, curly hair had been braided and looped into a large knot on the top of her head.

With a gesture indicating the whole section of *"Elimination,"* he said, "None of these are in our membership."

"Are these ... um ... were these the heads of real people?"

"Yes. They are the ones who changed their minds to sign. A copy of their heads are a record of their being here as candidates. I don't know how the crystal is involved in keeping them as a record, but it does. The ones I know are in the *'Current Members'* section."

It took a couple of aisles for Claude to find the heads of himself and Lissette among the current members.

"Here we are, or as we once were," he said, pointing to his head on the shelf.

She appraised him critically. "You look a little different. Now your nose is straight."

"The hook in my nose was a family trait."

"Your sister has the same nose."

"Yes, Mauvais had it straightened like mine. Also my sister's fingers were lengthened to play better. All of me has been improved. A male dancer has to be tall and strong to lift his partner. My body parts are improved, but how much of my insides are remade, I don't know."

The candle flickered and burned while she continued to look at more than a hundred heads. She recognized many from the ballroom. At the last head on the bottom shelf of the last aisle, she realized she hadn't seen Gazellia.

"Where is Gazellia?"

"Isn't she there?"

"Not that I can see."

Quickly he walked past the shelving, checking each face. "Odd, she isn't here. She should be here. These heads are a roster of our active membership. I have no idea why she isn't on the shelf."

"Maybe you don't recognize her."

"Remember, I saw her, knew her centuries ago. I remember her then. I know her now." He frowned. "There's no question about it. She has been removed."

"She said she wanted to talk to Mauvais. Maybe she took her own head—" Carolyn stopped, suddenly shaken by the ridiculous-sounding statement she was making. It would be funny if it wasn't so scary. She shivered.

On impulse she reached out and grabbed his hand. His skin was soft and warm like hers. The crowd in the ballroom all seemed flesh and blood. What part was human? What part robot? She shivered again.

He squeezed her hand. "You're tired. You've had a full day." He led her to the door and blew out the candle. "You need food, rest, a quiet time to think ... to review your future in the mirror if you wish ... and a good night's sleep. You will need your strength for tomorrow."

The crystal lit the way back to her room.

After escorting her through the open door, he bowed. "Rest well, lovely Carolyn. Keep the Laurel Crown close to you."

"Don't worry," she said. "I'm going to sleep in it."

"Then I bid you good-night."

As soon as he turned to walk down the dark hall, Carolyn looked up at the globe. "I'm real tired," she said. "I'll follow you to my room."

Once inside, she sank with a weary sigh into the chair across from the mirror. She watched her reflection begin to fade. *That's interesting,* she thought. *I didn't rap or knock or do anything to it.* As if in answer to her thought, she saw a slight glint reflected from the crown before the mirror went dark.

Like in a DVD movie, the gazebo appeared.

The crown gently squeezed. *Watch and learn.*

Immediately, she knew those thought-words came from the crown. "Okay," she said, her energy revived with curiosity.

The leopards were nowhere to been seen as Mauvais stepped up onto the concrete foundation and sat on a bench.

At the same time, carefully pulling her dress closer to keep it from catching on the branches, Gazellia sidestepped through another hedge opening.

With a wave and nod, Mauvais invited Gazellia to sit next to her on the bench.

"We expected you to come. We spent considerable past negs here discussing your assignments."

"Among other things." Gazellia sat down. "We know each other well. Just as you said, we have spent many negs together."

Mauvais swung one leg over to straddle the bench to face her. She leaned slightly forward and smiled. The echo softened.

"With fond memories, it is here we have allowed you to converse with us as an equal."

Gazellia avoided looking directly at Mauvais. "Oui. And have I not been most grateful? Have I not been a loyal subject as well as a trusted confidante? Have I not been useful to you over the centuries?"

"We cannot say otherwise. Until, of course, your rebellion against us. We were most gracious in our judgment and sentence. The possibility of your escape was determined by us to be most fair."

"That is the exact reason why I have come to speak to you. It did, indeed, occur to me you had arranged that I would do so." Gazellia's fingers trembled as she brushed away a trickle of sweat from her upper lip.

Carolyn watched Mauvais's irises turn from black to a warm amber. Another fairytale? But who is the villain here? Mauvais or—could it be Gazellia?

Gently the crown squeezed. *Shh. Watch and listen.*

Chapter 15

the mirror

"Okay." Carolyn leaned back as she watched Mauvais smile at Gazellia.

"We knew we would miss your company," Mauvais said. "And we did not desire you to be absent for any length of negs."

Gazellia pointed to the empty case. "And did you expect that the New One would be able to wear the crown?"

"No. That was most *un*expected. But we are most pleased to discover she is able. Now we can harness its power to ours."

Gazellia frowned. "She will not sign."

"Are you certain? We have never been denied, nor have we ever been mistaken."

"Mistaken you were with me."

"Ahh, yes," Mauvais said as she chuckled. "But here you are. A fool returned to her master."

Gazellia crossed her arms against her chest. "You may think of me as you wish, however I will do whatever it takes to shield the New One. She has captured my heart."

Mauvais's lips became a hard, thin line. "As you did mine, once."

"No. You have no heart."

Mauvais fingered her diamond pendant. "You are mistaken. We held great affection through the negs for you."

"Untrue. I remember quite accurately your history. Shall I remind you of it?" Gazellia asked.

"You mean your version of our personal history, which includes your deceit. This we would like to hear."

"Oui. I will oblige.

"You were known as Morna, first daughter of Mordred, a high druid priest at Stone Pillar, Solar Cap. The stones erected there for worship have long crumbled into dust."

Mauvais smiled. "But, my friend, His Majesty's rule continues throughout the universe. Those sacred stones may be dust, but that dust has been powerfully scattered throughout the galaxies."

"'Tis true," Gazellia said as she nodded. "There is yet to come a power to destroy King Baal's kingdom and your regency on Double Suns."

"There shall never be such." She patted Gazellia's hand. "Do continue. We are enjoying this repartee ... and this remembrance of our past."

"You became the first daughter. The one who is first is the one trained in the magic arts."

Carolyn saw Mauvais's eyes change from black to yellow with flecks of red. "Is Gazellia a witch, like Mauvais?" she asked the crown. But before it could answer, she thought, *But Gazellia says she's isn't.*

She is not. Listen and learn.

"Ahh, yes. My older sister, Briget refused learning sorcery and renounced the teachings of our father Mordred. She went to the other side by following Saint Patrick. I was the loyal one, therefore I became the first daughter."

Gazellia smoothed her skirt. "At the convent, I knew her as Bridget. The sisters added the letter D to symbolize her choosing to worship a higher power, one greater than King Baal's."

"You mean the nonsense about love conquering death? The physical in every realm of existence only changes from one molecular dimension to another. We have evolved to a higher source of energy, nothing else. You are foolish and stupid to believe otherwise."

"I may be foolish, perhaps stupid, but the one who wears the crown is neither."

Surprised by the reference to herself, Carolyn fingered its leaves. *What does this have to do with me? Or is this a you?*

Listen and learn.

"Gazellia, confess. You hate the superior technology that allows us to conquer space and nonhuman species. You are jealous of our shape-shifting abilities."

"Never was I jealous. I pitied you. Unlike your father, mine loved me. Your father was a murderer. He poisoned your mother to marry a woman of wealth. It was the new wife's land and castle that your father desired. He brought you and Bridget to live with—"

"Do you remember her name?"

"Hookah." Gazellia crooked her finger. "Like a hook used for catching prey. After Bridget ran away to the new religion, Mordred placed you first ... and above her in status with his followers ... the followers of Baal. As I recall, you cut off Hookah's head and dedicated it to Baal after Mordred died."

Mauvais licked her lips. "You remember well."

"And for that blood, King Baal honored you, and positioned you to be high priest in your father's place. At the Stone Pillar Fire Ceremony you dedicated your soul ... what you name as worthless cells to the gods and Baal. You still light a dedication candle upon entering the storage room for what you pretend to consider worthless parts."

"You forget one scene in the story about our family."

"What scene is that?"

"Our mother, Sheila, was a great dance worshiper. One who pleased the gods with her beauty and grace."

The chorus of echoes suddenly became a solitary soft voice. "You reminded us of her, resurrecting an affection which has never completely died."

With a shock, Carolyn realized she was hearing the voice of a young woman. It was musical—like notes played on a flute.

Mauvais's eyes closed and her chin dropped as if in a deep sleep. "Is that you Briget, speaking over the voice of us?" Her red lips turned pink, full and natural. "Aye. I, the one called Briget of old Stone Pillar, am still here surrounded by many, locked inside a circle of false worshipers. They have a message for you, Gazellia. Find the key to unlock the power-secret of the Laurel Crown, and you will be free forever. Bring the New One to sign the contract. Remove the crown from her head. Bring it to Mauvais, and your contract will be cancelled."

"No. You are a shifter. I dare not trust you."

Relief flooded Carolyn. "Yea!" she yelled at the mirror, her fist raised. "Take that, you witch."

Watch.

Suddenly Mauvais lifted her head—her nostrils flared. "Briget lives no more."

"The New One is quite alive, however ... wearing the crown."

Mauvais pointed her finger like a dagger at Gazellia's throat. "We will soon accomplish our goals as far as both are concerned."

Gazellia flinched. She touched the medallion hidden under her lace bodice. "Carolyn is special. You know the legend. Harming her could mean your death."

Mauvais's sharp fingernail pressed into Gazellia's throat. "You know what is in the storage room. You have been employed long enough to know what the MV Enterprises' policy is."

"Oui. But I believe the legend." She pushed her finger away.

"You are ever a fool. Your own life is a testimony to the selfishness, the corruption of your race. You speak of a human child as being special. Humans are exactly like you. You sold your life to have the life we created for you."

Mauvais sneered. "You are a perfect example of our mind-set method. You returned to us to sacrifice Carolyn to free yourself from your contract. You brought her here to make an exchange ... her life for yours."

Gazellia's eyes filled with tears. She pressed both hands against the medallion. "That is not true. I told you I love Carolyn." She pulled out the chain, cupping the medal in her hands. "You have wanted this. I will give it to you, if you do not force her to sign."

"We own you. We own everything on your body. And your body. We allowed you to keep the medallion because it suited our purposes. As soon as you are disassembled, it will swing from around our neck."

There was a long silence as Gazellia rubbed her fingers over the raised lettering. Finally, she spoke—her voice firm, quiet, deep.

"Long ago, I betrayed My Lady. In signing the contract, I exchanged one kind of prison for another much worse. Whatever goodness the Poor Clares put into me, I threw away. When I first saw the Laurel Crown in your possession, I remembered its legend and told it to you. As the negs passed, and I would return for parts and new assignments, I would spend time with you in the gazebo. But I always hated myself for what I did. Seeing the crown and thinking about its legend began to work in my heart. Oui, I am willing to exchange my life for Carolyn's. I will do whatever it takes to keep her from signing."

Gazellia kissed the medallion and pressed it to her heart. "You have made the choice. This is not yours until I am dead. And mine is this. For as long as I have breath in my body, I will protect Carolyn."

"You fool! You can do nothing." In Mauvais's cold fury, her shrill, echoing voice had an edge of controlled fear. "You have no power. And there is no escape for Carolyn whether or not she signs. Tomorrow both will be in my possession. And then she will witness your elimination."

The diamonds in the MVE turned bright red, flashing tiny sparks. "It will give us great pleasure to see you finally finished." She stood on the bench, her hands on her hips, glaring down at Gazellia. Her voice trembled, vibrating in its high pitch. "You can do nothing."

With her right hand, Gazellia gripped her medal and with the other she pointed to the fiery pendant. "Your anger, your fear betrays you. It is *you* who can do nothing. Not to me. Not to Carolyn." Her face was radiant. "You are afraid of the crown's power. You are afraid you cannot please *your* master. You believe the legend *is* true. You believe the crown has more power than you and the king who rules you, combined. 'Tis you who is afraid of Carolyn. And … *my* medallion."

She jumped to her feet and twirled, her blue silk skirt billowing out as she spun.

"Mon Dieu. *Magnifique!*" she shouted. "You will never make her a member or own the crown. It is *you* who will be finished in the end."

Mauvais's lips drew into a tight, vicious line. "Then prepare for your death. Once you signed, we owned you forever."

"Wrong, you are. You can do nothing without the king's permission. And he has not given it, yet. If he had, you would not be here talking to me."

Joyfully, Gazellia swung the medallion in front of Mauvais's face. "This protects me. It will never be yours."

Mauvais jumped down and tried to grab the medallion, but Gazellia was too quick. She side-stepped her, dancing backward, swinging the medallion as she teased, "Be careful, Mauvais. You cannot touch me without Baal's permission."

Mauvais grabbed Gazellia's shoulders and shoved her down on the bench. Her right hand gripped the chain around Gazellia's neck, twisting it tight. The metallic voice shrilled. "You think the crown can save you? You think the New One can continue to live without us?" The shriek became a soft hiss. "See how the powers of the universe belong to usss. See how the

New One will desire to become one of usss. See usss take you apart piece by piece. Yesss, this you will see."

With both hands Gazellia tried to break Mauvais's grip. "Mon amie, Bridget," she cried. "Are you inside anywhere still? If there is one cell left of you in this creature, have mercy, mon Dieu, upon me."

Instantly, Mauvais released the chain. Her features quickly melted into a shimmering, vibrating golden glow, which spread like liquid completely covering her black suit.

Dressed in a flowing white robe with a crescent silver moon hanging on turquoise beads around her neck, a young woman in her twenties stood like a hologram in front of Gazellia. A wide headband with silver half moons was twisted through long golden curls around her head. The benches, pillars, and shrubs of the maze bled through her shimmering figure.

Whoa! Carolyn stood up. *Who is she?*

Watch.

Gazellia took a deep breath, rubbing her throat, clearing it softly. "Merci. There is something of you left in Mauvais. Some particle of kindness."

"You expect too much of me, my friend. I am gone like a solar wind blown across a star exploded epochs ago." The voice vibrated as the figure danced.

"Mon amie." Gazellia's tears fell. "Oh, help the New One. Let her ride upon your wings of courage. Give her your victory. Do not let her fall," she sobbed. "Remember, he agape nikai panta." She held up the medallion. "Remember the Sisters of Clare. What you once were. Have mercy and do not let the crown fall under King Baal's power."

"I will do what I can." The shimmer dissolved into a bright spot that disappeared into one of the rays of suns.

Alone, Gazellia dropped to her knees, and, with her head bowed, cupped the medal between her hands.

"Oh, Great Majesty, I promise to do all I can to protect Carolyn to recompense for my many selfish acts, beginning with Milady. I threw away any chance for living a worthy life. Instead I have lived a betraying one. Whatever Mauvais does to me, I do deserve. Oh, Mighty One who gives everlasting mercy, reveal to Carolyn how to unlock the secret power of love that will free us from the tyranny of Mauvais. May she never rule again."

Sobbing quietly, she whispered, "Forgive me for serving evil. I return to serving you, the All Good. Give me grace. Set me free. Amen."

She lifted her head and held the medallion high. As the light hit, rainbows danced under the curved roof of the cupola.

"He agape nikai panta. 'Never forget us.' I thank you for those who loved me. I remember my beginning. I trust you with my end."

She rose, wiped her face, and slipped the medal inside her dress. Gathering her skirt close about her, she walked through the hedge opening.

Before Carolyn's mind could wrap around what she had just seen, the crown squeezed.

There is more to watch and learn.

Like a glitch in a DVD, for a second Carolyn saw the mirror turn black and then she saw the throne.

Chapter 16

mauvais

The birds were silent in the apple tree.

Carolyn watched rays stream from the globe into the cobras' heads. As soon as they reached them, a platform rose from the marble floor rotating the throne toward the back wall.

While it turned, the apple tree, furnishings and windows, disappeared. The back wall opened into a computer room where two gray-uniformed men appeared sitting at a large console of three-dimensional screens. The MVE logo was stitched on the backs of their uniforms and on their military caps. In front of the console a giant screen displayed the logo, duplicated on the smaller monitors.

By the time the platform had completely turned, Mauvais's shimmering form appeared seated on the throne.

"Connect me to King Baal."

"Yes, Director." They both touched the keyboards in front of them. On the monitors a series of stellar maps, views of the universe, galaxies, and solar systems flashed as fast as lightning during a thunderstorm. Milliseconds later, a map of a solar system, then a star, and then a close-up of a city appeared on screen.

A large, transparent dome covered the city. A system of elevated highways connected buildings of various sizes and shapes. The view enlarged and zeroed in on a pyramid structure made of steel girders. This structure towered above the other buildings. From within these triangular girders, a pulsating beacon of light radiated a glow outward throughout the city. Its reflection pulsed off the metal buildings. The view enlarged again, closer to the pulsating beacon of light.

"My Lady Regent," said one of the corpsman. "You may transmit your message."

"King Baal, a New One can wear the Laurel Crown."

The screen filled with hundreds of stars through a black space. A metallic voice, pleasant sounding, said, "Welcome, Mauvais," as the words clicked on screen and continued. "I am pleased you have recruited a New One capable of wearing the crown. Put her on."

Mauvais's face appeared in an upper left hand section. As she spoke, her words appeared underneath. "It pleases us that you are pleased, Your Majesty."

She snapped her fingers at the globe. And the scenes of what had transpired in the maze between Gazellia and Carolyn appeared.

"This New One is a child. We did not consider the crown would choose a child."

A beam of light from the globe cut a twenty-foot by twelve-foot opening between the monitors and corpsmen, and Mauvais.

In milliseconds, the triangular girders reappeared within the frame and dissolved into a golden cobra head. Its hood opened like a fan, which became shimmering white hair flowing on well-muscled shoulders. Fangs became white teeth behind golden lips. Fiery diamond eyes cooled into a deep amber color. Perfect in form, a giant golden man stepped out of the rectangle into the computer room.

The screens returned to the stars moving in black space. The words printed out as they were spoken on the monitors.

Mauvais stood and bowed low. "Your Majesty. We are delighted you have sent your spokesman to our humble dwelling."

"Accept him as myself in solid substance necessary for interaction with you. When you speak to him, you speak to me."

The golden man held out his hand to Mauvais. Although his lips moved, his printed words were smoothly voiced through the monitors. "I am Gog, a shape-shifter like you, employed by our great master."

She nodded to the giant. "We meet again."

"Yes, Mauvais. You were a druid priestess at Stone Pillar when solar cap, north-south-five-two-one was inhabited with giants eons ago. We were as one then, and now on Double Suns we are united in the same great cause."

She kissed Gog's hand. "Yes, Your Majesty. We do remember."

Gazillia's extensive file flashed on screen as certain lines glowed for emphasis.

```
   ^#^ neg-time: MV 666-239-461.
   Guilty of breaking the law of confidentiality.
   Guilty of rebellion against code of recruiter conduct.
   Guilty of insubordination on assignments.
   Guilty of noncompliance with district regents.
   Guilty of noncompliance to identification modulation improvements.
   Remanded to incarceration and exiled to Milky Way; Planet EART ^=sOLAR CAP nrt/soth 521.
```

Gog reached into the rectangle and pulled out the file.

"What changed her loyalty to us?" the computer voice asked as the words printed out.

"You sent the Laurel Crown to us in Vess neg-time," Mauvais said.

"Yes, I placed it under your protection as a reward for your loyal service."

Gog offered her the file. "You are evading my question. Perhaps you need to reacquaint yourself with her history."

Mauvais waved it off. "No, my king." She rubbed her palms together. "Upon receiving your charge to secure the crown, we attempted to wear it. We could not, nor could any of our other loyal members of your kingdom in Double Suns. When Gazellia attempted to place the Laurel Crown on her head, she remembered the legend and told it to us."

Mauvais lightly touched the arm of Gog. "Your Majesty, we could not understand why no one could wear the crown. It was for our loyalty to you, great king, that we chose to listen to her explanation of this mystery."

"Well you know this mystery-legend is a lie. It is my pure, perfect energy that empowers all. It is my eternal cause to perfect all universe species to achieve higher and higher levels of energy that fuel individual and corporate expansion."

"Agreed, Your Majesty. However, Gazellia had discarded this mind-set. Therefore, after her trial we banished her into a puzzle."

"How do you account for her restoration?"

"We cannot account for this occurrence." Mauvais hesitated. The echo quivered slightly. "Except ... possibly ... for the medallion."

"Explain."

"Yes, Your Majesty. Member recruiter Claude, MV 666-200-245, neglected to list her medallion as our property. At the time of her signing, we did not see this as a difficulty since all members are owned by us, soul and body. Therefore, we cannot account for Gazellia's release from prison. At her trial, her memory belief was stronger than our programming and our code red chip. On more than one occasion she attempted to join noncontracted specimens to our company."

"Are you saying the MV 666-239-461 brought unsworn humans into my kingdom? Explain why you did not delete this criminal member and confiscate the medal."

Mauvais's long fingers tightly clutched her diamond pendant. "We considered her past employment history of excellent recruiting methods. Therefore, we gave her privileges our other members did not receive."

Gog's lips thinned; his eyeteeth began to sharpen into points.

"What privileges without my authorization?" the monitor voice asked.

Her intertwined fingers grew white. "When she told us the legend, we desired to use her to be certain it contained not a molecule of truth."

She bowed slightly. "It was this great desire to serve you, my king, that prompted us to allow Gazellia to draw close. To our misfortune, in allowing her the privilege of keeping her medallion, it seemed to have resurfaced a section of her brain which we were unable to reprogram."

Red flecks appeared in Gog's amber eyes.

"Regent, you have broken our directive to confiscate all personal articles on members' bodies."

"True, Your Majesty. We judged our chip would overcome any residual memory."

She bowed slightly again. "My king, as your humble regent, and supreme judge of Double Suns Court, exiling Gazellia offered us a slight opportunity of discovering whether or not the legend is true."

Mauvais smiled. "We are pleased our judgment has proved itself valid. And, Your Majesty, may we add that Gazellia has come into our possession once more."

"An elimination procedure must be enacted immediately."

From the waist she bowed low before Gog. "My king, let us not eliminate too quickly. The child trusts Gazellia. We must turn that trust from her to us."

"I will hear your recommendations."

"We have not assigned this New One a number. You may access her history under Carolyn Farmer. Once she has signed our contract, we will correct her physical disabilities, reprogram her mind, and implant our chip. In completing these directives, we will discover the New One's ability to wear the crown. Thereupon, we will deliver the knowledge of this power to Your Majesty."

Mauvais bowed again and sat down.

"After all procedures have been completed on the New One, you will eliminate the MV 666-239-461. You will delete her molecular substance. She will be disassembled and disintegrated."

"Yes, my king."

"The medallion is to be melted and added to my treasury."

"Yes, my king."

"Should you fail in carrying out my directives, should you fail to complete the total recruitment of the new specimen, should you fail to wear the Laurel Crown ... you know the consequences."

"Yes, my king."

The crystal appeared on the large screen and monitors. Gog turned to the screen and tapped it. The globe bobbed and disappeared.

"Thank you, Your Majesty."

Gog stepped inside the rectangle. "Shape-shifter Mauvais, we enjoyed our visit."

In a millisecond, he crumpled inward into a gold dot that disappeared into the stars.

The computer screen went blank.

The gray uniformed man tapped the keyboard. "Transmission complete."

As soon as the platform started rotating, Mauvais's shimmering form dissolved, and the wall, draperies, and furniture reappeared as before. The birds in the apple tree were silent and unmoving.

The scene vanished.

Like an uncapped, shaken bottle of soda, Carolyn's brain exploded in umpteen different directions. Confusion. Fear. Guilt. Panic attack. Run.

Where? To whom? Gram? How can she help me? Home? How stupid I was to leave. Oh, my God! What a mess I've made of my life. All I wanted to do was to go someplace better. What have I gotten myself into? Jimmy was right. She touched the crown. *You had better tell me what to do,* she thought, *or I'm a goner.*

I chose you. I am with you. Trust me.

A coolness came over her, a stillness that calmed her heart and quieted her mind. Fear not. Trust me. That's what Gazellia kept saying. And I did. And here I am in a mess worse than the one I left. *Why should I trust you? Who are you?*

Love.

"Huh?" Carolyn shook her head. "What's love got to do with Mauvais? Gazellia? This nutty place?"

You are on a journey.

Carolyn looked at the mirror and pointed. "Some way I can go home through that?"

No answering thought came. She sighed. Her body ached. The green dress and silk underwear, which had felt smooth on her skin a short while ago, suddenly felt scratchy. *I'm tired. Got to rest. Oh, the bed will feel good.*

She limped to it and was leaning over to untie her shoes when the door swung open and Gazellia entered.

They both spoke at the same time.

"Mon amie. I am free. Free! My medallion protects me just as—"

"I saw you and Mauvais in the mirror … and, then—"

"Wait," Gazellia said. "You saw me and Mauvais?" She grabbed Carolyn's hands. "But what exactly did you see?"

"The conversation between you and her just before you came in. And then I saw her on the throne talking to King Baal and some giant … in outer space somewhere about the contract I'm supposed to sign and the crown and you and me and … and … *what* kind of person are you to bring me to a place like this … anyway?" Carolyn pulled her hands away. "And … we're not free. Mauvais is going to eliminate you after I sign … after she finds out how I work this." She lifted the crown slightly. "And then she's going to eliminate me too."

Trust me. Calm yourself.

Carolyn paid no attention to those thoughts. "What am I going to do? Gazellia, you promised you'd make every dream come true … you promised my life would change. New destiny ... new adventure ... discoveries." She pointed to her shoes. "And no more pain. Do you hear me?" she shouted. "No. More. Pain!"

Immediately Carolyn felt Gazellia's arms tight around her. "Oh, *ma chérie,* do not fear. The same words written on my medallion, the same words written on the crown you wear, those same words gives us the power to resist evil ... to believe love conquers ... love protects."

Carolyn nodded. "So okay. The crown keeps telling me the same thing. Fear not. Trust me. Just what you said in the cellar."

"'Tis true. Believe it. It is the power of eternal love that has victory over everything Mauvais stands for. All this belongs to us. To believe that breaks the chains of fear." She kissed Carolyn on the cheek. "*Ma chèrie,* thank you for being the special, special person you are."

"But ... I didn't do anything. I can't do anything."

"The crown does not agree. It chose you. And it was you who released me from prison to rediscover the truth I had forgotten. Merci, ma chérie."

In the warmth of Gazellia's arms, Carolyn felt the same comforting protection—just like when her mother hugged her after a horrible nightmare—reassuring her everything would be all right. But Mom was gone.

Carolyn wept. "Nothing's all right. Nothing. Mom is gone. And Dad too. And it's all my fault. There's no way I can do anything right."

"Ma chérie." Her fingers wiped away Carolyn's tears. "The crown will right whatever is wrong. We will trust the words on my medallion and on the crown. Though Mauvais summons all her resources, her powers against us, we must believe the legend."

The crown gently squeezed. *Fear not. I am the power behind the legend.*

"Come," Gazellia said, starting to pull on Carolyn's sash. "You are tired." She looked up at the globe. "You need to change, eat, and rest."

"The rest part sounds real good. I'm—" But before Carolyn could finish, the mirror began to vibrate violently.

Crashing through an explosion of glass, Jimmy flipped onto the marble floor, hitting his head with a smack.

Like a bullet out of a gun, Carolyn flew to his side. She crouched down and touched the cut on his forehead. "Oh, bro, you're hurt."

Chapter 17

the intruder

Gazellia bent over his glass-covered body. Using her silk skirt to protect her hands, she pulled off several large pieces of mirror. She pressed her fingers against his neck to feel a pulse. "He is alive."

They rolled him onto his back. Carefully Carolyn straightened his arms and Gazellia straightened his legs. Together they brushed away tiny slivers of glass from the creases in his clothes. His corduroy jeans and plaid shirt were spotted with blood from tiny cuts.

"Let's get him up on the bed," Carolyn said.

"Wait." He might have internal injuries." Gazellia's fingers probed his body with an expert touch. "No bones seem broken."

They watched him breathe.

Total shock registered in Carolyn's brain. *He came to rescue me and take me home. He's hurt because he risked his life for me. How absolutely, positively great is that!*

Gazellia sighed with relief. "Except for a few surface cuts on his knees, the rest of his skin is unbroken. The cut on his head is the worst."

"Do you think he'll need stitches? It looks pretty bad."

"First, we need supplies." Gazellia looked up at the crystal. "Antiseptic, towel, washcloth, a bandage, a bowl of water and ice," she commanded.

The crystal flashed and they appeared beside his body.

Carolyn cradled his head in her lap while Gazellia emptied the tube of antiseptic into the ice and water. She gave the towel to Carolyn to wrap his head. After soaking the washcloth, she pressed it to his gash, stopping the flow of blood.

Carolyn dipped a corner of the towel into the ice water and began dabbing at the small cuts on his freckled face.

"He will not need stitches," Gazellia said, rinsing and reapplying the washcloth. She looked up at Carolyn. "Not that Mauvais would be willing to provide medical help for your brother if he needed it."

With the towel Carolyn completed cleaning his left hand and went to his right. "Look what's tied to his wrist."

"Worry about that later."

His lids fluttered. He groaned, "Uhh ... uhh ..."

"The bleeding's stopped. I think he will be fine." Gazellia unrolled the gauze bandage and wrapped it around his head.

Carolyn looked at him cradled in her lap. What were they arguing about—what seemed a thousand years ago—just before the truck hit them? *How far away that all seems now,* she thought, leaning over to kiss him on the cheek. "Glad to see you, bro."

He reached out to her with trembling hands. "Is that really you, sis?"

"Yeah. It's me."

"Where am I?" He made an instinctive effort to rise. "Uhh ... my head."

"Don't move yet," she said, pulling him back down.

He pointed to the crown. "What is *that?*"

"It is a wondrous gift to Carolyn called the Laurel Crown. It has power—"

"Which I don't know how to use. It's complicated, bro."

"A water glass," Gazellia commanded. It flashed as she reached for it. "Fill." She lifted his head. "Here, drink this."

He took a couple of sips and pointed to the crystal. "What's that?"

"It materializes whatever we ask it to give," Gazellia said.

"Huh?"

"Um ... I don't know how it does what it does," Carolyn said, holding his head while Gazellia slipped her hand under his shoulder to lift him higher to the glass.

He squinted in the light as he looked around the room. With a sweep of his hand indicating its enormous size and rich contents, he asked Gazellia, "Does this belong to you?"

"No. You are in the home of Mauvais Vallee, the owner of the school."

"School? What school?"

They helped him sit up. "Oh, it's just too complicated to explain right now," Carolyn said. "It's just too mixed up."

Gazellia placed her arms under his shoulders. "Right now, you need to stand up. Perhaps, if you can walk a little ..."

He managed to take a few steps.

"Is your vision clear?" Gazellia asked. "You might have a concussion."

"I'm okay." He shrugged. "I've been hit worse in a game."

Carolyn watched him lean against Gazellia as he slowly walked around the bed.

"How'd you get here? Did you tell Mr. Reed about what happened? Does Gram know you're here?"

"No, didn't tell Gram you vanished with her." He held up the silk. "Mr. Reed helped me with this. Just followed the instructions."

"What instructions?" she asked.

"After you left, I figured there had to be a portal you guys went through. No way was I going to let you take off without me following." He raised the silk. "In here are the border pieces. I borrowed Mr. Reed's stamp magnifier to read the fine print on one." He stumbled over the French words: "Property of Mauvais Vallee. If found, return to L'Ecole Des Particuliers Arts, Les Deux Suns, Solar Une, ST 981."

"Oui, that is the school's address."

"That's not all," Jimmy said. "It gave directions. 'Wrap puzzle in red silk. Tie with cobra skin. Swing in circle three times and release.' Now I thought, *Where the h am I going to get a cobra skin?*"

Carolyn smiled. "I bet I know. Mr. Reed to the rescue."

"Yep. He took me to the mall for the silk. Went to a music store where you could buy skins to cover drums."

"So he does know what happened?" Carolyn asked.

"Are you kidding? Tell him my sister and some witch out of a puzzle disappeared? He'd think I was crazy. I told him I was helping you with a class project. Don't think he bought it. But doesn't matter. Guess he saw I was ... um ... ticked about you giving me the assignment and wanted to help." He sighed. "It wasn't cobra. Wasn't real skin either. Wasn't sure it would work. Had to try it. Told Reed I needed to be left alone to finish the project. I did what the piece said. And here I am."

She hugged him as tightly as she could. "Glad you could make it, bro."

"Quit it." He frowned at her. "What makes you think I'd wanna come?

You're nothing but trouble. But I had to. Not coming would've caused more trouble with Gram hysterical, the police asking questions, everybody hunting for you, thinking you'd been kidnapped or murdered or ... whatever. How the hell could I explain how you disappeared? I'd have ended up in a padded cell."

"Well ... thanks. I'm still glad you're here."

"Do not be too glad, Carolyn," Gazellia said. "His coming has completely changed our circumstances. We have protection. But he has no defense. After his trial, he will be exterminated."

"What trial?"

"Mauvais puts intruders on trial, Jimmy. None of us were invited." She looked at Carolyn, "Remember, mon amie, we crashed. We too are trespassers. She considers anyone who violates her space deserves execution."

"But you brought me. I didn't ask to come."

"Pity-Party, you lie. You asked to go."

"But ... I didn't know I'd be—"

Gazellia interrupted. "Although Mauvais is a tyrant, a despot, she is capricious, unpredictable like all murderers. Even Hitler, Stalin had friends and were loved by relatives."

She guided Jimmy to the side of the bed. "I have been one of Mauvais's favorites. And she covets my medallion and what is on Carolyn's head. Those are the protections you don't have, Jimmy."

"Well, give 'em to her and we'll all get outta here. You can take us back the way we came."

"Jimmy, in truth, 'tis not that simple." She pointed to the crystal. "It is already too late. She knows you are here. And she will use your life as a ransom to ... the word Mauvais would choose ... *persuade* ... Carolyn to sign her contract."

"Guess I jammed you guys up."

"No," Carolyn said. "I was in one before you came."

He rubbed his forehead. "I got a lotta questions ... and a big headache. How 'bout I lie down for a minute?"

They both helped him step up on the platform and eased him onto the bed. Taking a couple of pillows, Carolyn propped them behind him and with a sigh he relaxed against the headboard.

Carolyn sat next to him and, as she untied the silk around his wrist, the border pieces fell on the bed.

He opened his fist. "Did what this said." He chuckled slightly. "But couldn't have done it without Mr. Reed. Cellar ... supplies ... we can blame *him* for everything." He closed his eyes. "Oh, man, major headache."

Gazellia looked up at the crystal. "Two aspirin."

They dropped on the coverlet.

"Whoa." He squinted from the light. "Geez, we could use one of those at home."

"Yeah, it'd be great at Christmas."

After taking the aspirin with water from Gazellia, he leaned back against the headboard. "Just close my eyes for a sec—"

"Oui. Rest and let the aspirin take effect."

Gazellia wet the blood spots on her dress, smearing them into large blotches. "We need to change our clothes." She waved the crystal to go to Carolyn. "You first, then I."

Carolyn thought, *Why not ask?* "I want designer jeans, a new green sweater, the color of the dress, with a hoodie and a brown leather backpack."

"My dear," Gazellia said as she laughed. "It is programmed to give you elegant seventeenth-century clothes. You can only have yours."

"I want my old clothes back like new."

It flashed several times. Her old sweater and worn denims, cleaned and ironed, appeared folded at the end of the bed. It took her couple of minutes to undress. To slide into her jeans, she had to take off her shoes. She placed them bedside on the platform.

Meanwhile Gazellia had taken off her blue silk, removed her shoes, and laid them next to Carolyn's green dress, sash, and underwear.

In a white body stocking, she stood behind Carolyn. "Here, let me help you." She unhooked the pearl necklace and pulled the ribbon out of Carolyn's hair. She pointed to the pile of clothes. "Take these, and the bowl, towel, and washcloth as well." In the flash, they vanished.

"Bring my dance costume and shoes with which I entered." Another flash, and Gazellia's like new pink chiffon and toe shoes materialized on the bed.

Finished with the tasks, the crystal soared to the ceiling, casting its light like an overhead fixture in the large room.

Carolyn thought about the green silk. Will I ever wear anything as rich, as beautiful as that again? Probably not. But it'd sure be nice to, someday. Maybe my wedding dress—

The morning sun, slanting through stained glass windows in a church, made colored patterns on the guests' clothing as she walked up the center aisle with Mr. Reed beside her. At the sound of the wedding march, Gram and bro stood in the front pew. In a white satin dress like the green one, slowly she walked to its beat toward Claude. Nestled in her hair, the crown sparkled with green flashes from under her gossamer veil. Her heart fluttered as she gazed into Claude's deep blue eyes. His lips were moist with anticipation. He reached out and—

"Come back, mon amie. You are daydreaming."

"Yeah. Bummer."

"Hey, sis." He pointed to the ceiling. Can you make that give you anything you want?"

"Oui, within limits."

"What limits?"

"It is a temporary situation," Gazellia said. "Until Mauvais decrees otherwise, Carolyn is a guest and it will do what she says."

"Okay, sis. Tell it to send us home."

"Sorry I am, Jimmy. It is not programmed to obey that command. I repeat, Mauvais wants the crown, and you are a pawn in her getting it."

"And like *I* said. Give it to her, and we'll be outta here."

"Carolyn cannot do that. Mauvais will not let her go without knowing what it can do. The crown has honored your sister by choosing her."

"I'm not the loser you thought, bro."

"Can I see it close up?"

"Sure." Carolyn handed it to him.

He rubbed his fingers over the smooth gold and cut facets. "This is beautiful. I bet it's worth a million or two bucks."

Seeing it in his hands, she knew she had to challenge the truth of the legend. "Try it on."

At four inches above his head the crown became fixed in midair.

Carolyn watched him try again and again to pull it down, until finally he pulled his upper body off the bed. She could see the sharp leaf points press into his hands.

"Ow. What the h—"

He let go.

For a second, it hung in midair, and then slowly sailed to Carolyn. She grabbed it and put it on.

"Geez. Will you look at that! It *is* true. I *am* the only one who can wear it."

"Oui, you are the one who has been given a lock to a key you have yet to find."

He lay back down on the pillows. "Okay, sis. I'm a believer. Give me the story."

Carolyn described the whole scene at the gazebo, the legend, and what happened when she tried it on. After she had finished, he was quiet.

"I know it's weird, but it happened just like I said."

"Funny it picked you."

"Thanks a lot."

"What's this contract you're supposed to sign?"

"I don't know. I've never seen it."

Gazellia snapped her fingers. "Of course, mon amie. How stupid of me not to think of it before." She walked to stand under the crystal. "Baal contract for Carolyn Farmer."

The crystal flashed. And a folded parchment tied with cobra skin dropped out of the air from the ceiling into Gazellia's waiting hands.

Chapter 18

the contract

Gazellia spread the parchment on the bed, smoothing the creases so they could see the writing. "I wonder if it will be any different than the one I signed."

It was a long legal-sized document handwritten in English in broad black script. "Except for your name, mon amie, it seems the same as mine."

Carolyn began. "I, Carolyn Farmer, do solemnly swear the following: One, I willingly and freely surrender my body and soul, my material goods, present and future, to serve Mauvais Vallee Enterprises, Incorporated (herein MVE).

"Two, I swear to obey without question the director of MVE and to fulfill with all diligence the requirements of the MVE mind-set method of operation as a recruiter for MVE.

"Three, I swear never to disclose personal knowledge or information pertaining to MVE to anyone outside the membership of MVE.

"Four, I swear to submit myself to trial should I break any of Baal laws and ordinances and, furthermore, I swear to submit to any judgment resulting from my criminal behavior toward MVE."

Jimmy continued. "In consideration for the services rendered by employee-member, Carolyn Farmer, the following shall be provided by MVE: food, shelter, clothing, transportation, free education in the mind-set method, wealth, fame, relationships among fellow members, rewards for loyal service beyond assigned tasks, restoration to perfection in physical beauty, and preservation of physical life in perpetuity."

"Purpa ... what?" Carolyn asked.

"Perpetuity," Gazellia said. "It means eternal ... or forever."

"That's BS," Jimmy said. "How can ... um ... MVE make her live forever?"

"Mauvais has the technology to change our structure. To duplicate."

"That's what Claude said in the storage room."

"Understand, I do not know how this is done. Nor do I comprehend the science behind what Mauvais is able to accomplish. I do know that some of us are—the term she uses is *downloaded*—to keep our personalities, our very selves, intact when we need restoration. It is the future of humans on planet earth."

"You mean this Mauvais could take me ... and make another me?"

"Who'd want to make another you, bro? One's quite enough."

"Ha. Ha. Very funny."

"It is a method to control and to perfect *homo sapiens* by saving the best and discarding the rest of whatever is not desired. The philosophy of Darwinism ... survival of the fittest."

"If Carolyn signs, she becomes a machine ... like you?"

"A machine I am *not*, Jimmy. I explained, remember in the cellar? I am an earth-born human? True, parts of me have been improved, but I am not cloned, not downloaded, not brainwashed in the mind-set method."

"But why not you?" Carolyn asked.

"Because, in addition to being her favorite and wanting my medallion, Mauvais has hidden cells. They belong to Bridget. Someone I knew centuries ago at the convent. I believe there is still a remnant of kindness within her that chooses not to eliminate me or Claude ... or a few others as yet."

Jimmy pointed to the lines at the bottom of the parchment. "Here's where Carolyn, Mauvais, and a witness sign with the date."

Gazellia scanned the page. "There is no added clause about the Laurel Crown."

"Your Mauvais doesn't need to put in a special clause," Jimmy said. "You belong to MVE body and soul."

"And mind," Gazellia said. "Between the lines it means code red."

"Claude talked about code red ... something about a pod—"

"The crystal puts us to sleep when a part needs restoration. We feel no pain."

"Yeah, he said he recovered in his room."

"Oui, until our next assignment."

"What's a pod?" Jimmy asked.

"It is like an operating room where a patient goes in for surgery and the doctor uses a drug to induce sleep."

"That's like what happened to Mom and Dad in the hospital," Carolyn said. "And they died in there."

"Well, I guess that's it." He sighed. "I'm a goner."

"Have courage. The Sisters of Clare had a saying: the play is not over until the curtain closes on the last scene."

"But doesn't number one read, 'willingly and freely'?" Carolyn asked. "How can I 'willingly and freely' sign when it's blackmail?"

"Oui. That is the deception. You will 'willingly and freely' sign for his life. The kingdom of Baal is based on the belief that humans live for themselves ... that they will do anything to save their own skins."

He shrugged. "What's wrong with trying to save your own skin?"

"Nothing. As long as it does not hurt someone else in the process. Which is what I have done." She rolled up the parchment and handed it to Carolyn. "Ma chèrie, this is not what I intended for you. Or me. I betrayed Milady ... and you, also. I did not tell you about Mauvais. I asked you to trust me, but I was not worthy of your trust."

"Hey," Jimmy said. "You can't take all the credit. You didn't ask me to come."

Gazellia smiled. "No, you did what any loving brother would do. You wanted to protect your sister." She kissed Carolyn on both cheeks. "Ma chèrie, I trust you to do what is right. Whatever you decide, whether to sign or not, I am with you to the finish." She paused to caress the medallion. "Fortunate you are to have each other. More fortunate I am to have you both." She pulled the chain over her head and started to slip it over his.

He pushed against her hands. "No, I really couldn't—"

Gazellia pressed the medallion against his chest. "Please, let me do this. If Mauvais had intentions of harming me, she would have already done so. She has had many opportunities of terminating me."

He looked down at the medal shining in the candlelight and cleared his throat several times. "Thank you," he said quietly as he helped her slide it over his head.

The atmosphere in the room was thick with love and hope.

Gazellia broke the silence. "Perhaps a rest would do us all good." She took a pillow and propped it behind Carolyn against one of the four posters at the foot of the bed. She picked up her chiffon and toe shoes. "We can do nothing until Mauvais makes the first move," she said, changing into them. She eased herself into a high-backed chair next to the mirror. "Let us rest while we can."

Leaning back, Carolyn realized how tired she was. She moved the parchment and silk roll nearer to Jimmy.

Umm, she thought, *how good it is to stretch out.* She arched her feet and twisted her left ankle. They don't hurt. She wiggled her toes to make sure. Nothing hurts. Good-bye, torture traps. Hello, beautiful shoes. She looked up. Why not?

"You up there. Give me a pair of seventeenth-century, white leather pumps with two-inch heels, size five and a half, A."

The crystal shot a beam of light and dropped the silver box next to her.

He sat up. "What's that?"

"That's not what I asked for."

No flash.

"What's in there?"

"My toe shoes."

"You're kidding, right?"

"It is Mauvais's gift to Carolyn," Gazellia said. "They have power to make her dance."

"Aw, come on. No way she's a dancer."

"Don't have to be. Don't even have to be in them."

"This I gotta see."

"Okay. Watch." She opened the gold lid. Focusing on the shoes, she willed them out of the box like two emerging butterflies out of a cocoon. The ribbons, flapping like wings, lifted the shoes to the ceiling, circling them around the crystal.

"How are you doing that?"

His question broke her concentration.

Plunk, plunk, they dropped on the bed.

"They do what I think."

"Mon amie, you told me you wished to dance in them for real."

"My thinking is real. And it's total cool to watch them. If I can make it happen, what's wrong with that?"

"If they're hers, what's the diff how she uses them?"

"A matter of great importance, Jimmy. Mauvais uses magic and science for her own amusement. Power can be used for good or ill, depending on the heart of the owner."

"Yeah, look who's talking."

"My exact point, Jimmy. A lie can have great power, but in the end the truth has greater power."

Carolyn looked at the toe shoes. She had soared in them. Felt thrills beyond anything she could have imagined. *But this wasn't given in love,* she thought. *It was given to trap me into doing something I didn't understand.* The scenes in the mirror with Claude rose in her mind. It would have been wonderful if only it had been real. That was a lie too. My life in Detroit was the real thing. Gram did love me. Mr. Reed was there when I needed him. Yolanda wanted to be friends. I had the attitude. And big mouth is here next to me.

She pondered: *lies are based on selfish desires and false dreams. Somehow I knew dancing in these would be cheating.*

"Oui," Carolyn said. "That's for yes, and we ... meaning," she pointed to Jimmy, "we know that truth matters." She closed the lid. "I don't want them anymore. The crystal can take them back to Mauvais."

The crown grew warm. *Take what has been given to you to use for good.*

Carolyn sent her thought-question back to the crown. *You say they're mine, but how do I know what you just told me is really from you?*

"Mon amie, keep them. What Mauvais meant for an evil purpose, you can choose to use them for good."

Carolyn was astonished. She answered the question in my mind. *How can that be?*

"Mon amie, surprised you are, I would make such a suggestion?"

"Yeah. You did everything to keep me from accepting them."

"Because the gift was based on a lie. Keeping you free, protecting you was my desire. Now, you can use them as you will."

"Forget about the dumb shoes. Let's keep our focus on the ball. You know ... the contract? That's the game we're playing now, guys. You can do your philosophy thing later, after we're outta here."

He picked up the parchment lying next to Carolyn. "There might be something in here we've missed." He leaned forward, smoothing it out on the bed. "I'll read it again. Maybe an idea will come."

Carolyn watched the medal swing from his neck as he intently studied it. The crown and the medallion. Somehow they were connected. But how? How did they both protect?

After awhile, he rubbed his forehead and took off the bandage. He arched his back to relieve the strain from bending over.

"Any ideas yet?" Carolyn asked.

He slowly shook his head no.

As hers relaxed into the pillow, the crown gently squeezed. She responded. *Show us, tell us what to do.*

Only the slowly rotating light from the globe continued to flash in the still room.

Suddenly Jimmy picked up the cobra skin. "That's it!" he shouted. He held it up. "What brought me in will take me out." He wound them around the parchment leaving the ends loose and turned to Carolyn. "Now, tie these with three knots around my wrist."

"What good will that do?"

"Just *do* it."

"There. Now what?"

"I'm going home. And I'm going back the way I came, I hope."

"Wait, I don't want you to leave me."

"Don't you understand, sis? With me gone, Mauvais can't use me as ransom. You're free. You won't have to sign the contract."

"But even if you get home, she can keep me here forever. What kinda help is that?"

"My leaving makes the contract no good."

"Of course," Gazellia tapped her forehead in understanding. "Carolyn, you already know the future is not as you saw it in the mirror. Jimmy is here, not at home. This makes the contract void."

"Understand? No, I don't understand at all."

Jimmy took a deep breath and licked his lips. "Remember number three, where it's written, 'I swear never to disclose personal knowledge or information pertaining to MVE to anyone outside the membership of MVE?' There's no way you can fulfill number three of this agreement. Once, I'm on the other side, that is. Secrecy is one of her weapons. Secrecy is how she, or whoever is behind her, can enslave others."

He held up the medallion and parchment and pointed to the box.

"When I return with proof, the world will know what she's up to. I'll call all the newspapers, TV and radio stations. I'll show and tell on websites ...

whoever will watch, listen. I'll tell how she trapped you guys, what happened to me."

He picked up the border piece. "Here … the instructions, the contract, the skins, the toe shoes, the box. Proof about Mauvais and this place. That breaks clause number three. All her employees' contracts will be worthless. Those who want to be free can be free. After I'm gone, you can …" Jimmy waved the contract for emphasis. "… blackmail *her*. Tell her if she doesn't send you home, I'm coming after her with reinforcements. Gram. Mr. Reed. My football team … whoever—"

"But how will you come back? If she doesn't let us go, how will you find me?"

"Same as before. Whatever belongs to her acts like a homing device." He held up the contract and puzzle piece. "She will do anything to get back what she owns. You'll be easy to find. Don't worry, sis. I'll be back for you."

Carolyn looked around the room at the four-poster bed and the expensive furnishings. Her fingertips slid over the coverlet, reminding her of the moment she dived into it. *This beautiful room ended up being the real prison,* she thought. Her throat ached with longing. Oh, to be home smelling Gram's oatmeal cookies. Biting into one—warm and chewy. She pictured Gram at the top of the stairs, arms open wide, watching her run all the way up. *Maybe it's true after all: love can find a way.*

She swallowed hard. "Okay. See you. And give Gram a hug for me. Tell her … oh, you know what to tell her."

Gazellia kissed him on both cheeks. "God speed, Jimmy."

Most of the glass was on the marble floor and under the table. But in the lower part, held in the corner of a carved edge, a large triangular piece of mirror remained.

He crouched down, positioning himself so that the left side of his body touched its surface. He raised his right arm, ready for the downswing.

In a blinding flash, the crystal sailed from the ceiling, rotating red like a unit atop a police car. It flew within an inch from his face, blinding him, causing him to duck to protect himself.

The moment he ducked, Gazellia sprang into action. She grabbed his wrist, trying to tear the parchment out of his hand. He dropped the box and blocked her reach with his left arm. She dodged. And with her left shoulder she smacked him in the chest. Surprised by the blow, he stumbled back against the frame. It toppled over from the impact of his weight, shattering the large piece of glass as the frame hit the floor with a crash.

Taking her advantage, she came at him—head lowered like a tackle. With split-second timing, he sidestepped her. Her feet slid on the splinters and slick marble as she flew past him and fell on the frame.

Taking his advantage, he landed on her.

Carolyn watched them, straining, shoving, pushing against each other. Without thinking, she yelled, "Help!"

The leaf points of the crown squeezed. *Grab a pillow and cover the crystal.*

As soon as she blocked the light, Gazellia went limp.

Jimmy shoved her body off his.

Side by side they lay, weak and panting, while Carolyn held the pillow over the crystal.

A curl of smoke rose from underneath.

"Watch out!" He scrambled to his feet and stomped out the flames.

The red globe soared to the ceiling still rotating.

Gazellia grabbed his ankles and with a great heave pitched him to the floor. She pounced on him—her knee in the small of his back. He hit her chest with his elbow.

Carolyn looked up. I've got to stop that crystal. He can't hold her off much longer. I need something long. But what's long enough to reach it? She saw a porcelain vase. Hit it with that. She threw the vase as hard as she could. And within two feet of its mark, the vase vanished.

Her heart thundered in her ears. What can I do? She touched the crown. Oh, help us.

The crown squeezed. *Send me.*

That's it. It flew out of her hand. Gold-green leaves turned into a buzz saw. *Zzz zzz zat!* The leaf points cut through the globe as easily as an electric knife cuts through a ripe cantaloupe. It made a last flash and died.

For a second the dark halves hung suspended. And then they fell, shattering and joining the glass pieces on the marble floor. The crown boomeranged to her outstretched hand. It was hot. Instinctively, she dropped it. It bounced several times on its rim and rolled under the bed.

Jimmy groaned.

At the sound of his voice, she completely forgot the crown. She didn't feel the cuts from the glass on her bare feet as she ran to him.

"You okay?"

"Yeah."

Next to him, Gazellia propped herself up on her elbows. Her glazed expression was replaced by bewilderment. "Wha … what happened?

"You nearly killed him," Carolyn yelled. "That's what happened."

"Mon Dieu. Code red."

"I told you she was a robot." He wiped away a trickle of blood from a cut on his cheek.

"Forgive me. I could not help myself."

With her chiffon skirt she began wiping the sweat and blood from his face. "Please forgive me. Believe my sincere care for you."

"Oh, yeah? Show me where *you* bleed." He pushed her hands away from his face.

Carolyn scanned her from head to toe. "You're right, bro. There's not a mark on her."

"Like I said, she's a robot."

"I am *not*. Do not speak about me as though I am not present." Her almond eyes teared. "*Mes amis,* truthful I am. I beg you to believe me. I am *not* a machine. It is as I have told you. I *am* human. Truly, I *am*."

The door suddenly blew open.

Chapter 19

Code Red

The leopards paced back and forth across the wide threshold, their tails twitching low, their ears flat against their heads. Above them in the doorway sparkles of light converged into a shimmering cloud, out of which Mauvais stepped into the room. Her copper hair was a frizzed mass of electrified fury. The diamond tiara glittered in the light. The tight black leather glistened—oily, shiny.

Her finger dagger-pointed. "Intruder, how dare you break into our house? How dare you destroy our property? You will be punished for this criminal act."

She motioned to the cats. Instantly they padded to Jimmy and crouched over him.

Their amber coats rippled in anticipation of the command to leap onto their victim.

Jimmy curled into a ball, his arms protecting his head.

"Don't hurt him," Carolyn cried.

"He has broken into our house and must be punished." Mauvais snapped her fingers. From a slit in the air another globe dropped. It sailed to hover over his head.

On the floor beside him, Gazellia protectively put her arm over his chest. "You cannot touch him. 'Tis against Baal law."

"You dare interfere with our authority? We can eliminate you at any moment."

She snapped her fingers. Instantly, the crystal moved from over Jimmy to Gazellia. Its flash turned red and began to rotate.

Gazellia stood up, her glazed eyes on the crystal.

"You think, worthless human, you can protect him? Prove you have power greater than ours."

Gazellia continued to stand transfixed.

Do something, Carolyn directed the crown, expecting an immediate squeeze with a thought-response. There was none. She reached up to touch it and realized it was gone.

"Rightfully, we see the crown has abandoned you. How delicious. How perfect. You can do nothing."

Mauvais put her hands on the leopards' heads. "Do not move to defend your brother or we will release them."

"No," Carolyn cried. "It's not his fault. He followed me here to take me home."

"Your brother must be punished. Justice demands a person be imprisoned for breaking and entering. And for destroying private property."

"But he was trying to find me," she pleaded.

Mauvais snapped her fingers. "Collar and chain for the criminal."

From a slit in the air above Gazellia's head, a large iron collar and chain dropped on the marble floor. "Put it on him," she commanded.

Glassy-eyed, Gazellia picked them up.

Carolyn grabbed her wrist with one hand and tried to pull the collar and chain away with the other. "It's me, Carolyn. Please wake up."

Gazellia shoved her aside like a rag doll. She reached for Jimmy's head. He ducked. She tackled him. Like wrestlers they fought, countering, dodging, and moving across the room. But the match was uneven. She was a cold, powerful machine—a solid determined force field of energy.

Finally, she flipped him over and, with her full body pressed against his, she pinned his arms behind his back. She grabbed his hair with one hand and forced his head back. With the other hand she snapped the collar around his neck, and after that she twisted the chain around his wrists.

Panic enveloped Carolyn.

She looked at Mauvais. The frizzed red hair flanged out like the hood of a cobra ready to strike. In that second, she knew she had no choice. "All right! All right! I'll do anything you want ... only please don't take him. Please let him go."

"So you will do anything we wish, will you?"

"Yes," she said, feeling totally defeated. "I promise. Anything."

"If we let your brother go, will you sign? Will you use the crown to do our bidding?"

Bro's life is worth more than a million crowns.

"Yes ... I'll sign."

Mauvais's lips twisted in triumph. "A wise decision."

With the snap of her fingers, the collar and chain disappeared. The red light changed to white and stopped rotating. It dimmed and soared to the ceiling.

Gazellia collapsed—out cold.

Mauvais smoothed her frizzed hair under her tiara. "We have been most kind to the three of you in spite of your criminal activities. New One, we continue to offer you the privileges of joining our company freely. And, because of our generosity, we offer your brother the same opportunity."

She pointed to the crystal. "We observe all that takes place in our domain. We do not fault you for the circumstances that have befallen you. Therefore, our kind hearts have considered your plight. And we do wish, above all else, to bring your resistance to our authority to one of desire for our company." She pointed to Carolyn's bleeding feet. "Without pain, we can replace those."

With a shock, for the first time Carolyn felt the stinging cuts. What was the use to resist such power? She looked at Jimmy. He's innocent. He came for me out of love, no matter how big his big mouth is. She looked at Gazellia, laid out on the marble floor, eyes closed, breathing quietly, still knocked out by the crystal. She played a dangerous game—and lost. But she's still alive. We all are. As Gram says, "It's not over 'til it's over."

"Okay. I said I'd sign. But I keep the feet I've got."

"We agree at present." Mauvais's gaze shifted to Jimmy. "What say you?"

"Huh!" he scoffed. "What say I? You're holding all the cards."

"Excellent." With a sweeping motion, Mauvais waved to the cats. Immediately they lay lengthwise on each side of Gazellia and began licking her face.

"Two new contracts. Carolyn Farmer and Jimmy Farmer," commanded Mauvais. "Pen. Ink. Scissors. Towel and ointment."

The crystal flashed and dropped them on the bed.

"New One, we are thoughtful. We are merciful. We are generous. Wipe the blood off your feet and apply the ointment. After you are finished, give it to your brother."

Carolyn limped to the bed and sat on its edge. Carefully she pulled out the slivers—trying not to show how much it hurt. She opened the jar and applied the ointment. She felt instant relief. In moments the cuts closed. Pain gone. Skin smooth.

She gave him the jar. While she laced her shoes, he rubbed it on his forehead and several cuts. They healed in seconds.

"New One, we take considerable care of our members. Our science is beyond your comprehension. As members you will become accustomed to the extraordinary, the supernatural. For us at MVE, the astonishing is quite ordinary."

Like a queen, she held out her hand to Jimmy. "Come. You are now a New One with your own contract. As soon as your sister cuts the skins from your wrist, you will be free to sign as well."

Gazellia struggled to raise herself to her elbows. "No, mes amis. Do not sign," she whispered. "Mauvais, you say you are merciful. The crown is gone. Send them home." Weakly she pushed against the cats' faces. "Take them away."

They stopped licking but remained one on each side of her.

"We have allowed you to remain assembled because you have served us well. We have granted you privileges by bending our laws to keep you in our company. You have exceeded the patience of our mercy. Give us a reason to keep you intact."

"In memory of your sister, Bridget. You are sisters from the same mother. Have mercy and send them home."

"Immaterial. We will no longer accept your insubordination. We will download and replicate you exactly." Her boots crushed the glass as she crossed to Gazellia.

"Pod."

It flashed and a glass container appeared beside Gazellia.

Carolyn's desperate thoughts shot into the cosmos. Where are you, Laurel Crown? Help us.

Under the bed. Refuse to sign.

"Wait," she cried. "I promised I'd sign. And he will too. But if you do this, I won't." She pointed the scissors at the crystal. "I don't care if that thing drops a thousand contracts. I'll cut them into little pieces."

"Oh, you will, will you? We will watch what you can do."

"We can do plenty. Come on." Jimmy grabbed Carolyn's hand and pulled her off the bed.

"Get outta the way," he shouted to Gazellia.

With a mighty heave, they pushed over the pod as far away from Gazellia they could. The cats jumped out the way as the glass shattered with a crash.

Mauvais snapped her fingers.

"Cover your eyes!" Carolyn yelled.

Gazellia pulled her skirt over her face.

"Oh, no, you don't." Jimmy punched at the bobbing globe as Carolyn tried to stab it with the scissors.

It flashed and they disappeared from her hand.

"You can do nothing, worthless humans."

Mauvais snapped her fingers. "Pod."

Another glass case appeared next to Gazellia.

"If you want them to live, you will get into it."

"He agape nikai panta!" Gazellia shouted. "Remember me." She stepped through the glass. And inside, stood stiff as a cadaver.

Anger rose in Carolyn like a blazing forest fire. "I'll never sign. Never. Never. Never!" Her words were swallowed in the wind that slammed the door shut.

"Now there is no escape," the words reverberated throughout the room.

Jimmy grabbed Carolyn's arm. "Run to the bed."

They made a mad dash and scrambled under.

A tornado ripped through the room. Chairs, tables, vases, porcelains, and candlesticks flew through the air, ricocheting off walls and the ceiling. It ripped the drapes from the windows and tore the coverlet, bedding, and pillows to shreds. A blizzard of flying feathers turned the red room into a storm of white.

As quickly as the tornado had struck, it stopped. Every piece that had been flying fell to the floor. In place of the roar of wind and objects crashing, a silence filled the room. It was more terrible, more sinister than the whirlwind which had destroyed everything in its path but the bed.

Huddled together, they waited.

Like snow, the white, swirling goose down and feathers gently settled to form a white blanket over every broken object strewn about the room. From underneath, Carolyn watched a few feathers give a final twirl before they came to rest on the platform.

Carefully, Jimmy inched his way forward to look out from under.

"Is she gone?"

"Don't see her boots. Or the cats."

"Can you see Gazellia?"

"No. I have to get out."

The feathers muffled his crunching steps. "Gazellia," he softly called. "Gazellia." But there was no reply. He waved Carolyn out. "Help me look."

As she crawled toward the edge, she felt a sharp jab on the side of her arm. It was the crown.

Relief flooded her. She almost asked aloud, are you okay?

Do not fear.

"That's what you keep telling me. Easy for you to say," she mumbled.

After standing up and putting it on, she asked, "Now what?"

"Let's look for the pod," he said.

No thought-direction came into her mind.

"Don't stand there like a dummy. What're you waiting for?"

Feathers flew as they sifted through chunks of wood, broken crockery, and torn fabric. Glass was everywhere, inches deep. There were no large pieces.

Where is she? Carolyn wondered.

Gazellia is with me. She is unseen as I am unseen. Her outsides remain. Those you will find.

"There." She pointed.

Protruding from under a torn seat cushion was Gazellia's foot in a pink toe shoe. Six inches away, one of her chiffon clad arms was wedged between a broken table leg and chair back.

Carolyn lifted a broken table top and under it was Gazellia's head. Her glassy, brown eyes stared, unseeing. She had been torn into parts exactly like the ones Carolyn had seen in the storage room.

"I knew she was a robot," Jimmy said. "Just a machine. No blood. No guts. Not real."

The crown squeezed gently. *Not true.*

"The crown says she's real."

"Doesn't matter. We gotta get outta here. It's our only chance." He held up the tattered parchment tied to his wrist. "I still have the contract. But I lost the edge piece. Come on, help me find it. With the frame and a piece of mirror, we can go back."

Have courage. I chose you to be my warrior.

"No. I have to stay. I don't know why, but I do."

"You can't help her!" he shouted. "We've got to help ourselves."

I will help you. Trust me.

"Don't just stand there." Jimmy picked up the twisted end of a broken candelabra. "Come on. Help me look for the piece."

Carolyn watched him desperately sifting and sorting.

Bro, she thought, *you're wasting your time. We have a snowball's chance in July of returning home.*

She looked at Gazellia's head on the seat cushion. Tenderly Carolyn closed her eyelids. With them closed, she seemed asleep—dreaming of something blissful.

"I will never forget you, beautiful lady," she whispered. Her lips lightly brushed Gazellia's cheek. "You're gone ... gone to a place without pain and trouble ... a place of peace and rest."

And joy, she thought. *Joy. That's what we'd shared a few short hours ago when we'd danced and laughed, believing we were free. But what you believed wasn't true. In the end, your medallion did nothing to protect—*

Wait. Bro is the one wearing the medallion. Both the medallion and the crown were with us under the bed. The wind didn't touch us. The legend must be true. It must be. We are a part of some cosmic divine plan. Even if bro could find that piece, the way back is the wrong way. Forward is the only way to go.

The sound of a distant rumble began.

"Hey, bro. We'd better get under the bed."

"Yeah, I heard it. But I gotta find a piece of mirror."

"Forget it. There's no way you're going back."

She watched him throw the candelabra across the room in disgust.

"You're right. We're cooked. Dead meat. Done deal. Gram will call the police. Mr. Reed will be a suspect. They'll dig around in the cellar for our bodies. Our photos will end up on milk cartons for years. Gram will never know what happened to us."

"Just get under the bed, will ya'?"

"Okay."

They crawled under.

Chapter 20

the trial

Faint at first, then growing in volume, the sound, the rhythm of a moving army stomped—left, right, left, right, left right—

From under the bed Carolyn could see sixty pairs of black boots marching into the room. A gray army in rows of four quick-crunched across the floor to position themselves around the bed.

"Halt." The computer voice was crisp, definite.

She saw the boots stamp twice in military style—then heels clicked together.

Silently she prayed, *Whatever power you hold ... whatever you can do for us, please, please do it.*

The leaf points pressed against her scalp. *Do not fear. Face them.*

"The crown is with us," she whispered. "We've got to face them."

Slowly she inched her way out from under the bed with Jimmy following.

Immediately she recognized Claude and Lissette in the first row and all those behind them from the ballroom. They were the same beautiful people. However, gone were the gorgeous silk gowns and brocaded suits. Instead, they wore wool uniforms with the MVE cobra logo on their shoulders, collars, and hat brims. They stood at attention, eyes unseeing, focused straight ahead. All of them carried lances resting on their left shoulders. Tiny flags with the logo hung below their sharp steel points.

In unison they mouthed, "Attention. Attention. Carolyn Farmer and Jimmy Farmer, you are under arrest. You are commanded to appear before the Supreme Court Justice Mauvais Vallee."

Without a word, the four in the front row lowered their standards. In quick military steps they moved forward until the sharp tips of their shafts were pointed directly at the chests of Carolyn and Jimmy.

After a couple of sharp jabs, they chorused, "You will proceed to the Supreme Court."

"Okay, okay," Jimmy said, as they continued to jab. "We're going. We're going."

Walking down the hall, Carolyn lightly touched the crown for assurance and comfort.

She glanced sideways at Claude's stern face beside her. *He sure has changed. From handsome-fantastic to wooden-plastic. Inside, the handsome prince is really a frog.*

At the far end of the oval room the gold throne was gone—the apple tree barren. Only the wallpaper and fancy moldings around the windows attested to the room's former richness.

About forty feet from the apple tree, the first military row, which included Carolyn and Jimmy, halted. Behind them, the fifty-six rapped their lance ends twice on the marble floor.

"Attention. Attention. All parties to hear the case of Carolyn Farmer and Jimmy Farmer shall enter this court. Prosecution shall proceed with its charges against the offenders. Defense shall proceed with evidence on their behalf. The Supreme Court of Mauvais Vallee Enterprises, Incorporated is now called into session," the army mouthed together with the echo.

In front of the tree, a black metallic platform began to rise with a large computer screen the size of a football stadium sign. Also on the platform was a high-backed leather chair behind a tall, mahogany judge's bench. Carved on its front was a shield with the MVE logo. A witness stand made of wooden posts and iron railings was positioned to its left. Facing the bench and stand were two long tables and chairs with an aisle between.

From many a TV crime series, Carolyn recognized the table on left side was for the defense, right side for the prosecution.

As the platform rose, fifty-six soldiers paced themselves around the oval room. When all had stopped, the tree vanished, and in its place an open door materialized.

Every eye focused on the door. Sixty hands raised in preparation to salute.

Carolyn saw the crystal flash and from behind her heard the sound of a bugle.

In a judge's robe with chevrons of black diamonds in logos on sleeves and shoulders, with the cats on both sides of her, Mauvais stepped through and paused. Her red hair was smoothly curled under a logo-encrusted ruby tiara.

"Attention. Attention. Salute Her Honor, Supreme Court Justice Mauvais Vallee presiding."

She returned their salute and pulled on the leopards' chains. As soon as their chains disappeared, their sleek coats began to dissolve.

Carolyn watched them morph. With each one, paws, legs, and head melted together into two separate cassocked figures. One was dressed in cranberry wool, the other the same shade of green as Carolyn's dress had been. The slightly taller figure carried a black ledger with an invisible hand through its red sleeve.

She wiped her sweaty hands on her jeans. *Stay calm,* she thought. *Remember, fear not.* Immediately like a hug, the crown squeezed—warm and gentle.

"Attention. Attention. Salute, Prosecutor Bersha and Defender Zetta." The words echoed and mouths chorused.

Sixty hands gave a smart salute.

"Attention. Attention. Salute, Master of the Court Gog."

Carolyn squinted as radiating golden rays appeared on screen. They converged into one bright beam shooting out from the screen to the floor. From it, yellow smoke began to spiral upward into a large cloud. Stepping out of it, Gog stood, covered in layered pieces of silver steel. His left hand rested on a sheathed sword hanging from a belt of diamonds. A helmet of colored stones with a visor of glowing red plates covered his head. Atop his silver helmet, with its closed visor, the rubies in the MVE logo pulsed rhythmically with the rubies in the hilt.

After Gog positioned himself behind her, Mauvais sat on the judge's chair and the robes went to their respective tables.

"Attention. Attention. Court is in session with the honorable Mauvais Vallee, presiding judge now in attendance. All will be seated."

Defend yourself.

"I'll sit when I want to," Carolyn said. "You've no right to try us. We haven't done anything."

Mauvais hit the wooden gavel on its pad. "Silence."

She pointed to Lissette. "Seat the defendants."

After they had been jabbed and pushed down by Lissette's lance, Carolyn leaned over to see what was under the pointed green hood. But all that was visible was an iron mask with two narrow slits—one at the top, one at the bottom. Stamped on its surface was a man's face.

The gavel hit the pad. "Without permission from this court you will not speak."

Mauvais pointed first to the green robe and then to the cranberry one. "Defender Zetta has been appointed to present your cases. The other is Prosecutor Bersha."

Invisible hands within cranberry sleeves opened the black ledger. The robe stood, bowed. "We are ready, Your Honor." The words came directly from inside the robe.

"You may proceed."

"If it please, Your Honor. We have positive proof that Jimmy Farmer, with criminal intent, did break into the premises of Mauvais Vallee Enterprises and did willfully destroy certain properties belonging to same. We have proof that his sister, Carolyn Farmer, did with criminal intent destroy certain properties belonging to Mauvais Vallee. As a result of the wanton destruction of Vallee properties, a murder was committed. We charge these two guilty of crimes against Mauvais Vallee Enterprises. If it please the court, these defendants, if found guilty, must receive the maximum penalty: death by combat."

"How do the defendants plead?"

The green figure stood. "They are innocent of all charges, Your Honor," the computer voice said before the robe sat down.

"Prosecutor Bersha, you may proceed with your evidence."

Opening the ledger, Bersha stated, "Charge one. Jimmy Farmer did, by trespassing onto Vallee property, destroy one priceless magic mirror thousands of years old.

"Charge two. Jimmy Farmer, now under the protection and hospitality of the gracious and kind director-principal, did take the contract intended for his sister, Carolyn Farmer. We charge he did mean to steal this contract and return to his earth-habitation for the sole purpose of slandering the good name of Mauvais Vallee, thereby ruining the reputation of Mauvais Vallee Enterprises.

"Charge three. Jimmy Farmer did resist by physical force an employee of Vallee Enterprises, one MV 666-239-451, herein to be referred to as

Gazellia. This resistance did develop into a violent assault resulting in the destruction of said employee."

"But he was only trying to—" Carolyn interrupted.

"Silence." The gavel hit the pad. "You have not been called upon to speak. However, since you are determined to interrupt these proceedings, Prosecutor Bersha shall skip charges four and five and go directly to your charges."

"Yes, Your Honor." Invisible hands lifted the ledger closer to the hood.

"Charge six. We, the prosecution representing Mauvais Vallee Enterprises, do accuse one Carolyn Farmer, while under the protective hospitality of Mauvais Vallee, of shattering one crystal communicator, causing damage and harm to private property. Such wanton destruction of the crystal communicator resulted in the disjointing and death of said employee, Gazellia.

"Charge seven. The prosecution accuses Carolyn Farmer of stealing certain properties belonging to Mauvais Vallee. These properties include one pair of red toe shoes and one gold and emerald crown taken from the gazebo. This gold and emerald crown, hereto known as the Laurel Crown, was used by Carolyn Farmer as a weapon, resulting in a violent consequence.

"All evidence points to the collusive acts of Jimmy and Carolyn Farmer to commit violence against the state of Mauvais Vallee Enterprises."

Invisible hands slammed together the covers of the ledger.

With a wave of a sleeve, Bersha turned to where the three sat. "Your turn, Counselor."

Under the cranberry hood, Carolyn saw the iron mask was stamped with a female face.

Zetta stood. "Your Honor, my colleague and learned member of this bar of justice has not provided one shred of evidence. What proof has the prosecution offered? Why nothing. Reading the charges from a book does not constitute evidence. Justice demands evidence. Unless such evidence can be brought forth, showing beyond a shadow of a doubt that these two are guilty—they must, under Baal law, be released."

Zetta bowed and sat down.

"Prosecutor Bersha, what proofs do you offer as evidence against the defendants?" Mauvais asked.

"Your Honor, may we exercise the privilege of using the crystal to provide necessary proof?"

"You may proceed."

Even though the hands were invisible, Carolyn heard a distinct couple of snaps.

The crystal shot a ray of light in front of the bench. A cart appeared with a silk red tasseled cover.

The sleeve waved to Lissette who then pushed the cart in front of the defense table.

"Here." Bersha's invisible hand threw back the cover. "Evidence."

A triangular piece of mirror lifted in space, then slowly dropped back on the cart.

A glass bowl hung, then returned to the cart.

"Third, the toe shoes taken without permission."

The lid lifted and the toe shoes wiggled slightly as they turned for all to see. After that, invisible hands fitted them into the box and closed the lid.

"Fourth." Bersha's sleeves indicated Carolyn. "The Laurel Crown was taken by the defendant without permission from the owner Mauvais Vallee. All can see the MVE property is now on the head of the defendant for the sole purpose of destroying the kingdom of Baal and the king's director-principal of Mauvais Vallee Enterprises."

"I object, Your Honor," Zetta said.

"On what grounds?"

"Carolyn Farmer is a guest of Mauvais Vallee Enterprises with full privileges accorded as such. The shoes were a gift of hospitality from Mauvais Vallee to the defendant. Your ledger records the agreement given to Carolyn Farmer of her ownership of the shoes."

The light danced off the diamond chevrons as Mauvais leaned forward.

"Correct. The evidence of the red shoes is inadmissible. In addition, the Laurel Crown has not left the domain of Vallee Enterprises."

"Does Bersha have conclusive proof of the intent to steal an MVE article in the possession of either defendant?"

"Yes, Your Honor. Double proof. I call Jimmy Farmer to the witness stand. May we remind Your Honor the defendant is hostile."

Jimmy gripped the arms of his chair. "Yeah, hostile as hell. I ain't movin'."

Lissette's lance jabbed Jimmy hard in the ribs.

He stood. "Okay. Okay. I'm going."

"Lift up your right arm," Bersha said.

The sleeve pointed to the dangling contract. "There is the first of two proofs. Notice this is the contract the defendant stole with the intent of escaping. Notice the three knots around the wrist. Positive proof the defendant stole property belonging to Mauvais Vallee with the intent to cause the destruction of MVE."

Expertly the sharp tip of Lissette's lance cut the skins. The tattered contract fell to floor.

Invisible hands picked it up and put it on the judge's bench.

"Do you deny," the computer voice continued, "your intention to steal the contract in order to keep your sister from signing? Do you deny you tried to escape with it to ruin Mauvais Vallee Enterprises?"

"No. I don't deny it. I'm *proud* of it." He smiled at Carolyn. "I came to find her and take her home. I'll do *whatever* it takes to make that happen."

"The words from his own lips condemn him."

With the tip of her lance, Lissette deftly lifted the medallion.

"There is the second evidence of thievery, Your Honor. All employees of Mauvais Enterprises are the property of MVE. This was stolen from one Gazellia. Therefore, according to Baal law, any outsider who takes property under any circumstances from MVE has committed a criminal act."

After the sleeve motioned for Lissette to withdraw the tip, the medallion dropped back on his chest.

"The defendant is a thief and must be dealt with accordingly."

Zetta stood. "While it is true that the medallion was owned by a Vallee employee, let the court hear what Jimmy Farmer has to say. How did you acquire the medallion?"

"Gazellia gave it to me. She *wanted* me to have it."

Bersha glided to the prosecutor's table and opened the ledger.

"Not only is the intruder a thief, but he is an outrageous liar. No one in this court would believe that a contracted employee would dare give what she did not own. This is impossible to believe. The evidence is quite clear. You stole it from her body."

"That's not true. She *did* give it to me."

"Prove it."

"Carolyn is my witness."

"Lies. You are both criminals. You support each other with lies."

The crown squeezed. *Defend with accusation.*

"You're the liar." Carolyn pointed to the broken globe. "You saw it from the crystal."

"Property which you and your brother destroyed."

"I didn't do anything." Her voice was low and tight. "The Laurel Crown destroyed your crystal."

"Ahh, yes, the Laurel Crown. Out of your lips you condemn yourself also. Like your brother you have taken what does not belong to you. And used it not only to destroy the crystal, but to murder an employee as well. You are a thief and a murderer."

Before Carolyn could protest further, Zetta interrupted.

"We object. Though we do not deny the evidence the prosecutor has provided, in the case of Carolyn Farmer we do contend that she is a victim of circumstance. While her brother may be guilty of certain charges, there is no proof, except by hearsay evidence, that links our client to any wrongdoing. There is not one witness who can corroborate the charges of the prosecution. Therefore, all charges against our client, Carolyn Farmer, must be dismissed."

Bersha nodded twice to Claude who quickly boot-stepped out the door.

Carolyn's heart pounded so hard she was surprised it made no sound in the silent room. She could see beads of sweat on Jimmy's forehead. She smiled at him with all the confidence she could pull up from inside.

He smiled back and gave her a double thumbs-up sign.

The heel clicks made Carolyn turn and watch as Claude carried in a large red bag. He placed it the cart, and, with a nod to Bersha, retreated to stand near the prosecutor's table.

Invisible hands opened the bag and pulled out a head.

Instantly, she knew this head was not Gazellia's from the bedroom. The eyes were rounder, the lips and nose fuller, the cheeks fatter. This was the missing head from the storage room.

"Here is the witness, Your Honor." Bersha set the head upright on the cart, facing Mauvais.

"Gazellia, you are called to speak the truth about the defendant, Carolyn Farmer."

At first the jaw moved up and down without a sound. Next came a series of grunts—*uh* ... *uh* ... *uh*—with more up and down movement. Finally, a pinched mechanical squeak came.

"I am Gazellia, MV 666-239-461, an employee of Mauvais Vallee Enterprises. I was assigned to protect and reeducate the defendant, Carolyn Farmer. In the course of discharging my duties, I was destroyed as a consequence of criminal acts by Carolyn and Jimmy Farmer. They murdered me. I charge them with my death. And I hold this court accountable for justice and the subsequent punishment due them." The mouth closed.

"That's not Gazellia!" Carolyn shouted. "She would never say that!"

"Examine the witness yourself," Bersha said. "Ask under what circumstance she came to be in her present dismembered state."

"No! That's not her. If she *is* dead, she *can't* talk."

The Laurel Crown squeezed. *Gazellia is alive.*

"Jimmy," she clasped her hands over her head, shaking them in victory, "she's alive. I know it. I know it!"

The gavel slammed down. "Silence in the courtroom."

"Your Honor," Bersha said, "we have presented irrefutable evidence of the criminal behavior of Carolyn and Jimmy Farmer. You have heard the testimony of the witness, Gazellia. Neither counsel for the defense nor the clients have offered any proof of their innocence. Both have acted criminally. Therefore, both must be judged guilty and punished by this court."

"Does Counselor Zetta have any evidence of innocence for either party on any of the charges?"

"None, Your Honor."

"In that case, it is the determination of this court that both defendants are not equal in guilt. Carolyn Farmer's action was brought about by her brother's trespass into Vallee domain. As a consequence of this intrusion, a chain of events led the defendant into the present circumstances. Therefore, it is the judgment of this court that two sentences be handed down."

The gavel came down. *Bam. Bam. Bam.*

"Jimmy Farmer, because you have broken into and attempted to steal the property of Mauvais Vallee, you shall be put into a pit with two hungry leopards to be torn apart. This is to be carried out immediately after this court is adjourned."

Bam. Bam. Bam.

"Carolyn Farmer, after you watch your brother's sentence being carried out, you will be taken to an arena where you will be suited with armor, sword, and shield. There you will enter into combat against the warrior champion of Mauvais Vallee Enterprises. However, this court is not without mercy. Do the defendants now throw themselves on the mercy of the court and proclaim their guilt?"

Never. Fear not.

"Never. We're not afraid of you."

"Listen," Jimmy said, "I didn't come all this way for my sister to let *you* scare me." He gave Mauvais the finger. "Up yours." He grabbed Carolyn's hand. "I'm with you in this."

In sync, the M and V on both the helmet and tiara melted into two slithering snakes sliding in the same rhythm, pulsing together—one atop the curved silver surface and the other through red curls.

Mauvais leaned forward with a slight smile. "Before we carry out your sentences, do you have anything further to say to this court? We will consider a last request."

Carolyn was shocked. *We've been sentenced. We're going to die. What more is there to say? To ask?*

Ask for the toe shoes. Ask to write a letter to your grandmother.

"We want to write a letter saying good-bye to our grandmother. And I want to take my toe shoes wherever I'm going to ... whatever."

"Due to our gracious mercy, your requests are granted. You have one earth hour."

Bam.

"Court is adjourned."

Mauvais pointed to Lissette. "Remove them from the platform."

Quick-marching to them, with her lance tip she forced them to stand and to step off.

At the same time, Gog pulled Mauvais's chair back as she rose. Quickly Zetta and Bersha glided around the tables to stand beside Mauvais.

She clapped.

And in reverse order, they left; the door vanished; the screen and platform descended into the marble floor; and the barren tree appeared.

Simultaneously, Claude and Lissette marched out with the gray army.

After all had exited, two soldiers returned.

One carried a small mahogany writing desk with a double ink stand that he placed in front of them. The other set the gold and silver box, a quill pen, and lined paper on it. The doors closed after they left.

Chapter 21

the pit

Jimmy leaned against the tree. "We're finished."

"No, we're not. The crown told me what to do."

"Oh, yeah? Ask it how to stay alive."

Take me off and look into my center.

At first Carolyn could only see Jimmy's face in the wreath. Then a veil-like gauze curtain dropped and parted.

Twelve trees with colored fruit and shiny green leaves lined a gold-bricked path to a pearl gate three stories high. It was hinged in gold and set into a transparent, crystalline wall. On both sides of the gate the wall was set with multicolored jewels in various designs: crosses, circles, flames, wings, and scrolls. Over the gate, large emerald Xs, with its one right side like a slanted P, bordered the top edges of the wall. Long-stemmed red and white roses in clear golden vases stood at each side of the gate. The flowers gently swayed from the slight breeze that wafted through the courtyard.

Carolyn inhaled the sweet rose scent. "Umm. Umm. Lovely."

"Where's that smell coming from?" he asked.

"From its center."

She held it up. "Come. Look."

He pressed his head next to hers.

"I don't see anything."

He must believe to see.

"Can you smell the roses?"

"Yeah. But I don't see anything."

One who does not believe in the supernatural cannot see the supernatural.

"But I didn't believe in it either."

"Hey. Who you talkin' to?"

"The crown. I told you. It's been putting thoughts into my head ever since I got the puzzle. At first I thought it was Gazellia."

"Yeah. Well, it was. I was there in the cellar, remember?"

The pure in heart are always a part of me. Gazellia is with me.

"The crown says, Gazellia is with it—"

"Dead like we'll be soon be with the *it* you're talking to."

Put me on your head and close your eyes.

The leaf tips were feather light.

She closed her eyes. And the twelve trees, gates, walls, and golden pavers remained in her mind.

Standing in front of the gate, Gazellia waved to her. She was dressed in floor-length white linen. On its hem, sleeves, and collar, the Xps were embroidered in gold.

Mon amie, it is I.

"I see you! I see Gazellia," Carolyn yelled.

"Give it to me," he said.

She did.

"Don't see anything. Maybe if I put it on."

Four inches above his head it seemed frozen in midair. "What's wrong with *my* head?"

Pride and anger.

"It says, 'Pride and anger.'"

"Oh, yeah? What about yours?" He handed it back to her.

I choose the hurting. I look upon the heart. I see into the future.

She didn't know how to explain what the thoughts meant. "I guess, it's ... because I was ... I don't know why."

Look into my center.

She held it up.

Inside, a shaft of light with two luminous wings flew in all directions. At one point it hovered upside down and dropped a branch with green leaves at Gazellia's feet.

"Whoa. Who are you?" Carolyn asked.

The spirit of love who conquers all things. Even death. He agape nikai panta.

"It says it is love."

"Great. Maybe we'll just have to *love* ourselves into staying alive."

She put it back on her head.

"Sorry my brother's sarcastic. But how *do* we stay alive?"

Trust and obey. There is no other way but to trust and obey.

"We have to trust it and do what it says."

"As if I got a choice."

Write your letter.

"We should write to Gram."

"You do it. I got no clue what to say."

She dipped a quill into the ink and started.

"Umm. Dear Gram. Jimmy and I have gone on a short trip. We'll be back soon. Don't worry. We're fine. We love you. Carolyn."

She offered the pen. "Here."

"Nah. You sign for me."

Place the letter in my center.

It was like posting an envelope into a mail slot.

"Okay, sis. I'm the next order of business. Ask it how I'm not going to end up cat food."

"Please help bro. What can he do against the leopards?"

Give him the toe shoes. He has the medallion. Tell him to use them both.

"Well? What did it say?"

"Use the toe shoes." She opened the box and gave them to him.

"Even if I could, there's no way I'm putting these on. No way!"

He does not have to wear them.

"You're not supposed to wear them."

"So?" He looked at them cupped in his hands. "How then?"

Remember they will move where you will them to move.

She focused her whole being, her whole mind-energy, on the shoes. *Rise,* her thoughts commanded.

From inside one of the toe shoes a pair of ribbons unrolled.

Move to the right.

Its heel lifted in his hands.

She pictured them flying.

They darted and dipped around the room like a pair of cardinals.

The crystal sailed after them and began to flash.

It cannot take what is legally yours.

She lifted her fist at the crystal and yelled, "They belong to me! You can't touch my property."

Send me.

She knew exactly what to do.

Zzz-zzz-zat. The two halves crashed to the floor.

He jumped to catch the toe shoes just as she reached for the crown.

"I've got it—*them,*" they both said at the same time.

The crown felt like a welcome, warm hug around her head.

He looked at the toe shoes. "Hmm, maybe ... maybe I got a chance, slim at best, but a chance. Cats are cats. They love to play chase. Make 'em run, exhaust 'em, hypnotize 'em. It's worth a try."

He wound the ribbons tightly around the arches and slipped each one into a rear pocket.

"Okay, David. Now what are you going to do against Goliath in the shiny steel suit?"

"Haven't the slightest. But the crown knows. I ... we will trust and obey."

The size of a sandy football field behind the school had been swept smooth. As the army marched across it, clouds of dust lifted in the hot air. The corps' footprints cut through its surface, marking a large circle in the middle of the field. There they stood waiting. Their sharp metal tips sparkled in the double suns. Two corpsmen stepped away from the front line as Claude and Lissette jabbed Carolyn and Jimmy into the center of the armed circle.

A large square had been drawn in the sand.

Lissette used her standard to point. "Carolyn, you over there, behind that line." And then to Jimmy Lissette said,, "You over there, behind that line."

Carolyn hesitated, not wanting to leave his side. Immediately she felt the sharp point of the lance in her back. "Move," came the cold command.

"I'll take her there," Claude said. From behind, quickly he gripped her under both elbows, half lifting, half shoving her to the mark. He stood beside her and whispered, "Now is not the time to argue."

Meanwhile, Lissette forced Jimmy to stand across the square opposite Carolyn.

With a flourish, the bugler sounded a summons.

There was a low rumbling and Carolyn felt the ground vibrate. A large line appeared in the sand, splitting the square in half. She heard a creaking, cranking noise. The line became a fissure that widened. Soon all the sand from above poured into a twenty foot by twenty foot deep pit. From below, clouds of dust boiled upward like steam.

Carolyn heard a metal door slide open from a hidden cage beneath. The first larger leopard leaped into the pit. Circling round at the bottom of the pit, he came to the side walls where Carolyn and Jimmy stood at its edge above him. Digging his claws into the dirt, he jumped as high as he could. Over and over he tried to climb his way up to them, but fell back as the walls were too high—the sides too straight. The smaller one followed cautiously, sniffing the air and her companion's footprints. The second cat watched calmly as the other circled in frustration.

"Jump or be pushed," Lissette said.

He jumped and landed on his heels in a mound of soft sand.

The startled cats froze, their attention riveted on him.

Tell Jimmy that in football the best defense is an offense. Use strategy.

Carolyn shouted, "Use football strategy. Don't show fear."

Stealthily, barely moving forward, the larger leopard crouched low. Every muscle was ready for the kill.

Jimmy bent over in an aggressive stance—legs far apart, elbows on knees. "Hut, one, two, three," he huffed.

Surprised, tails twitching, they stood still—yellow eyes riveted on him.

"Lie down," he commanded, imitating his coach.

Neither leopard moved.

With his right palm he gestured. "Lie *down*."

The moment his hand moved, the larger cat's lips curled back, exposing his teeth. His left front paw lifted, sharp claws fully extended. Ever so slowly, he advanced.

"Try the shoes."

With as little movement as possible, Jimmy pulled the toe shoes out from his back pockets. Slowly he unwound the ribbons, letting them swing as he did so.

The large cat's eyes shifted to the ribbons. His ears swung forward. The other cat's eyes also left his face and focused on the dancing ribbons.

"Niiice kitties, beeyouuutiful kittties," he cooed softly. "See what I have here? Wouldn't you like to play with the pretty ribbons?"

Jimmy increased the tempo, making the ribbons hop, wiggle, and waggle over the sand. The larger cat's head jerked up and down following the ribbons. And just as he jumped to get them, Jimmy did a quick step back, yanking the shoes high. He forced him to miss the ends by inches. He repeated the action. Again the cat pounced. And missed. Jimmy spun, causing the ribbons to fly. The cat bounded after them. Except for his size, he was like a young kitten playing a game of chase.

Meanwhile, the smaller one had not moved from her spot.

"Can you focus on just one of the shoes?"

"I'll try."

He tossed it in the air.

Carolyn concentrated, seeing it spin in her mind. And it spun, soaring and dipping over the cat's head.

The male bounded after it, trying to catch it with his front paws.

"Give it to him," he shouted, "while I work with the other one!"

She focused her mind to dangle it in front of the large cat's nose within easy reach.

Joyfully, the male scooped it up in his mouth and pranced proudly to a corner. There, like a kitten with catnip, he happily amused himself with the shoe. He jumped and tumbled over it, playfully tossing it in the air and chasing it to where it landed.

The smaller leopard's attention now went back to Jimmy.

"Do that with the other shoe."

She concentrated, lifting it high and twirling it over the cat's head.

The female completely ignored the spinning shoe. Her eyes never left Jimmy's face. Slowly she began to creep toward him. As she came closer, she lowered her head and tail. The muscles under her spotted coat rippled in anticipation.

I've got to do something, Carolyn thought.

The shoe fell to the ground. "Don't move!" she shouted. "I'm coming in."

Instantly she felt a sharp pain around her head.

Do not jump in, came the command. *Tell Jimmy to take off the medallion.*

"Take off the medallion."

Immediately the crown released its painful hold.

Tell him to face the medallion toward one and then the other. Tell him to say, "He agape nikai panta. God protects me. I command you to do me no harm."

The moment he did, a beam of light shot from the face of the medal directly into the face of the cat.

Startled, the female first tried to duck, and then she ran away. But it followed her, widening to cover her body. Totally wrapped in brightness, she relaxed, yawned, stretched, tucked her head under her paws, and fell asleep.

He walked over to the corner where the larger cat was still playing with the shoe. He faced the medallion toward him and repeated the words. Within seconds, covered in light, he too fell asleep.

Turn the medallion toward himself.

She understood exactly what the crown intended—protection for him and the cats. The power behind the crown doesn't want to destroy the leopards. They're just cats being cats. It's Mauvais that shape-shifts them into demons.

"Turn it toward you."

He did. And it enveloped him with sparkles and flashing.

"Our power is greater than yours." The words shrieked from all directions.

The larger cat began to elongate, expanding himself into a cranberry robe. The other into green. Invisible hands held curved sabers with sharp forked ends. Bersha and Zetta stood in front of Jimmy

"Now what?" he screamed.

Open the medallion.

"Open the medallion."

"How?"

Unscrew the top.

She repeated the command.

As he began to twist the top, the medal grew in his hands into a disk with finely serrated edges—its tips razor sharp.

She spoke the thought. "Throw it."

As it spun out of his hand, the two robes crossed their sabers in defense.

Sparks flew as the disk bounced off—metal against metal. It ricocheted into the walls, causing clumps of earth to hit the ground before they landed at his feet.

The moment he reached to pick it up, a handle appeared in its center. The disk grew to cover his body.

Screeching like banshees, the robes flew at him.

As they whizzed past, their sword edges clipped the metal disk.

The shield and his body became one—turning, twisting, repelling their attacks.

The ground began to vibrate.

"We are everywhere. You cannot escape our power."

Clouds of dust rose from the pit floor as the walls started to cave in. Jimmy kept deflecting the saber thrusts from the flying banshees.

Claude shoved his lance at Carolyn. "Throw him this."

"Oh, no, you don't, brother," Lissette screamed. "I won't be eliminated because you're a traitor to Mauvais." And with the blunt end of her standard, she hit him squarely in the back with such force that he fell into the pit.

It took one swipe from Bersha to slice the lance in two. And another quick slash across Claude's neck to sever his head.

Shimmering liquid spurted his from neck and head as he fell—limbs askew—making a glistening pool on the ground.

Jimmy hit Bersha as hard as he could with the shield's edge. It tore into the robe, ripping it up the center. Both robe and saber instantly vanished.

From behind, Zetta's sword slashed Jimmy across the back of his neck.

To Carolyn's horror, she watched blood spurt like a fountain as he fell face down in the dirt.

The pressure on her head from the crown kept Carolyn from passing out. Like the impact moment the truck hit their car, every cell in her body went into shock. She dropped to her knees in despair.

He is not dead. He is with Gazellia.

She watched the iron doors close over her last view of her brother sprawled in a pool of blood next to Claude's head.

Chapter 22

Victory

"Well done, employee Lissette," the echo boomed. "You shall be rewarded for your loyalty to us."

Carolyn's gut wrenched. "How could you?" she screamed at Lissette. "You sent your own brother to his death."

Lissette mouthed with all the corps, "Exactly like you did, stupid human."

Overwhelming guilt flooded Carolyn. True. If it hadn't been for me, this never would have happened. We would all be together … home.

She sobbed, "Why does everybody I love die?"

From the top of her head to the soles of her feet, a warm blanket of love engulfed her, seeping into every pore of her body.

I know your end from your beginning. I redeem the anguished soul. They are not dead. They live. I chose you to be my warrior. If you make me your friend, it matters not who your enemy is. Trust and obey.

With those thoughts, a calmness began to penetrate her mind and cool her body. She took a deep breath. Okay. I'll try. Help me to trust you.

I accept your willingness. Accuse them.

Sudden strength poured into her. "You're the ones who killed my brother," she shouted. "You killed Gazellia. Not me." She pointed to Lissette. "You shoved Claude into the pit. Not me."

"Jimmy Farmer's sentence has been carried out. Yours now begins."

Say, "You will be vanquished."

Carolyn shook her fists in Lissette's face. "You … Mauvais … you all will be vanquished … destroyed."

The echo shrilled, "No power is great enough. Like your brother, you will cease to exist."

"Liar! Coward! Murderer! Nothing you have ever said is true. You are the criminal. You are the murderer. My brother lives. Gazellia lives in spite of you."

Suddenly a roaring wind came from four different directions. It whipped the sand into a tornado of stinging, black dirt. Lissette bent down covering her face with her arms.

Carolyn squeezed her eyes shut, but she did not flinch or cower. She raised her fists and shouted into the wind, "Liar! Murderer! Coward!"

The roar changed into a screeching wind. "How dare you call us a coward! We shall witness which one of us is to be feared. Prepare for battle. Prepare yourself for death."

Abruptly the wind died. The swirling dust subsided while the corps, coughing, hacking, brushing themselves off, positioned themselves again in a double circle. Lissette waved to the bugler. He gave a short trumpet trill.

Beside the shut iron doors, a platform rose in a billow of dust. On it stood a painted green wooden hut—the size of a large clothes closet.

"You'll change in here." Lissette shoved Carolyn inside.

In the close quarters to the left of the door, an armor chest piece hung by its leather shoulder straps on two wooden pegs. Dull, pockmarked with rust, the old armor had not been cleaned, she guessed, for centuries. But from its fresh scratches, dents, and dings, it had been used recently.

Next to the armor, a dirty chain-mail tunic, separate leggings, and gloves hung on another wooden peg. Above the armor and chain mail, a wooden shelf held a rusty helmet. Its hinged visor had three slits for two eyes and a nose. A few green scraggly feathers were left in the groove on top of the dented helmet. In front of it, a sword hilt of emerald and gold stuck out of a black leather sheath attached to a leather belt. Underneath the shelf, a triangular concave shield covered in green leather leaned against the wall. Inside the shield was a wide leather strap. Beside it leaned a rust-tipped lance.

Lissette took the tunic off the pegs. "Get into your armor," she commanded.

"No way. I'm not getting into a dirty wire cage."

Lissette shrugged. "Up to you. How you die, whether sooner or later, makes no difference to me."

Chest armor. Sword. Shield. Lance.

"I'll wear the chest armor. I'll take the sword, shield, and lance. The rest stays."

While Lissette cinched the leather straps of the chest armor over her shoulders and behind her back, Carolyn buckled the belt around her waist. The sword hung down her left side. She twisted her upper body and moved her arms to see if she could maneuver. Although the rough edges rubbed under her arms and across her ribs, she could manage the weight. She picked up the shield. It was heavier than any school books she had ever carried in her backpack.

No way can I use this, she thought.

Put your left arm and shoulder through the leather strap and lift.

She braced her back against the hut wall. Sliding her left arm and shoulder through the leather, she lifted the shield. Suddenly it became almost weightless. Its curved surface covered her body from below the belt to her neck. She reached over and picked up the lance. It too was light.

Tell Lissette to hold the lance.

"Here, hold this," she said.

Outside the hut, she struggled to unsheathe the sword. The shield kept getting in the way, and her right arm wasn't long enough to pull it all the way out.

Use your left hand to pull the scabbard down, while your right hand pulls the hilt up and out.

On the second try, she smoothly pulled it out. Once it was free, it seemed light in her hand. Its blade was double-edged stainless steel. She swished it through the air just like she had seen Robin Hood duel with the Sheriff of Nottingham in a movie.

Sheathe it and take the lance.

Rivulets of sweat ran down her face. On the fourth try, she was able to find the slit and slide it back into its scabbard.

She took a deep breath. Facing an enemy she had to kill registered in her brain. Terror filled her gut. And with it a mix of sorrow and anger. *Jimmy is dead. So are Claude and Gazellia.* Pain beyond any pain she had experienced before—like the blade she had just sheathed—pierced her chest. *Everything I touch ends in death.* Terror changed to fire which blazed into a rage directed at the crown. *Who are you? What are you? You want me to trust you? Right?*

Her angry sobs came in short breathless gulps. "I've been doing it," she screamed. I *have!* I *have*! I don't know how much more of this I can take."

The familiar gentle squeeze came. Like being under a cooling shower, she felt suddenly calm. *The legend will prove true. You are ready.*

She turned to Lissette. "Give me the lance."

Lissette turned it tip down and thrust it into the soft sand. She snapped her heels, then marched across the arena to a similar hut painted red. On its roof an MVE pennant drooped in the heat.

Alongside the hut, a page-groom in gray held the bridle of a huge black stallion decked in red silk. On his back, silver cobra-headed studs with diamonds adorned the red leather saddle and silver stirrups. The horse whinnied, tossing and shaking his black mane impatiently. His hooves nervously struck the ground. The groom *whoa-ed* and gently patted the horse's nose and neck, trying to calm the shifting, high-strung animal. The horse stomped and whinnied, almost throwing the groom to the ground. He yelled, and two other grooms came running out of the hut. All three, dwarfed by the huge animal, clung to the bridle. They struggled to keep the horse from rearing up.

You will ride also, for you are my champion. I have chosen you for my cause against evil on Double Suns. You will have victory in me. For I am against Baal and all those who love his power and submit to him.

"But why me? Why didn't you choose bro? He's stronger than me."

For that reason. He is proud of his strength.

"I don't understand, but if there is a secret to your power, please tell me what it is ... how you work." She felt the back of her throat squeeze tight with pain. "If this is a dream, I want to wake up."

Extend your right hand, palm up.

Before she saw them, she felt the reins. First a breath, and then a soft push on her shoulder, a whinny, and then another breath and push. Without turning she could smell horse. He stepped forward and dropped his head over her shoulder. His soft lips mouthed the reins in her hand. She reached up and stroked his white forehead and soft brown nose. His brown eyes sparkled.

"Hello there. What's your name?"

He blew through his nose and lips a ruffling, horsey acknowledgment of her question.

Victory.

"Hi, Victory," she said, patting him on his neck. His white coat glistened in the suns. He stood quietly as she slowly walked around him. She stroked his neck, his shoulders, and his rump. His long white tail swished as she passed.

He resembled an Arabian stallion—twice as tall as she was from his hooves to his shoulders. Only his eyes, eye lashes, and the insides of his nose were brown. In tiny Greek letters tattooed on his upper right shoulder were the words "He agape nikai panta." She examined the saddle—green leather with gold stirrups higher than her shoulders.

"How do I get on?"

Tell Victory to bow.

After her command, he lowered himself to his knees, enabling her to reach the stirrups.

Take the reins in your left hand. Grab the horn. Place your left foot into the stirrup on his left side. Swing your right leg over his back and sit in the saddle.

After a mighty pull up, she swung her leg over.

The broad saddle was hot, hard, and uncomfortable.

She didn't expect the sudden jerk as he stood up. She lurched backward, gripping the pummel tightly to keep from falling off.

He pulled his head down and shifted his body under her until she regained her seat—then stood still.

"Whew. Thanks, Victory."

He whinnied softly and shook his head up and down, causing his white mane to swing.

"Now what?"

Use your knees to grip his sides. Pull the reins to the right or to the left across his neck and with your heels gently tap him.

It took several circles around the hut for her to understand that he could sense what she wanted almost before she asked. He walked, trotted, and finally galloped around the hut, expertly shifting his body under her, helping her to stay in the saddle.

As he trotted by the lance, he angled closer so she could lean over and pull it out of the sand. *He knows just what to do,* she thought. *I can trust him.*

When Gog rides toward you, lift your lance and hit him squarely in the chest.

Her stomach somersaulted. "I've never been in a fight … not physical … really. Um … I don't think—"

The fight is not yours, it is mine.

She licked her dry lips. "But … it's my body you're using. And … I'm in it."

True. I have chosen you. I know your courage. You are my accomplice.

"But why me?" she asked. "Why me?"

"You are a criminal and must be punished." The words came from all directions.

Do you love them enough to fight for them?

Do I?

She saw her brother's body in a pool of blood beside Claude. She doubled over from the pain in her chest.

"I don't know if I love them enough. I just know I can't leave them here. If I can help them, I'm willing."

You have found the key to unlock my secret: love conquers all things … fear … even death.

She felt resolve rise from within, strengthening her to sit upright in the saddle. With her sleeve, she wiped away the tears and sweat and took a deep breath. The worst that can happen is the best that can happen. I'll be with them.

"I guess I'm as ready as I'll ever be."

Squinting into the bright sunlight, she saw the opposite hut door open.

The stallion whinnied, stomped, and then stood still. It seemed as if the three had finally calmed him.

She wondered at the change in the horse's manner. He moved in such a way to make her think someone was beside him. The left stirrup dropped as the saddle slid slightly sideways on his back. As she watched, one of the grooms handed the reins to nothing. There they hung in exactly the proper position a hand would be for a rider.

How can I hit an invisible target?

A gentle press on her forehead.

"This hour you will be laid low," Carolyn shouted. "Your authority will end. Your power will cease. And what you have built will be destroyed."

She was astonished the moment those words left her lips. The courage to say them had welled up from deep inside her gut. She and the crown had become one.

Silence. Ominous. Deadly.

Mauvais has sent the tormentors. I will allow them to send you into battle.

In the haze of dust and heat, like a mirage, she saw a black pool emerge in the center of the field.

Buzz. Buzz. Black horseflies. They swarmed, zoomed, and dive-bombed her and Victory. He snorted and stomped his hooves as they nipped his fetlocks. His tail snapped them off his back. They stung and bit his tender nose and ears.

She laid the lance across the saddle so she could frantically wave them off. One landed on her eyelid and bit. "Ow!" Another landed on her cheek. "Ow! Ouch!" She slapped it away. More came. A black horde, they multiplied faster than both could manage to wave and flick them off.

The maze.

With no more than the verbal command, he complied with a quick walk that developed into a fast trot. With the reins still in her hand, she used the lance for balance like a tight-rope walker as he cantered across the arena.

He was in full gallop, nearing the far end, when a corpsman leaped out in front of him. With incredible ease, Victory high-jumped over and past him. Her rear hit the saddle with a hard, painful thwack when his hooves hit the ground.

"Whoa, Victory. Take it easy. I'm not used to riding."

Behind them the black cloud fanned out, covering each soldier from caps to shoes in flies. Swatting desperately, four members were driven from the field. They ran after Victory and Carolyn while the rest continued to stand, not bothered in the least by the biting insects.

He galloped around the building to the front, stopping short of the maze entrance. Once they entered, the flies disappeared.

The hedge row tops were now at her waist and she could clearly see the cupola with the iron MVE in its center. She shifted the lance lengthwise under her arm because it was too wide across the saddle to go between the hedges. She leaned forward, pulling the reins across his neck. Behind them after every turn the hedges changed positions. Under the shade of the cupola they waited.

She heard a rustling. Four corpsmen—two men, two women—pushed their way through the branches. They collapsed on the cool cement. Their uniforms were torn and stained with perspiration, and three had lost their military caps. Every part of their uncovered bodies was bitten and bleeding.

Seeing their swollen bites, she realized hers were gone.

Immediately she recognized them from the ballroom.

"You're Michelle," Carolyn said. "I think you wore yellow. And you're Carlos and Raymond." She looked at the other woman. "But I don't remember you."

Victory lowered his head and smelled Michelle's hair.

"Thanks for leading us here," she said, stroking his nose.

Carolyn turned around in the saddle to look behind. "Any more coming?"

"No. We are the only ones left that are like Gazellia and Claude," Michelle said.

"Why'd you follow us?"

"Because you are wearing the Laurel Crown," Carlos replied.

The other lady stood and dusted herself off. "Let me introduce myself. My name is Porcelain. When you all had the conversation about Mauvais, I remained silent. But I hate Mauvais and what she has done. I also take my stand with the one who wears the Laurel Crown."

"I thought you guys were robots. I thought Claude was one too."

"Poor Claude," Carlos said. "Like Gazellia and him, we will meet the same fate unless the crown intervenes. It was their hope and ours that it would. We had all agreed to follow it should it ever prove itself true."

"But we are alive," Michelle said, "because of Mauvais's weakness for human companionship. She was not always evil. Her stepmother hated her. She had a terrible life. I think she kept us human because there is something inside her that still seeks affection."

"We knew her at Stone Pillar too," Carlos said.

Michelle rubbed Victory's nose. "I think that is why Gazellia was sentenced to the puzzle instead of being eliminated."

"And why she has kept us alive as well," Porcelain said.

"No matter," Michelle said. "Whatever the reasons, we are here to assist you and the crown however we can."

"I don't know what you guys can do," Carolyn said. "I don't even know what I'm supposed to do. But thanks, I can use all the help I can get."

The crown gently squeezed. *Gog comes.*

Carolyn's heart lurched. She stammered, "H-he's coming."

Michelle blew Carolyn a kiss. "May God protect you as you ride Victory and destroy Mauvais," she said.

Chapter 23

GOG

It was in watching the four run to hide in the hedges that Carolyn realized they were not in a maze anymore. They had changed from curves and angles to form three straight rows. Starting at the gazebo, these ran parallel to each other for about a hundred yards. Here and there, outside the long rows, clumps of bushes remained in circles.

Face our enemy.

She turned Victory to the rows.

A glint of light reflected off silver metal. Quicker than the silver flash, she knew Mauvais's warrior was positioning himself at the other end of the hedge rows. At the far end, she could see a dazzling, ten-foot warrior sitting astride the black stallion.

Four simultaneous trumpet blasts sounded.

"I guess this is it." She took a deep breath and lowered her lance.

From opposite ends they galloped toward each other. She leaned forward in the saddle, bracing herself for the impact after her lance would hit the warrior.

Closer and closer thundering hooves galloped. Just three yards from where the horses were close enough that their lances would clash, Michelle and Raymond jumped out of the middle hedge and into the black stallion's path.

"Wahoo! Wahoo!" they yelled, waving their arms wildly in front of him.

Startled, front legs rearing, churning in midair, the stallion's hind legs skittered backward.

Meanwhile Victory galloped past them to the end of the right lane.

By the time Victory had stopped at the end of the row and turned, the warrior had recovered control. Viciously he kicked the stallion with spiked spurs into a frenzied gallop after Michelle and Raymond.

The stallion was upon Michelle in seconds. And with sword drawn, Gog slashed and hacked her into tiny bits. Blood and pieces darkened in the sand.

Horrified, Carolyn screamed for him to stop, all the while furiously kicking and hitting Victory with the reins. But he would not budge. He stood solid, firm at the end of the lane. No matter what she did to him from the saddle, he would not move. Desperate, angry because he wouldn't obey, she was about to get down when the crown painfully squeezed her head. This was the second time it had given her pain.

Do not dismount. Your heart is right to defend. But the power to conquer belongs to me. We cannot win without you obeying me.

"But you *were* with me when Jimmy was in the pit. You did nothing. Nothing!" she shouted. "At least Claude tried. Now they're dead … and you still want me to obey you?"

Yes. I know their end and yours from the beginning. Believe. Obey. All will be well.

The image of Gazellia waving to her from inside the courtyard came into her mind.

"Okay. I won't get down."

Immediately it released its hold and her body instantly cooled.

I am the protector.

An assurance welled up in her beyond her understanding. Somehow she knew that those words were a true answer, even though she couldn't quite grasp what they meant. She knew there was no going back without bro. Forward, like it or not, was still the right direction.

She focused on the warrior and stallion frantically charging in and out of the hedges looking for Raymond.

She wondered, *What is it like inside a complete suit of armor … and in this heat? How does an experienced knight do battle?*

And with those questions in mind, she studied how Gog rode—how he used his lance and sword to search and cut. His biggest problem, she decided, was his mount. Because his horse was difficult to control, Gog swayed in the saddle. A couple of times when he leaned down with his sword to swipe a hedge, the stallion reared, almost throwing him off. Furious, he was brutal with his spurs. Blood flowed from his stallion's flanks.

If somehow I can catch him off balance, she thought, I might be able to unseat him.

Unable to find Raymond, the warrior returned to the far lane opposite her. He jerked the bridle bit in the stallion's mouth—making it bleed. The horse whinnied in pain. He lowered his lance and spurred the stallion forward.

Without any voice command or heel pressure from her, Victory lunged into a fast gallop. She positioned her lance, guessing where his chest plate might be.

Midway—

Gog hit her squarely in her shield, splintering his lance.

The blow rocked her back in the saddle. Victory wheeled, shifting his weight under her as she grabbed the saddle horn. After teetering for several seconds, and with him countering under her, she was able to regain her seat.

She leaned over and patted his neck. "Thanks. You did great."

Slowly he trotted to the end of the lane, turned, and stood quietly.

Meanwhile the warrior drew his sword. As his sharp spurs cut into the stallion's bleeding flanks, the horse took off in a frenzied gallop—his hooves throwing clumps of dirt in the air.

The Laurel Crown squeezed. And she felt her body tingle with a powerful surge of electricity. She knew exactly what to do.

Just as the stallion galloped toward them, she reversed her lance. With her knees slightly bent in a batter's stance, she stood in the stirrups. With both hands she gripped its broad end like a bat ready to swing. At precisely the moment the warrior thundered past, she ducked his sword and—*whack!* She cracked him across his back, hitting his shoulder armor plates with its blunt end.

Down he went, toppled over by the force of her blow and the forward weight of his armor. On the way down, his right spur hung up in a stirrup. Spooked by the dragging, clanging armor, the stallion kicked and kicked. Finally, he freed himself. Bucking to the end of the lane, he jumped through the gazebo and was gone.

Out of the center hedge, Raymond, Carlos, and Porcelain flung themselves on Gog. While Raymond wrapped his body around his helmet, Carlos and Porcelain each grabbed an arm.

"Use the crown," Raymond shouted to Carolyn.

She reached and pulled hard. "I can't take it off," she shouted back.

"Then use your sword!" he cried.

The warrior staggered to his feet with Raymond still clinging to his helmet. Ten feet up, the three dangled as Gog shook himself. Then with a fast twist, he swung his arms, flinging Porcelain and Carlos to the ground. He reached behind his helmet, and with chain-mail hands grabbed Raymond by the neck. He pulled Raymond over his helmet and smashed him to the ground, instantly breaking his neck. He picked up Porcelain and Carlos and cracked their heads together like two china dolls. He dropped both on top of Raymond. All three were dead.

An anguish rose in Carolyn—an anguish so intense, so fierce, that she would do anything to destroy this evil force. Nothing in the universe could stop her from trying to kill this horrible monster.

"Prepare to meet your doom," the echoes shrieked.

In a giant stride he was over her, his sword ready to strike.

Again, she knew exactly what to do. She hit him squarely in the chest with her lance. The metal tip bent; the wood was shattered by the force of her hit.

Victory reared and with front hooves striking out forced Gog to back up.

For a split second, she was surprised she wasn't unseated. It was as if she had been glued to the saddle.

Once more, the warrior advanced to strike her.

Victory spun and then danced backward, giving her time to pull her sword from its scabbard.

The sharp steel edges flashed in the suns as she raised it to strike him.

At that exact moment, the warrior stabbed Victory in the chest.

Time stood still—the universe hung suspended—

Then she felt Victory go down to his knees.

The crown cut deep into her forehead, but she felt no pain.

As he fell and rolled over, she jumped out of the saddle. When her feet hit the ground, Victory vanished.

And the warrior was again towering over her.

She swung her sword as hard as she could, striking it against his side, putting a dent in his armor. She felt the wind whistle past her cheek as his blade barely missed her, hitting her shield. But it did not penetrate. She darted left, right, striking him with a force she knew was not her own. Over and over she whacked at him with the flat of her blade; she swung, hacking at his armor with the sharp edges of her sword. She hit him everywhere she could—on the legs, on the thighs, at the waist.

Her size, her speed, her lack of heavy armor had a distinct advantage. She was light and fast. He was big and slow. Dodging, darting around him, she kept hitting him, hacking away until a dent opened into a large hole in his right thigh. She plunged her sword into it up to its hilt and twisted. She felt the blade go into nothing. The leg was hollow. She pulled the sword out of the hole.

From above, she saw his metal fingers coming at her like a giant claw. It clamped around her shield and chest piece. His glove squeezed. Her chest armor began to creak. He threw down his sword and with both gloves squeezed. Her armor began to buckle. She looked into his eye slits. Blackness.

Her chest piece and shield began to crush her ribs. Her lungs screamed in pain. Desperate, she thrust her sword into his left eye slit. And lifted.

The visor flipped up. And the sword was wrenched out of her hand. It sailed over his helmet and dropped somewhere in the bushes.

Her brain began to mist over from lack of oxygen. Jimmy's face swam before her. She groaned and touched the crown. I've done everything I can.

From far away she heard the sound of ricocheting metal.

Clink. Clank.

It became louder. And louder.

Smack! Bang!

And suddenly air was pouring into her lungs.

Her foggy mind cleared in seconds. The crown was gone from her head. And then she knew. It was ringing its way down inside the armor, metal against metal.

From deep within Gog came dark and terrible wails. Long howls of agony echoed through the maze.

"Aaahhheee. Aaahhheee."

His metal fingers opened and dropped her into the hedge.

The broken branches cushioned her fall. Springing to her feet, she accidentally stepped on the sword. She picked it up ready to fight.

"Aaahhheee."

Starting from his feet—slowly at first, then more rapidly—she watched him being corkscrewed, twisted from bottom to top as easily as a thin sheet of foil. The two ends were then knotted three times into a mangle of chain mail and chunks of plate.

From inside every crack and crevice, smoke-like tendrils uncoiled, turning into black eel-like snakes. Thousands of them slithered and squirmed over the mass of jumbled metal.

The sword flew out of her hand.

It sliced off their heads as quickly and as easily as a Ninja knife.

Their disconnected bodies continued to squirm as the massive jumble of metal melted into a pool of black ooze.

When the sword was finished, it boomeranged. Instinctively, she reached out and caught it by the hilt.

From the muck—first spinning rapidly and then slowing down—the crown rose clean to hover over her head.

She watched the slimy stuff dissolve into the ground without leaving a trace that Gog had ever existed.

The crown felt cool on her forehead.

Joy and relief flooded her whole being. It was over.

Now, to get to the pearl gate inside the jeweled wall to bring back bro, Gazellia, and the rest.

We are not finished. Go to the gazebo.

Under the cupola, Carolyn eased her every-muscle-aching-body onto a bench. She put the dented sword and crumpled shield next to her. The tight chest piece was unbearable. She reached up and unbuckled the leather straps. They dropped with a clank onto the concrete. She inhaled, stretching her lungs in an exquisite, deep breath. She looked down at the gouged metal from Gog's grip.

I survived. I'm alive.

Images flooded her mind: Gog snapping Raymond's neck. Hacking Michelle into pieces. Blood and shimmering liquid spurting everywhere—the eels, the muck, the mess. She vomited until she was empty. She wiped her face on her sleeves.

Her shaking hands lightly touched the crown.

"Enough already. I can't take any more."

A kaleidoscope of faces spun through her mind. Jimmy. Gazellia. Claude.

They are there, safe. They are waiting for you to come for them.

"Do I have to die to get there?"

The circlet grew warm.

"I don't know what to do."

Instantly she did know. In quick succession she stacked the shield, chest piece, and sword on the bench. She placed the crown on top. Then stepped away. She watched the emeralds glow—a million green sparks fly. And wherever one landed, the metal changed from rust to silver. The dents and gouges smoothed, making the chest piece, shield, and blade brand new.

Get dressed. We have work to do.

Once she had slipped on the crown, she buckled the leather straps of the armor. It fit her perfectly. She sheathed her sword and lifted the shield. Etched into its curved surface were the Greek words underneath the laurel leaves.

Hold up the shield and see your reflection.

Her face filled the spaces between the etching. The letters and leaves were a part of her gray eyes and soft features. Her blond hair curled around the emerald-gold on her head. She leaned the shield against the bench and moved back. From the top of her head to the soles of her shoes, she shimmered—vibrating light expanding in all directions.

"Whoa!"

My knight is splendid.

"If only Mom and Dad could see me now … and Gram. Oh, and Kelley. She was my best friend in Seattle."

I send you Victory.

Before Carolyn saw his reflection, she smelled his horsey breath. He nuzzled her neck.

"Oh, I'm so glad to see you." She turned and kissed him on the nose. "I thought you were dead. Where were you?"

Outside the pearl gate.

The crown squeezed.

Mauvais comes.

Carolyn felt a cool calmness permeate her whole body. She slid her arm into the shield.

"Victory, bow!" she commanded. He bent down. It was good to be on him again.

She put her feet in his stirrups as he shifted, facing her to the row of hedges.

Chapter 24

Destroyer

At the rows' far end, Carolyn saw a red glow moving up, down, and swinging sideways.

Forty feet long and ten feet in diameter, a jointed, segmented machine came undulating toward them. At the front of the snaky cylinder, ten heads—one higher than the others, bobbed on long necks. The largest above the rest was the cobra's. A ruby and diamond tiara pulsed on its head. Of the remaining heads, a human male and female were attached together on one neck. The rest, on their own necks, were egg-shaped ovals with slits for eyes and mouths. From along its metal sides, black light emanated through holes like fuzzy legs. Twigs, rocks, and grains of sand were sucked up into its moving hoses. Raymond, and the remains of the others, were vacuumed up as easily as dust on a carpet.

From every direction Carolyn heard a low, metallic hum, which grew louder as the cobra-headed machine approached.

She felt a cold wind move through the gazebo.

"Foolish human. This is your last chance. Save your life. Join us. Sign the contract and you can have your freedom."

Carolyn drew her sword. "All who destroy are destroyed in the end. So shall it be for you. The destroyer destroyed."

An iridescent black veil fell over the gazebo like a blanket. Carolyn could feel its pull, trying to draw her body out of the saddle into its darkness. She tightened her legs around Victory with all her strength. She gripped the hilt of the sword, ready for some kind of attack.

Instead, in her mind's eye it was as if she were a giant holding a glass-like globe, looking down into it at herself seated on Victory in miniature.

"There is no energy like mine in the universe," the metallic voice hummed. "I will share this with you. Relinquish the crown and you will become my new regent on the planet of Double Suns."

The electricity that she had plugged into when she had danced now surged through her fingertips as she looked into the dark globe.

Her mind-scene changed. The gazebo with herself on Victory vanished. In its place, Gazellia and Jimmy bowed low before her seated on Mauvais's golden throne. Her long blond curls were intertwined with diamond stars held by a silver band with a quarter moon on her forehead. Gazellia's medallion hung from her neck.

The sight of Gazellia and Jimmy sent waves of happiness like another power surge through her brain.

"I have the ability to replicate any human you desire … mother, father, grandmother. Your family can be reconstructed as a reward for your employment."

Inside the globe the dining room in Seattle materialized. Carolyn recognized the Christmas arrangement of holly and the red placemats on the table. The turkey platter and serving dishes were full. Her mother lit a couple of white candles on the table. Her father, Jimmy, and she herself pulled out the chairs and sat down.

At the sight of them around the table, her heart ached with longing.

Oh, to go back to then, she thought. *How wonderful it would be to live it again. Only this time, no fighting with Jimmy in the back seat. If I could undo that, I would give anything.*

"Whatever you desire can be yours. I can reprogram past memories to successful outcomes. You need only to swear your devotion. I, King Baal, will provide countless pleasures beyond your present comprehension if you will bow down to me."

Suddenly Victory shifted under her.

Reprogram past memories? Like shaken bubbles in a bottle of soda water her thoughts rose. How would that really undo the past? The past would still be the past. Would I really be happy with robots that looked like Mom and Dad and Jimmy? If you can remake my mind, who would I become? The *me* of me would be blown away.

"No way," she shouted, "are you getting into *my* brain!"

She made several thrusts into the veil, but nothing changed—the blade swished through what seemed to be black nothingness.

"You have sealed your fate."

The dark blanket and its pull on Carolyn vanished. But before she could take a breath, the cobra and its attached heads swayed in front of her.

The jaws of the cobra opened like white gates. In a quick lurch and one snap, the fangs shut behind her and Victory. They were inside its head.

Like a command center inside a nuclear submarine, the walls inside the head were covered with dials. Around them in consoles, video screens flashed images from different nations as well as stars and galaxies. Light from the outside streamed into multiple tiny holes through the snake-metal scales. These enabled her to see into the narrow neck passages that connected the cobra compartment—branching off to the other heads.

The hum grew more intense as the head swayed. Her senses reeled from the smell of sulphur and machine oil. She gagged from the nausea. But there was nothing in her stomach to empty out. Everything had been dumped after Gog's defeat. She forced herself to swallow hard several times. Okay. She took a deep breath. I'm okay. She patted Victory's neck. "We're okay."

She felt something brush against her cheek like a sticky web. Instinctively, she brushed it away. She felt another. Wherever it touched her, she felt it burn.

Your shield.

Carolyn lifted it and ducked under.

As the head swayed, Victory shifted under her, keeping his balance in the rocking room.

Your sword.

With the shield over her face, she struck out, chopping as best she could at the sticky strand. The millisecond the edge of the sword touched it, it dissolved.

The hum increased until Carolyn thought her brain would explode. Holding up the shield and striking with the sword, she was incapable of shutting out the vibrating sound.

The crown squeezed. And Carolyn felt as though tender hands covered her ears. The hum was muffled, but she could still hear it.

Under the shield's cover, she felt Victory walk slowly forward and stop.

She lowered it and leaned over him to peer down a precipice. Below them, the open segments, somehow hinged together, moved slightly. She could see down the cobra's neck into its body. The leg holes, lined up on each side of the sections, emitted oscillating fibrous threads that crisscrossed each other.

The head shook.

And they were pitched into the webbing.

Ew!

Sticky ooze covered her exposed skin—burning, stinging every pore. A thick gel filled her nostrils, cutting off her breath. Suspended in thick mucus, she was helpless.

Slowly she felt the crown expand around her forehead and slide down her face. Its leaf edges skimmed off the goo as easily as a knife scrapes grease off a plate. She could see the Greek letters growing larger. It slipped over her body and around the shield and sword. It continued pushing the secretion away until Victory was clean and dry.

The crown stood on its leaf edges. Like a circus horse through a ring, Victory jumped through the circlet.

Instantly they were in front of the pearl gate.

It took a couple moments for Carolyn to realize: I'm not dead, and the shock of where she was.

And—there they were: Gazellia, Jimmy, Claude, and who's the other woman?

"Mon amie. Dear one. Delighted I am you have come."

"Hey, sis, better late than never." He gave her a thumbs-up.

She laughed. "Told you, bro, you'd be stuck and want my help someday."

Claude reached up to take her shield. "Let me help you down."

Carolyn sheathed her sword and swung her leg over Victory.

As soon as her feet hit the gold bricks, Jimmy grabbed her arm and pulled her close.

She hugged him while he thumped her chest piece and kissed her cheek. She kissed him back and noted his gray eyes filled with tears.

A tall, slim woman dressed in a linen toga with a purple belt offered her hand. "I don't think we've met. I'm Bridget."

"I'm glad to meet you."

As Carolyn clasped her hand, she wondered ... The red hair. The shape of her nose ... and eyes ...

"You look like Mauvais … a little …" She paused, not wanting to offend. "But … um … You must be okay. You're with us, right?"

Bridget leaned forward to kiss Carolyn on both cheeks.

"Indeed I am, mistress. And glad of it." Her voice was soft and thick with a Celtic lilt. "Inside of time, I was the sister of our enemy. We came from the same mother. But unlike Mauvais, I walked a different path. Glad that I did. Sad I was that she did not."

"When I saw Gazellia earlier through the crown, was I inside or outside of time?"

"Then you were inside. Here you are outside," Bridget said.

"But where is *here?*"

"Mistress, you have come through a portal where one can reenter time and space. But once past this gate, one is permanently, forever, a citizen in the city of light. Life in perfection is there. No hunger. No pain. No tears. Joy. Peace. Love beyond measure. Every dream fulfilled. It is the eternal city the prophets and sages of old described."

"How come you're still in front of the gate?" Carolyn asked.

"Because of my many prayers. My utmost desire was to participate in the destruction of my evil sister. The sisters where Gazellia and I first met had a saying, *hope springs eternal.* My hope has been realized. My prayers answered. The legend is true. And it has brought us together to end Mauvais."

"The only way we can go home is to go back and defeat her," Jimmy said. "We've got the winning team. Let's go for it."

"Oui, mon amie. The crown chose you to lead us."

"Come on, Victory. We gotta turn around and go back." Carolyn pulled on his mane, indicating she wanted him to bow.

He didn't move.

The scene of Jimmy's body in a pool of blood came into her mind. But like a film in reverse, she saw the medallion shrinking from a disk with serrated edges—deflecting the banshees to its normal size.

Send it.

Carolyn didn't quite get what the crown meant.

I give you authority to bring the medallion. Set your mind on it like the toe shoes.

She closed her eyes and concentrated. In her mind, as she spun it on its chain like a helicopter propeller, it lifted. She heard the sound of it drop at his feet before she opened her eyes.

Jimmy picked it up. "It followed me."

"Uh, not exactly, bro. I thought it here like I made the toe shoes work and somehow the crown … um … we brought it."

"Cool. Bring armor. Bring guns. Think a horse for each of us."

"Jimmy," Bridget said, "she cannot do that because those are inside time, as is Carolyn. You … we have come here through a different way by what is called death. Inside time, our bodies are still where we were last."

"You mean I'm not real?"

"You are real, Jimmy, just removed from the earth-physical into another dimension … soul and spirit. A body-energy change."

"Lady, you're nuts. I ain't dead. My sister is here. Gazellia is here and Claude. And I'm feeling …" He rubbed the medal. "This." His finger poked her arm. "And you!"

"Yes. It is thus with the saints behind the gate as well. However, I am not to return with you. I am to go on through the gate. The legend has proved itself true. The Almighty One allowed me to receive the joy of knowing the ones who will destroy Mauvais."

Bridget caressed the shield. "This has been renewed by God's grace. And thus it shall ever be used by the saints inside time wherever needed."

She bowed her head. "Greater Than All Kings, protect your warriors in their battle against the evil one. May they live again to honor and serve you … to accomplish the destinies you had in mind for them from before the beginning of time."

She lifted the shield while Carolyn slipped her arm through the strap. "Your brother, Gazellia, and Claude will return with you to the moment before the portal opened."

Jimmy slipped medallion over his head. "I'm ready."

"Mon amie, united we are with you."

When Victory jumped through the ring, she bent her knees for a soft landing. Immediately she felt the crown encircle her head. Quickly she looked behind for the three of them. She recognized each by their outlines. The medal swung from around the neck of a transparent Jimmy.

Guck hit Carolyn's face. It stung her cheeks, her mouth. She ducked under the shield as they swayed inside the metal-snake section.

Send the medallion.

The second Carolyn's thought unscrewed its top, the serrated edges buzz-sawed through the section, leaving a large gash in Mauvais's snaky-metal side.

The oozy webbing gushed like a river of pus out of a stomach wound.

The humming grew louder.

The buzz saw cut larger.

Jimmy, Gazellia, Claude, and then Carolyn on Victory were swept out the hole from the force of flowing slime.

The jaws of the cobra yawned—its fangs neatly chomped that metal section free. Like projectiles, it spit out its remnants, spewing them across the lanes and bushes.

Victory charged into a gallop as Carolyn raised her shield against the shrapnel. Sparks flew off—metal against metal. Once out of range, she watched the remaining pieces fly through the outlines of Jimmy and the rest. Undisturbed by the debris, they ran after Victory down the lane.

With the wounded section gone, the remaining ones closed.

The hydra heads shook as the cobra swung around to view Carolyn and the others at the far end of the lane. Still on its tail and humming, it paused.

"It's thinking," Jimmy said, "what to do."

"Impossible. It does not think," Gazellia said. "It serves Baal. It does what he orders."

"Do you think it can see you guys?" Carolyn asked.

"You can see me, right, sis?"

"Barely ... um ... like a ghost. It's more like I can feel you." She pointed to the medal. "*That* I see clearly."

He fingered the medallion. "So send this to lop off its heads."

"No," Claude said. That would only make it multiply. Mauvais replicated our parts. It can clone any part of itself."

"I was in its head." Carolyn said. "It's a machine. It eats energy. If we could just find a way to pull its plug. We could kill it."

"Mes amis, let us ask the one who has the answer. The one who is on our side. The crown."

Carolyn pulled it off and held it up. "Help us."

What do you want me to do?

She was shocked by the question. And angry.

"Do what we can't. You killed Gog. Now we want you to destroy Mauvais."

Both are servants of King Baal.

She shook the crown in frustration. "Then get rid of him too!" she yelled. "And send Jimmy and me home … earth time … whatever … back. Back!"

Pull off a leaf and eat it. Give one to each of them.

The moment the skin of her fingers touched a leaf edge, the emeralds and gold disappeared. She popped the leaf in her mouth and chewed.

Bittersweet. Fire hot. She exhaled to cool her tongue. And a blue flame shot out.

She and the crown were one. She knew exactly what to do.

She pulled off three more leaves. "Eat," she commanded.

Three blue flaming torches stood where Jimmy and the others had been.

When she put the crown on her head, none of the leaves were missing. It was again a circlet of emeralds and gold.

She dropped her shield and pulled her sword. With a gentle heel tap, Victory trotted down the lane with the torches following.

A dark, iridescent veil descended over the gazebo and covered Mauvais.

Victory and the rest stopped at its edge.

Blow!

Carolyn inhaled sharply and blew as hard as she could. Fire burst out of her mouth like a blow torch.

The three also blew. Four funnels converged to strike fangs, eyes, and neck. Ignoring the putrid smell of sulphur and burning metal, they continued to shoot projectiles of fire at the head—melting it, vaporizing it into the black veil.

Lower on the neck the oval heads began to smoke, then burn, and finally disintegrate and also disappear into the veil.

As they continued to blow, one by one the lower sections exploded, their shrapnel vanishing into the black.

The dark cloud began to spread over them.

They blew, but the fire from their mouths was stopped by a luminous wall.

Incredible heat began to flow through her body. She felt herself being lifted out of the saddle. Below her she caught a glimpse of Victory and the others. And the roof of the cupola was under her feet.

She felt the crown squeeze. Flying faster than her mind could grasp, she caught glimpses of clouds, stars, asteroids, and brilliant solar rays spiraling into rainbows.

Looking down while slowly descending, she saw a Plexiglas dome over a city of elevated highways and steel girders.

A crash through, like before? she wondered.

The bittersweet taste of hot fire rose in her mouth. Heat from the soles of her feet to the top of her head filled every pore of her being.

Blow!

Sharply she exhaled.

And—flames. Red. Blue. Purple. Like missiles launching from bays, they shot from her mouth, shield, sword, and chest piece.

The crown lifted and spun enormous lightning bolts downward.

The dome cracked and split open. A blazing thunderbolt struck the beacon of light in the center of the pyramid. It exploded into a gigantic ball of fire. The highways and girders hit by the missiles and bolts collapsed into each other. A mushroom cloud of debris rose into space.

The spinning crown whipped it into a hurricane and hurled it out into the cosmos until it became a pin prick of light.

Carolyn watched it vanish completely.

The destroyer is destroyed.

Carolyn hung suspended in the vastness of space. Her body felt no hard edges. She was wrapped in a cocoon of softness, held like a baby in a down-filled blanket. Yet she knew she still had on her armor. Held the shield. Gripped the sword. The band around her head was gentle, soothing. And she realized the heat was gone. In its place, a cooling peace filled her every pore.

Joy. Immeasurable, indescribable overwhelmed her senses. Oh, to be forever in this state of being. She and the crown—the wonder of being one. Knowing creator and creation. Triumph and glory and love. Experienced.

Chapter 25

the proof

In the timelessness of moments, she returned to the gazebo. The crown on her head, dressed in armor, her sword sheathed, she descended.

She shouted on her way down, "King Baal's gone! Dead! Finished!"

Gazellia hugged her first. "Praise the Great One who delivered us from our enemy."

Jimmy gave Carolyn a quick kiss. "Couldn't have done it better myself."

"Oh, yeah," she said. "Next time there's a King Baal somewhere, it's your turn."

He pointed to the crown, "Now how about you get us outta here and back to where we belong?"

"Total cool. You're talking to it."

'Yeah, well, I'm ready to leave any ... excuse the expression ... *time.*"

All must be fully restored.

With that thought Carolyn realized, even though she sensed their presence, they were still like ghosts. She had felt her brother's kiss and Gazellia's hug, but beyond her understanding they still looked like outlines.

"You know you're not ... um ... normal."

"Hey, sis, you think you are?"

"I think what Carolyn means is, we need to return to where we were," Claude said. "We need our bodies. My sister Lissette might be waiting for us back at the school. With King Baal dead, she is free from her contract. She might still be alive."

"Oui. We need to be whole again."

The sight of the iron door clanging shut over Jimmy and Claude and the bedroom with parts of Gazellia strewn about came into her mind.

"Let's go. We've got to return to the places you were last," she said.

Up the lane, Carolyn heard voices. The outlines of Raymond, Carlos, Michelle, and Porcelain rose from the ground. They clapped and cheered and lightly touched Victory's sides as he trotted by them.

"Awesome!" Carolyn yelled. "Follow us."

In the arena behind the school, empty uniforms lay crumpled on the ground.

Walking behind Victory, Claude said, "I'll look for Lissette." He inspected several rows near the green hut. "I can't distinguish which one was hers. She has gone the way of Baal. Sad. We were identical except in heart."

"She was a great pianist," Carlos said. "Porcelain and I danced many times while she played."

"We did try to persuade her to our side. But to no avail," Michelle said. "I'm sorry, Claude."

Until they reached the pit, the only sound was the clopping of Victory's hooves.

Carolyn looked down at the iron door.

Blow!

She did, aiming the torch from her mouth around its edges until it melted down the sides.

Both corpses lay face down in the dirt. The pool of blood by Jimmy's head was dark brown.

"Jimmy, Claude, jump in," she said.

Immediately each outline dissolved into its respective body.

Throw me in.

"He agape nikai panta!" she shouted, spinning it down.

From the leaves, thick smoke poured over their bodies. Sparks snapped like miniature lightning bolts within the white cloud.

The thought came and she blew.

Instead of flames, her breath was a cool wind driving the smoke upward to vanish into the air.

Even knowing what was going to happen didn't prepare Carolyn for the shock of seeing her brother's gray eyes and freckled face looking up at her. If she hadn't known better, she could have sworn his death was a figment of her imagination. But when he turned to shake Claude's hand and slap his shoulder with a "Man, oh man, we made it"—and there was no cut on the back of his head—she knew that what she had witnessed was for real.

Claude smiled, blue eyes twinkling. He brushed the dirt off his uniform. "Good to be myself again."

"I'm ready, sis. Blow us outta here."

She exhaled.

No fire. No wind. Her breath was normal.

She laughed. "Guess you guys are too heavy to lift."

Use Victory.

She dismounted and dropped his reins over the wall.

"Grab 'em, and when I back him up, he'll pull you out."

In quick succession they scrambled up.

Jimmy patted Victory's neck. "Thanks. Couldn't have done it without you."

Claude put his arm around Carolyn. "Appreciate your help."

"What about Raymond, Carlos, Porcelain, and me?" Michelle asked. "We were chopped up into pieces and sucked up by Mauvais."

I will restore. Their cells are in the ground.

Immediately Carolyn knew what to do.

She pointed to each. "Put your arms around each other."

She laid down the shield and scooped up the sand. "I'm going to throw dirt on you."

She lifted the crown and it sailed to hover over them.

As the particles fell, the crown spun. Each grain became a golden sparkle descending over their outlines. They became smoky streams that curled around them.

Carolyn inhaled deeply and blew.

Like a cool breeze against a morning fog, the smoke dissipated.

The four danced and squealed in delight. They jabbed and pinched each other. "Hurrah! Praise our Greatest Majesty!" they exclaimed over and over.

The crown returned to her head.

"Now it's Gazellia's turn," she said, reaching down to pick up some sand.

No. Her remains are in the bedroom. Take the shield.

Once there, Carolyn and Jimmy led the rest through the debris. Pieces of Gazellia were in the same position: foot under a piece of candlestick, arms wedged between a broken table leg and chair back. Tenderly, gently, Carolyn lifted Gazellia's head from where she had left it on the seat cushion.

Gazellia put her hands over Carolyn's. "My dear, many of my appendages Mauvais replaced. Stated I have many times that I am fully human. But, mon amie, I am not certain 'tis true."

"Doesn't matter," Claude said, "whether we were cyborgs or not. The crown has proved it can create whatever is missing."

Jimmy snapped his fingers and in sing-song repeated a couple of times, "Better together, we get her together."

Gazellia laughed. "Oui, mes amis. Available I am to be whole again."

Carolyn put Gazellia's head on the bed. Jimmy and the others picked up the rest and placed them in order. When all ends touched, they stepped back.

Carolyn expected the crown to lift from her head to spin out smoke and lightning bolts.

It didn't move. It didn't squeeze. No thoughts came.

On the bed, Gazellia's outline sat next to her body. "Correct I was to consider the crown would not renew me. My betrayal was deliberate. Raised I was with the truth of honor and love. My sisters taught me well. My choices were made from the wickedness in my heart. Yours from ignorance."

"You're forgetting the legend," Claude said. "The king's intention was wicked also."

"That's right," Michelle said. "Remember, later the king prayed and dedicated it to the Loving Creator."

He did more than that.

"What else did the king do?" Carolyn asked.

Gazellia sighed. "He was willing to sacrifice his life for his daughter's husband. A man he never wanted her to have. It was a sacrifice of purer love. This I did not do for Milady. I could have confessed my criminal acts and taken her place. I did not."

"Listen," Jimmy said. "We all got things we're sorry about. What's the big deal?" He pointed to the crown. "Take it off, sis, and throw it. And let's get outta here."

The idea of home raised a lump in her throat. Her choice. Her old world versus Double Suns with Gazellia and Claude. The crown on her head. The pearl gate. Fire in her mouth and power.

"Betwixt and between," Gram would say.

"Jimmy, what if I don't go back with you?"

"What do you mean? You got to go back."

"No. I want to stay with the crown. It's used me in awesome … beyond, beyond … ways I could never accomplish at home. You don't need me, really. I don't know why it chose me, but it did. I'm not meant to go back."

He put both his hands on her shoulders and lightly shook her. "No way," he said. "You've got to come home with me." He stepped back and crossed his arms. "Besides, how do you know this is real? How do you know that you're not just dreaming?"

"Come on, bro. I'd never have you rescue me in a dream. And see you killed? And fight a giant? And fly through outer space? In my wildest imagination, I couldn't think all that up. I don't have the brain power to do it. And what about the puzzle? That was no dream, bro."

He chewed his lower lip. "Yeah. Well. If you stay, I stay. I'm not leavin' without you." He smacked his right hand into his left palm. "Where you go, I go."

Carolyn was surprised by the emphatic pronouncement. His wanting to follow her had nothing to do with explaining to the police and Gram what had happened. It had nothing to do with the fear of going to jail. Or to be locked up in some mental institution. Gazellia was right. He loves me. He's willing to give up everything to stay with me.

Give me to him.

With both hands, Carolyn lifted the crown. "Here," she said. "Put it on."

He hesitated at first, and then he slid it easily over his head.

"Will ya' look at that! I can wear it."

"How does it feel?" Carolyn asked.

"Light. Warm. Doesn't hurt." He laughed. "Makes me feel good. Like I did something."

"Is it telling you anything?"

She saw his gray eyes widen.

"Yeah. Sis, take off your armor, shield, and sword and pile it on Gazellia's body."

She waited for further instructions.

He was silent.

"Go on."

He smiled. "Now I understand. First you do what it tells you. When you've done that, it tells you the next thing."

She stacked everything on Gazellia's body.

Jimmy lifted the crown and placed it on top.

"We're to join hands and touch her body," he said. "Including Gazellia's ghost."

Jimmy bowed his head.

And in unison from everyone the words came: "Greatest Majesty. Loving Creator. Forgive us of our wicked desires, our selfish plans, our betrayals, our weaknesses. We declare over Gazellia, he agape nikai panta for her services and willing sacrifices over the centuries to find the one who could wear your crown. Restore her according to the promise in your legend."

A magnetic field—an electrical force—switched on around them.

Under Carolyn's hands a surge of power traveled up her arms. She knew the electricity spreading into every cell of her body was going through theirs as well.

The voltage increased. The emeralds flashed.

Except for Gazellia, they pulled their hands away.

The intense heat drove them backward.

Gazellia's outline melted into the glowing armor.

They stood as close as they dared.

Neither the bed nor the room was aflame.

The emeralds turned from deep green to pink and then to bright red. Miniature bolts of lightning cracked and flashed around the fiery leaves. A spiral of white smoke rose from the center of the crown. Faster and faster, countless white shining tendrils rolled and curled over her body—until she was completely hidden inside a white cocoon.

Carolyn didn't know how long they stood watching. Finally she nudged Jimmy and pointed. "Look, it's beginning to reverse itself."

Unwinding exactly as they had wrapped, the thick strands rolled back into the crown's center. As the emeralds cooled, they returned to their original deep green color.

It rose and returned to Carolyn's head.

Gazellia's lids flickered. Her hands twitched. She lifted her arms and stretched, yawning and blinking as if coming out of a deep sleep.

Her movements shifted the armor onto the bed.

Carolyn reached for her as she stood up. They held each tightly, laughing, crying, and jumping up and down.

Jimmy and the others also group-hugged Gazellia with exclamations of praise and joy to the Almighty Creator.

"My dear … as dear to me as a daughter. You said you would stay with us?" She patted Jimmy's shoulder. "And you also, my friend, promised to stay as well?"

Before Carolyn could nod yes, the crown squeezed.

You and Jimmy will return home.

Jimmy smiled and shook his head. "No. We can't. We're supposed to go back."

"*You* heard the crown."

He chuckled. "Yeah. I guess I've learned how to listen."

Picturing the jammed room with Jimmy snoring beside her, his mess, his smelly shoes, registered intense disappointment. Ramrod-Riguez. Yolanda and the track. The prison of Gram's rules.

Her thoughts argued. I know Gram'll miss us. But you could bring her here too. I thought I was your champion. We're a great team conquering … whoever you want me to. We could go to other planets where other kings try to enslave … um … others. How about us fighting evil on earth? Please, don't make me go back to the place where I was.

Once you return, you will remember what we have accomplished together. What truth you speak about me will be like flames from your mouth. Tell them the meaning of he agape nikai panta. Tell them about the pearl gate. I am the Laurel Crown who gives love to the abandoned, liberty to slaves, forgiveness to the guilty, and life to the dead. I will always be with you. Go home.

"How?"

Climb the apple tree. Jump off its highest branch.

Chapter 26

home

The sweet scent of apple blossoms filled the ballroom. The birds darted among the white flowers. A robin perched on Carolyn's shoulder as she stood under a fragrant bough. She shooed him off. He flew to a window.

"Let him out," she said. "Let 'em all out."

"Done," Jimmy said.

Each ran to a window and pushed open the casement.

A flurry of wings and out they flew into the late afternoon sunlight.

"Wild again they soon will be like the Creator meant," Gazellia said. "It will be wonderful to hear them singing early in the morning."

"What are you going to do once we're gone?" Carolyn asked.

"Mon amie, the crown spoke to me as well. I, like you and Jimmy, will speak to others about its powers. What I was taught at Sainte Clare, I will proclaim to all who wish to be truly free. We have a school. We will teach what we have learned."

"We were recruiters for Mauvais," Michelle said. "Now we are recruiters for the legend."

"If there are other King Baals or Mauvaises," Claude said, "we have the weapons to destroy them. The crown's armor, shield, and sword."

"Don't forget," Raymond said, "we have each other as its warriors."

"And," Gazellia said, "the mind to resist the worst in ourselves for the good of others. The secret of true sacrifice."

"I'd like to see Victory before we go," Carolyn said.

"My dear, do you not know he is at the pearl gate waiting to be used?"

Carolyn sighed. "When you see him, kiss him on the nose for me. Okay?"

Gazellia lifted Carolyn's chin. Lightly she kissed her on both cheeks. "My precious, dear Carolyn. You are special. Never forget us."

"I love you," Carolyn whispered.

"Je t'aime, aussi."

Carolyn smiled at them. "Take care of Gazellia for me, will you?"

One by one they came and kissed her and Jimmy on both cheeks. "Adieu. Good bye. God bless."

Jimmy climbed first, testing each fork and branch.

Carolyn followed.

The topmost was too thin to support both at once.

"I'll jump first," Jimmy said.

For a second he hesitated, and then he flung himself off. And vanished.

The branch swayed as Carolyn looked down.

Gazellia made the sign of the cross.

And Carolyn jumped.

Her feet hit the cellar floor.

"Ow!" Jimmy said, his rear smacking the butcher's table.

She felt for the crown. It was gone.

Mr. Reed opened the trap door. "What's goin' on with you two? I heard you guys crashin' around clear outside. You beatin' each other up?"

"No. We're okay," Jimmy said. "We just got carried away."

Carolyn laughed.

"Well, Eunice wants both of you *pronto.*" He looked at Jimmy. "I didn't tell her about our trip to the store. If you want to, we can keep it between us."

"Thanks. We'll be right up."

"I'll tell Eunice."

"I wonder what time it is." Carolyn said.

"Who cares about that?" He pointed to her head. "What happened to the crown?"

"I don't know where it went."

"We got nothin' to show for where we've been?"

She picked up the parchment from the table. "We have this. And we've got each other."

"Yeah, well, besides you and a piece of paper, I'd rather have tangible evidence to prove where we've been."

She sighed. "We'd better go."

It was almost dark. Eunice sat opposite Mr. Reed at the kitchen table. When she saw Carolyn, she got up and flipped on the light.

"*Where* have you been? You know you're supposed to be home well before dark. You promised you'd leave a note. You've given me a terrible fright." She smacked Jimmy on the chest. "And as for you, I expected better. You're older. You're the man in this house. You're to look after your sister."

Jimmy chuckled. "Believe me, Gram. I most certainly have."

"He really does care about me."

Eunice crossed her arms. "Of course he does, child."

Carolyn gave her a bear hug. "I'm sorry, Gram. We started working on the puzzle and didn't realize how fast time went."

"Nonsense." Eunice pushed her away. "Mr. Reed checked down there three hours ago. After working all day, I just couldn't walk anymore."

"I checked the whole neighborhood lookin' for you both. Came back two minutes ago an' heard the crashin'."

"Sorry we worried you," Jimmy said.

"*Worried* isn't the right word," Eunice said. "*Scared* is. Ten more minutes and I would have called the police."

"We're sorry, Gram." Carolyn touched her shoulder. "We are, really."

"I'm the one who's sorry I gave you that puzzle. I thought it would change your sour attitude. It certainly has taught you some things. Thoughtlessness. No consideration for my feelings." She shook her head. "I don't know … I just don't know how I can ever trust the two of you."

Carolyn didn't know what to say. How could she explain? How could she show how much she had changed inside?"

In the kitchen light she caught a glint of gold where Jimmy's shirt was open at the neck.

The medallion!

She knew what she would say.

"Gram, we've been to a planet called Double Suns …"